FIREWORKS

FIREWORKS

ALICE LIN

Underlined

GetUnderlined.com

Educators and librarians, for a variety of teaching tools, visit us at
RHTeachersLibrarians.com

Library of Congress Cataloging-in-Publication Data is available upon request.
ISBN 978-0-593-56535-3 (trade) — ISBN 978-0-593-56536-0 (ebook)

The text of this book is set in 11-point Fairfield LT Std.
Interior design by Jaclyn Whalen

Printed in the United States of America
10 9 8 7 6 5 4 3 2 1
First Edition

Oh. My. Sweet. Tea. Someone ring the proverbial gong. Karnival might host their first world tour this summer! Everyone's talking about it on the fancafé (big thanks to JennyKPops for translating), but there hasn't been an official announcement. Does anyone know if this is legit? DM me if you have insider knowledge. In the meantime, I'm refreshing the fancafé every three seconds and selling my kidney so I can afford a ticket.

#karnival #fireworks #kiteismybias #xiaomingislove #karnivalstan #someonepinchme #suddenlyanorgandonor #willkillfortickets

1

There's nothing more satisfying than stretching your arms out after a three-hour exam, confident you nailed the last question.

I roll my shoulders and look around at my classmates as they crack their knuckles and massage the kinks out of their hands, each and every one of us eager to abandon the little folding desk chairs we've been confined to all morning. Our proctor organizes our exam booklets into one neat pile on his desk before glancing at his watch.

"You're dismissed," he says without making eye contact.

All at once, every occupied chair in the room screeches back against the floor. Footsteps shuffle toward the door, trailed by a cacophony of ringtones and alarms. I make a small victory fist as I exit the library and head over to the language wing to retrieve my things for next period.

Something unusual, though not entirely unfamiliar, is in the air. It's not dust or mold, or the potheads and vapers who sneak off to the bathroom during study hall.

It's the smell of freedom.

I am done. No more late-night study sessions hunched over a six-hundred-page book! No more cramps in my hand as my writing devolves into chicken scratch with every tick of the clock! No more AP exams! All that's left is finals, but no amount of free bubble tea can make me care—not when I'll be kissing high school goodbye next month.

Summer vacation can't come too soon. I can't wait to unwind at the beach, get my sun-kissed glow on with my toes in the sand and a bowl of shaved ice in my hand.

Of course, Stephanie will be joining me. It's her duty as my best friend to help me fulfill my summer itinerary. Who else is going to rub me down with sunscreen in those hard-to-reach places? Definitely not some opportunistic creep ogling me from behind his aviators.

Up ahead I see Stephanie waiting at my locker.

"You have that dreamy look in your eyes again," she says. "It's terrifying."

"Hello to you, too." I brush her aside, twist my lock open, and check my reflection in the little mirror mounted on the locker door. I dab my face with an oil-absorbing sheet and click my teeth at how greasy my hair is. I kept touching it during the exam, after someone pointed out the powdery residue of my dry shampoo—one of the disadvantages of having black hair.

Stephanie also just got out of an exam. Unlike me, she took the time to curl her hair and dress as if she's ready for a lunch date, with her denim dress and lacy off-white blouse; whereas I'm in a sweatshirt and leggings, the epitome of cozy.

"How was world history?" I ask while searching for my red lip tint, lost in my backpack.

Compared to the calculus and biology exams Stephanie took earlier this week, world history must've been nothing more than a brain teaser.

"Like taking an afternoon coffee break," Stephanie says, pantomiming a yawn. "How was comparative gov?"

"It was a race against the clock, but I know I scored at least a four." All that last-minute cramming paid off. "You could've taken it blindfolded with time to spare."

Counting today's, Stephanie has taken a grand total of five AP exams, three more than me. The last two weeks would've been hell for anyone else, but for her, standardized tests are like drugs. She derives a masochistic pleasure from tricky multiple-choice questions and convoluted word problems that leave other people scratching their head.

Stephanie leans against an adjacent locker with a cheeky grin on her face.

"Oh boy, what is it?" I prep myself for what's to come.

"Lawrence wants to take you to prom," she says.

"Isn't he dating Ariel?" I ask.

Prom is next week, and I have no intention of going, regardless of who wants me as their date. I love formfitting dresses and high heels that make me taller than five foot two, but I'm not about to shell out hundreds of dollars to look like a superstar. And dancing? Not my thing.

Besides, I already turned down Kellie Blair, and that was emotionally draining.

Beauty and brains aside, Kellie is ambitious and compassionate. Not only did she serve as student council president all four years, but she founded the Children's Hospital Volunteer Club and revived the Environmental Club, which had fallen by the wayside after continuous harassment from climate-change skeptics. While I know a lot about her accomplishments, we only had an occasional class together and collaborated on a handful of student council events.

So when she asked me to meet her on the football field the

other day and gave me a box of cookies that spelled BE MY GIRL & GO TO PROM WITH ME? I was as flabbergasted as I was flattered.

I almost said yes, but I just . . . didn't feel it.

"According to the juicy grapevine, Ariel broke up with Lawrence to date Mia, and now he's frantic for a date," Stephanie explains as I give up on the lip tint, grab my notebooks, and slam my locker shut.

"Hurray! I'm his backup!" I give myself a round of applause.

Slowly we make our way to honors English at the opposite end of the school.

"More important, did your mom finish altering your dress?" I ask.

"She'll have it done by tomorrow. Cross your fingers it fits."

Stephanie has been dreaming of prom ever since we became best friends in eighth grade, going so far as to design her own dress. Her ideal dress has changed more times than I can count with my fingers and toes. After an unreasonably long phone call, where I had to talk and pee at the same time because she wouldn't let me hang up, Stephanie finally decided on an off-shoulder emerald gown that flares out at the knees. Her mom, who runs a tailoring service, made Stephanie's dream dress a reality and is currently putting the finishing touches on it.

"I wouldn't worry about it," I assure her.

We reach Room 284 ten minutes after the bell, and Ms. Greene is too nose-deep in her book to notice. She can disguise the book with a fake Toni Morrison cover, but everyone knows she's reading another steamy bodice ripper with sexy fallen angels warring against bloodthirsty demons.

The end of the year is almost upon us, and Ms. Greene has made it abundantly clear that she doesn't want to teach anymore. For the last couple of days, her classes have turned into study halls. At least she's honest and doesn't bore us to tears with documentaries as Dr. Campbell does. The guy takes himself too seriously because he has a PhD.

As Stephanie and I settle into the back row, Ester, who should be in art right now, slips in after us. Ms. Greene doesn't bat an eye as Ester clomps over in her combat boots and claims the desk in front of me, her legs spread wider than necessary as she straddles the chair backward.

"Someone here paid a visit to the salon," I say, looking Ester over with approval. Overnight she got rid of her auburn highlights and dyed her hair back to its natural color. Her hair now falls to the middle of her neck in tight black waves.

"I wanted to spice things up, lose the long hair. Mom threw a fit when she saw the perm," Ester says through a mouthful of bubble gum. "So, did you hear?"

"You have to be more specific than that," I say. "Just a bit."

"Karnival might do a world tour this summer. Before it was just rumors, but it seriously might happen now. The three of us have to go. No matter what!"

"What do you mean by *might*?" I ask.

"There hasn't been an official announcement." Ester shrugs. "I bet they're delaying it on purpose to rile everyone up—publicity stunt, you know."

"No announcement means no one knows when tickets go on sale, and isn't it late to be planning a world tour? It's already May. . . . What if their concert falls on a day I made plans for?"

"Lu." Ester fixes me with an incredulous look. Her liberal use of eyeliner makes her gaze even more pointed. The gray contact lenses don't help. "The Jersey Shore is going to be here this summer, next summer, and the summer after that."

"A hurricane could wipe it out. You never know," Stephanie chimes in.

"Not helping!" Ester tells Stephanie to zip it with a theatrical flourish of her hand before returning her attention to me. "As I was saying before I was *rudely* interrupted, you can hit the beach whenever you want. How many chances will you get to see Karnival live?"

"But we don't know if they're performing. That's my point. *Whoosh!*" I swing my hand over my head to emphasize the *whoosh*.

Ester shoves her phone into my face. She has Karnival's Twitter pulled up. Five hours ago, they tweeted, *Stay tuned, Fireworks*. Whatever that means.

"Let me know when tickets go on sale. Then we'll talk," I say.

"I wish you'd be as excited as I am." Pouting, Ester sinks into her chair. "You're the one who introduced me to Karnival, and look what I've become. I used to be a devout Catholic. All I do now is pray to Karnival every night."

"You okay with all the hyperbole?" I crack a smile as Ester pops her bubble gum and playfully shoots me a wounded look.

Ester's the furthest thing from a Catholic, but it's true that, while I don't think she worships Karnival, I did introduce her to them.

She didn't even know what K-pop was until last year.

Her life was nothing but anime soundtracks until she came over to my house the first time to work on an assignment. I played TWICE, BTS, and EXO while we dissected the literary representation of women in Kate Chopin's *The Awakening*. She liked the music enough to ask me who the singers were, but it was after she listened to Karnival that she died from an eargasm and was reborn a Firework.

Fireworks is the name of Karnival's fan club. Membership

comes with certain perks, like early ticketing for fan meets and access to exclusive merchandise, but registration is restricted to fans in South Korea, much to Ester's disdain in this unfair world. You can find other online communities, ones that are friendlier toward global fans, but according to Ester, it's not the same as being part of the official fan club—which I understand.

I used to be quite the fanatic when Karnival debuted two years ago with "Lights Fantastic." It was the most downloaded song in South Korea in the first week of its release. The song's catchy, leaning more toward old-school funk than pop, but the MV is what won me over. Having five living definitions of eye candy serenade me with smooth vocals and even smoother dance moves—how could I resist putting these guys on replay?

For months my browser history was an endless log of image searches, fan forums, gossip blogs, and websites, all in Korean (which I can't read). Every night I fell asleep to Karnival's music, and after Stephanie grew sick of them, I bribed her to listen with me during our sleepovers.

It embarrasses me to admit this, but I used to dream up these scenarios where I'd be out and about like any other day, and by chance I'd bump into all five Karnival members—on the streets, at a coffee shop or bookstore, in an elevator, sometimes on a postapocalyptic space colony—and unwittingly I'd find myself in the center of a Karnival love pentagon. I further fed my obsession by buying posters and stickers at obscene prices, no thanks to international shipping fees. One time I almost begged my mom to get me life-size cardboard cutouts of my favorite group members.

And then, after a year of thirsting over unobtainable guys, I mellowed out. With college on the horizon, I realized I was wasting too much time and energy on a bunch of guys I'd never get to know beyond what they wanted me to know.

Well, except for the one I do know. Or at least, I used to know . . .

"Can you at least watch the 'Lights Fantastic' MV with me?" Ester says, extending one earbud to me. She cuts me off before I can ask why. "So you can fall in love with them all over again."

Thoughts of strangulation darken my mind as Ester sings along to "Meteor Shower" on our ride home. Every time she hits a high note, she sounds like a screeching pterodactyl on the brink of death. The veins in Stephanie's hands are popping as she grips the steering wheel and fights the urge to drive us into a utility pole.

I angle the rearview mirror toward me and watch Ester in the backseat as she rocks her body to the music. Her movements are wild, violent even. If she waves her arms any faster, she might dent the ceiling. For a moment, I am convinced that a demonic possession is taking place and that perhaps I should call a crisis hotline or order a bottle of holy water off Etsy, but then I remember that this is normal for Ester, so I let her do her thing.

Minutes later we pull up to my house: a dark teal bungalow with a cracked driveway and a bed of tulips and daffodils out front. I have one foot out of the car when my next-door neighbor pops out from behind the rose hedge dividing her house from mine.

"Good afternoon, Mrs. Xu." I wave at her as Ester stands awkwardly close to me.

Mrs. Xu waves back before fanning herself with her gardening hat. "Connie told me a senior asked her to prom today. Do you know a Lawrence in your grade?"

"Doesn't ring any bells." I shake my head as Stephanie coughs into her hand to mask her laughter. "Did Connie agree to go with him?"

"You know my daughter. She likes soccer, not boys."

"She knows what she wants." I give Mrs. Xu a thumbs-up before skipping up the steps to my front porch.

"I fried some scallion pancakes earlier," Mrs. Xu says, waving hello to Stephanie and Ester. "Want me to bring some over? There's enough for everyone."

"We're fine, thank you," Stephanie answers for me as I fish for the house key.

Ester giggles nervously behind me as I unlock the door.

One by one we shuffle in. I take off my shoes and dump my backpack onto the floor, grateful for the relief. Soon the three of us are chilling on the living room sofa, our legs stretched out on the coffee table. No one else is home to correct our bad manners.

"Are you always going to be this shy around Mrs. Xu?" I ask Ester.

Shy is the last word I'd use to describe someone who pushes the boundaries of our school dress code daily with fake-leather miniskirts that upset all the conservative moms who drive by in their minivans.

"Can you blame me? It's unbelievable!" Ester exclaims, throwing up her arms. "To think her son, the kid you grew up with, is *the* Kite."

"We know. It's not like you haven't said this before," Stephanie says, disappearing into the kitchen to pour herself a glass of water. "Isn't Kite your least favorite member?"

"I don't have a *least* favorite," Ester says, aghast at the thought. "Wayne is my bias. I like everyone else equally."

So, as I said, Karnival consists of five members.

There's O-Kei, one of two main vocalists, born in Incheon, South Korea, and twenty years old as of this January, making him the oldest member and by default the group leader.

Yoosung is the other main vocalist and the second oldest, born in Seoul and a resident of Australia for six years before returning to his home country to pursue music.

Then we have Xiaoming, the rapper and best dancer of the group (depending on who you ask). He hails from Taiwan and learned Korean for three years before his debut. He turned nineteen last month, two weeks before Wayne.

Wayne is a sub vocalist and the best dancer (also depending on who you ask). Fans refer to him as a "spicy maple cookie" because he seems intimidating on the outside but is sweet and soft on the inside. Being Korean Canadian has something to do with it, too.

Finally, there's Kite.

Kite is many things. He's the youngest member, at eighteen years old. He's a sub vocalist and a gifted pianist. He's an old classmate, an old friend, and my former next-door neighbor who is very much talked about to this day despite his absence.

"Does Mrs. Xu know anything about Karnival doing a world tour?" Ester asks as she tries and fails to sound uninterested. "Is Kite visiting anytime soon? If he is, maybe he could bring Wayne, and I could get a selfie—"

I reach for the pillow on the nearby recliner and bop Ester over the head with it, in time for her stomach to start growling. Mine does the same. I regret not taking Mrs. Xu up on her offer of scallion pancakes.

Stephanie returns with a glass of water and a take-out menu. "Let's order pizza."

"A splendid idea." I whip my phone out from my back pocket. "Tell me what toppings you want or forever hold your peace."

"I want pineapple and bacon with a drizzle of Wayne," Ester says, wriggling her brows, "if you catch my drift. Yum yum."

I bop Ester once more.

At night when I'm dreaming
I see a phantom image of you, pale and shimmering
Your dress is like a cape, weightless and dark as midnight
We leave everything behind and fly to a new world

Lyrics from "Lights Fantastic," cowritten by O-Kei, Kite, and
industry hitmaker Kang Jihyun, translated from Korean.

2

"Are you sure you don't want to take the night off?" Aunt Mei asks for the third time.

"Trust me. I wouldn't be here if I didn't want to be," I assure her.

Aunt Mei purses her lips, ready to ask the same question for the fourth time, until a group of guys in identical college sweatshirts file in through the front door. We greet them from behind the register: "Welcome to Dāngrán Bakery!"

One guy acknowledges us with a small nod before picking up a tray and a pair of tongs from the self-service station near the entrance. Like many people before him, he lays a sheet of wax paper onto the tray and begins to peruse our selection of savory breads and pastries, limited at this hour of night. His friends come straight to the counter, bypassing all the carbohydrates to stare at the digital menu mounted above us that lists all the beverages we have to offer.

After an intense study, one guy says, "Can I get two large taro milk teas?"

Aunt Mei hands me a ticket and I get to work.

Mom and Aunt Mei opened Dāngrán Bakery nearly a decade ago. It's your typical Asian bakery that sells coffee and bubble tea, situated between a nail salon and a Vietnamese sandwich shop in a modest strip mall. Mom manages a small but loyal kitchen staff, and business has been strong since our grand opening. I occasionally help out when I'm not bogged down by school, club activities, and community service. Mom doesn't like having me around too often; she thinks I should be at the movies, playing video games, or hanging out with my friends, doing "whatever it is teenage girls do." I like to do all that, but I also like to help my family.

Placing the two drinks into a to-go carrier, I slide the order across the counter into the customer's waiting hands. Aunt Mei rings up more people, and then the bakery empties out.

Aunt Mei checks the time. It's almost eight-thirty.

"We have a half hour until closing. You can go home if you want," she offers.

"There's nothing to do at home. I might as well stay and clean," I say.

Tonight is prom night. Stephanie and Ester are unavailable until further notice. Since I elected not to attend, the only thing waiting for me at home is season one of *My Hero Academia* and more food and travel channels on YouTube.

"Enchanted Forest" is this year's prom theme. Our school reserved a banquet hall at the Hyatt. The venue is replete with lanterns, fairy glow jars, paper butterflies, topiary animals, and other faux foliage. Kellie outdid herself with the indoor gazebo she fashioned out of a patio tent, some string lights, and white tulle.

Stephanie and Ester have been posting to Instagram all night long, from the moment they got ready at home to the moment they stepped onto the dance floor and realized dancing in heels isn't as easy as it looks.

Both are stunning in their evening gowns. Stephanie's custom mermaid dress fits her perfectly. She could be mistaken for Le Ha Anh's younger sister, with her plump red lips and long black hair pinned back with jeweled ornaments. Meanwhile, Ester, who wouldn't be caught dead without her fishnets, is unrecognizable in a teal modern-day interpretation of a baro't saya, with a titillating low-cut back and a detachable sheer shawl with pearl beadwork. I had no idea what a baro't saya was until Ester explained it to me, and now I'm a teeny bit more educated in Philippine culture.

Personally, I would've chosen a sapphire-blue or porcelain-white qipao. Aunt Mei would've bought me one if I'd gone to prom.

Regret nips at me like a harmless bug bite. Being a reluctant dancer is a flimsy excuse for missing out on a once-in-a-lifetime experience, especially since Ester, who hates dolling herself up, ended up going and looking like a fairy-tale princess. I'm sure I would've enjoyed myself without the dancing, and it's not as though I couldn't afford to attend. . . .

I don't know.

Prom is meant to be special. It should live up to your expectations and elicit a smile when the nostalgia rolls in at your ten-year high school reunion. Stephanie's been dreaming about this night for years, not because she wants it to be the most romantic night of her life, but because she wants to be the belle of the ball.

She can be quite the show-off.

Going to prom with someone I'm head over heels for would've made it worthwhile for me. But I'm not head over heels for anyone, which I guess is the ultimate reason I decided not to go. Kellie's promposal was sweet, but if prom can't be everything I want it to be, then I'm better off without it.

Mom saunters through the kitchen doors, and I nearly mistake her for Aunt Mei. They are identical twins. They share the same oval face, the same wide nose and pointed chin. You have to learn their personalities to differentiate them. Aunt Mei is a sugar cookie, whereas Mom is more like a sweet pork bun coated in sharp cheddar.

"Honey, go next door and buy me a banh mi," Mom says, holding out a ten-dollar bill.

"You know they're not going to let us pay." I head out without taking the money.

We have this unspoken arrangement with the Vietnamese shop: they get a discount on all bakery purchases, and in return, we get free sandwiches.

I step inside Pho King Delight and find Connie Xu at a corner table, her mouth a vacuum as she slurps a bowl of pho. Her oversized hoodie is tugged all the way down to her nose, but her neon yellow soccer cleats give her away.

Meanwhile, Jason's busy wiping tables. I sneak up from behind and tap him on the shoulder, ducking low when he looks back.

He sighs. "Lulu, I know you're there."

I stand to full height. "It was worth a try."

"Suffer the consequences!" Jason springs into action, locking me in a choke hold before I can sidestep him. He ruffles my hair with a sweaty palm as I squirm against him. "What are you doing here? Shouldn't you be at prom?"

"Not everyone goes to prom. Plenty of people I know stayed home. Now let go!"

"No need to yell. I've got customers here," Jason says, granting me my freedom. "Let me guess: two ham banh mis with extra jalapeños for Ms. Li?"

"Yes, and slice them in half!" I say, loud enough for Jason to hear me as he disappears into the kitchen, leaving me with Connie.

I've known Connie since she was in diapers, back when I was taller than her, however momentary it was. Only two years apart, we used to have playdates—hosting tea parties for our stuffed animals, molding candy sushi out of the worst things possible for our teeth, pretending the floor was lava—and then she discovered her love for soccer. After that, all her free time went toward perfecting her game and kicking mud into her opponent's face. I never acquired a taste for mud; naturally we parted ways.

"Hey," I say with a timid wave.

"Hey," she says without looking up.

Connie's always been on the quiet side: hard to read and deliberate with her words. I suppose she has to be, now that her brother is famous.

Kite's real name is Kai Xu. He debuted under a stage name, like most members of Karnival. We attended the same preschool and were classmates until he dropped out of eighth grade to become a K-pop trainee with Dream Drop Media. The story of how he got scouted is one of luck. After clicking through a series of recommended videos, a talent agent stumbled across Kite's YouTube channel—all thirteen videos of his piano renditions of hit singles by big K-pop artists—and invited him to audition in LA.

An hour before his audition, Kite called me to ask if I would wish him good luck. His nerves were getting the best of him. He thought being Chinese American would disqualify him and that nobody would want someone who wasn't already fluent in Korean, not even a small but reputable label like Dream Drop.

Memorizing lyrics was one thing, but writing them was another, he said.

Despite his self-doubt, he got a callback and moved to South Korea shortly after. He hasn't been home since. His parents have gone to visit him twice in the last four years.

It hurt to see him go.

In elementary school, I liked having him around.

Knowing he was around.

Every weekday morning we waited at the same bus stop, and every weekday afternoon we walked home together. We went trick-or-treating together every Halloween, and at the end of the night we'd pool all our candy into one huge pile. I let him have his chocolate, and he let me have my fruity candy. Connie took whatever was left, in addition to her own stash.

Kite was my go-to person whenever we had to pair up in class. And I was his. We refused to work with others. It got to the point where our fifth-grade teacher had to assign partners. He called us inseparable—that is, until he separated us.

Kite and I spent less time together in middle school. He met new people, and so did I. Being neighbors saved our friendship from deteriorating altogether—long enough for Kite to say goodbye not only to me but to everyone and everything else he left behind for a new life in a new country.

For what it's worth, I was the first person he told when Dream Drop reached out to him. Calling me from LA before his audition must count for something.

I wanted to keep in touch, but his training schedule and confidentiality agreement, which barred him from having any unauthorized social media presence, made coordinating a phone call nearly impossible. This was before you factored in the thirteen-hour time difference.

We exchanged emails here and there the first year he was

gone. He took a whole month to respond to one email I sent, and then he stopped responding altogether. Anything I hear about him now comes either from the internet or from Mrs. Xu.

But I'm happy Kite is out there living his dream. He wanted to be a singer ever since fifth grade, when he discovered 2PM and SHINee. He was the one who introduced me to K-pop, proving to me that heaven does exist on earth.

I'd be lying if I said I didn't feel a little special having a personal history with Kite. But it does have its drawbacks. Over the years people have befriended me in order to get close to Kite. They lost interest in me as soon as they realized I couldn't fulfill their fantasies.

Now imagine being Connie.

There was an incident last year where the Xus were bombarded with fan mail for weeks on end after someone leaked Kite's home address. The letters they received could fill a bathtub. The mailman started joking about how the Xus better send Connie to Hogwarts before a burly giant broke down their door. Nobody was laughing, however, when some fans stalked Connie on her way home and begged her to deliver their love letters to Kite.

Dream Drop released a statement instructing fans to stop harassing Kite's family, which didn't deter the extreme ones, the sasaengs. It took multiple attempts to get the police to act, and when they did, it was because our neighbors filed a collective complaint about how teenage girls were setting up camp on our street and creating a public disturbance.

"I heard that Lawrence asked you to prom." Connie breaks the silence between us.

I blink away my surprise. "He didn't ask me, but I heard he wanted to."

"Looks like I dodged a bullet." Connie slips some money onto the table and starts to leave. "See you later," she says before going out the door.

Jason emerges from the kitchen with a baguette sticking out of a paper bag.

I cross my arms. "What took so long? Did you have to go out and buy jalapeños?"

"Nope, just taking my sweet time, hoping you and Connie would find something to talk about," he says with a sly grin.

"You're not playing matchmaker, are you? Just because I go both ways doesn't—"

"I just want to hear Connie's voice once in a while. She eats here more than you, but it's always your voice buzzing in my head. Kind of like a mosquito you can't get rid of."

"Oh, please. As if anyone could get rid of wǒ."

"What does wǒ mean?"

"It means *me*. This is elementary Chinese, Jason."

"Did I mention you're like a mosquito I can't get rid of?"

I help Mom and Aunt Mei close up, and we get home around ten. We share the banh mis and have them with some lemon balm tea.

Before I call it a night, the doorbell rings. I find Ester outside in her baro't saya, her updo about to come undone. She welcomes herself inside.

"I take it prom went well?" I follow Ester as she charges into my room and motions me to unbutton the clasp around her neck that holds her dress up.

"Better than expected. Kellie won prom queen. You would've earned bragging rights if you'd been her date." Ester lets her dress fall to her ankles. "Steph and I were going to drive down to Kellie's beach house for prom weekend, but something came up."

I rummage through my closet for an extra pair of pajamas and set them aside on my vanity. I already know Ester plans to sleep over.

"Damn, Ester." I watch as she brushes her hair and helps herself to my makeup wipes. "Don't leave me in suspense. What happened?"

"So I'm in the bathroom, reapplying my mascara—"

"I love the color, by the way."

"Me too! Who knew teal could look this sexy?" Not missing a beat, she picks up from where she left off. "So I'm in the bathroom, reapplying my mascara, getting ready to leave, when Steph asks if I heard any news about Karnival. I check Twitter, and people are going crazy about Kite setting his Instagram to private."

Only three members are on Instagram: Xiaoming, Wayne, and Kite. They opened their accounts back in February after getting approval from Dream Drop.

"Do you know why?" I ask. "It wasn't that long ago he opened an account."

"No one knows. I doubt it means anything good. Why open an account, only to make it private? Maybe someone hacked it? Ugh, this better be a publicity stunt and not the beginning of some scandal."

I grimace. "I hope you're right—wait, did you bail on prom weekend just to tell me this? You could've told me over the phone."

Ester is stunned into silence. Common sense isn't so common when you're a Firework, apparently. "Well, it's not like I wanted to stay at Kellie's beach house that badly. I don't really belong in Kellie's circle anyway."

"Is Stephanie mad that you ditched her?"

"Nope, she seemed relieved."

Probably because she won't have to listen to Karnival on the way to the shore.

A sinking feeling unsettles my stomach: Stephanie may have been spared, but I'm not so lucky.

POSTED BY MYLIGHTKITE ON MAY 19.

I'd like to be a voice of reason, now that Fireworks are freaking out over Kite disabling his Instagram. Karnival should've explained why, to minimize the confusion, but they also don't owe us an explanation. We all know how crazy the fandom can get. Sasaengs were probably harassing Kite with DMs, and now Kite's taking a break from social media. Remember when that girl sent Xiaoming a nude photo with her fan letter, or when people hounded Kite's family with fan mail? That type of invasive behavior takes a toll on idols. They're humans, too. This means we Fireworks need to step up! True fans respect their idols.

#lovemeansrespect #stopsasaengs #stanwithkite
#fireworksstaystrong

3

Can someone call an ambulance? I'm about to keel over.

What's the point of graduating high school if your school can't be bothered to make sure the HVAC is working during the ceremony so you don't die from heatstroke?

"Glad that's over," Ester says, sighing, as we reconvene outside the ceremony hall to savor the fresh air, our ruby-red graduation gowns billowing behind us. "Whoever installed that crappy sound system needs to be terminated—yesterday! I couldn't understand a single word during the valedictorian's speech."

"Kellie worked hard on it, and how does the school reward her? With a screechy mic," Stephanie huffs, unpinning her graduation cap from her hair to fan out her wilted curls. "I'm still reeling over the fact that she asked you out," she tacks on, eyeballing me as I shed my gown to reveal the midi dress underneath. "What does she see in you?"

"I ask myself the same thing." I fold up my gown and tuck it under my arm.

As runner-up for salutatorian, Stephanie has more in common with Kellie than I do. I would have thought Stephanie was Kellie's type. I don't know why Kellie asked me out, but that ship has sailed, and there's no use dwelling on it. I'm sure Kellie's already put it behind her, and I'm sure everyone here is ready to put high school behind them.

I know I am.

I said my goodbyes prior to the ceremony. My yearbook is littered with signatures, most of them some variation of *It was fun having you as a student* or *It was fun having class together*. The longest ones are, of course, from Ester and Stephanie. They each took up half a page—after I told them to write in ten-point letters. Both signed their names with their own display of self-importance: Ester Tan with big and bold capitalization and Stephanie Nguyen with fancy cursive and elongated downstrokes.

On the last page of my yearbook, I reserved a spot for Ms. Hopkins, my favorite history teacher, and Mr. Knopf, the coolest student teacher I've ever had. I hope college professors are like them. I took a photo with them on the last day of school; I wasn't sure if I'd see them tonight, and it looks like I made the right call.

It's well past sunset, and the area is so poorly lit, I can hardly see two steps ahead of me. I pity whoever saved group photos for after the ceremony. I use the flashlight on my phone to navigate the sea of families around me. Carefully I climb over a stone barricade to cut through the parking lot.

Stephanie and Ester have forgotten where their parents parked, and as it turns out, so have I—even though our families parked next to each other. Since no one wants to own up to it by texting our parents, we aimlessly search for a familiar license plate, our patience thinning into exasperation until I spot a magenta star flashing in the distance.

Aunt Mei predicted my memory lapse and came prepared with the glow-in-the-dark wand I used to play with as a kid. Why she still has it is beyond me. Nevertheless, I follow the star, and at last, our families are together.

"We were about to send out a search party," Mom says as Aunt

Mei taps me on the nose with the tip of the wand before opening her arms for a hug.

Then I'm hugging my mom, Stephanie's mom, Ester's mom, and Ester's older sister (who once tricked me and Ester into believing that Karnival was disbanding by creating a fake Wiki page). The dads, sans my own, congratulate me with a pat on the back, their smiles stiff but well-meaning. *You survived the shark-infested waters of high school; on to the next adventure,* they imply with their stoicism. Mr. Tan and Mr. Nguyen are not talkative people, so a pat on the back from them is very touching.

But that doesn't stop Ester from bursting into sobs as she smacks her dad for being an unfeeling robot on this momentous night.

"Don't act like it's all over!" she cries, tugging at his shirtsleeve the way a dog clamps down on someone's pants and thrashes it with all its might. He rubs her back and brings a handkerchief to her nose. She misses and shoots a web of snot into his hand.

"You're such a crybaby," says her sister. "Wait until college, when it's *really* over."

"Come on, we have a dinner reservation," Mom says, starting the car.

"See you at the restaurant." Stephanie flicks the end of my cap, knocking it askew. "By the way, I got Ester's ugly cry on camera," she says, waving her phone in triumph.

Ester is easy to pick on, because she wears her heart like a rainbow pin on her shirt, but I know Stephanie. Her eyes are glossy with unshed tears, and the cover of darkness can't hide them from me.

In the car, I wipe the sweat from my pits with a tissue and roll the windows down, welcoming the evening breeze as it cools my skin and combs through my hair. Aunt Mei looks back at me from the front passenger seat and hands me a red envelope.

"From Mrs. Xu," she says. "Don't forget to thank her."

I open the envelope and find a crisp one-hundred-dollar bill inside, along with a note: CONGRATULATIONS, LULU. YOU EARNED IT!

I seriously did.

Four years of commuting the same route every weekday without being tardy; four years of studying my way through honors and AP classes; four years of working toward this very moment when I can finally tell myself I earned it.

This September I'll be starting my first semester at Rutgers University, double-majoring in Chinese and economics while minoring in Korean. That's the plan for now, at least. I had my choice of Penn State and UC Santa Barbara but didn't score any scholarships—not that I'm gutted over it, because Ester will be with me. We're staying home and commuting to campus this year, but we're hoping to room together sophomore year.

Ester's heart is set on computer science; Stephanie's is set on Barnard's English department. Of the three of us, Stephanie is the only one who knows what she wants to do after graduation. She wants to go into technical writing. I didn't know that was a profession until she explained it to me. Guess I never put much thought into who writes instruction manuals.

Stephanie will only be two hours away, but I'll miss her—as much as I would if she had gone with UC Berkeley, her second choice. All the more reason why she has to help me fulfill my summer itinerary, and I'm not asking for much: I want to hit the beach, embark on an eating spree in New York City, and get high off sugar at Hersheypark. I'm not dragging her to the Moroccan desert or forcing her to go paragliding with me in Switzerland.

That would be Ester.

"Dad called earlier," Mom says, stopping at a red light. Stephanie's family pulls up in the next lane and honks at us. "He said he tried calling you, but your phone was off."

"It wouldn't have been off had he bothered to remember when the ceremony started and that California is three hours behind," I grumble, checking my phone for any new voice mails, only to find my inbox empty. "Does he want me to call him back?"

"Not unless you want to."

"I don't."

Dad's with his family in California, and I'm with my family on the other side of the country. The divorce was ages ago, and I don't need a cheating scumbag for a dad.

Everything's peachy.

The light turns green, and the car jolts forward as Mom presses the gas pedal. I wave at Ester as her family zooms past in their minivan with "Lights Fantastic" on blast.

Whatever makes her happy, I tell myself.

We hit another series of traffic lights before arriving at a dim sum restaurant reminiscent of an imperial palace in the Forbidden City, with its pyramidal roof and towering pillars painted a tacky red, the symbol of good luck. Despite the wannabe-royal décor, which seems to be compensating for something the restaurant lacks, the food here is phenomenal—and authentic. Mom loves their shumai and egg-custard tarts, says the flavor reminds her of Taiwan.

As soon as Mom cuts the engine, I leap out of the car and race Stephanie and Ester up the concrete flight of stairs to the lion statues flanking the entrance to the restaurant. Stephanie's ahead by a few steps, but I quickly catch up to her and we reach the door at the exact same time. Ester stands several feet behind us, having given up midway.

Sometimes I let Stephanie win. Sometimes she lets me win. Ever since our families started coming here, Ester loses on purpose.

Every time.

After I gorge myself with shrimp dumplings, stewed chicken feet, and coconut pudding, our parents let Stephanie, Ester, and me take one of the cars so we can prepare for a last-minute sleepover. Stephanie's house has a furnished basement with two sofa beds, one of which is reserved solely for Ester, because she rolls around in her sleep and hogs the blanket.

We stop at my house first. I scurry inside and shove everything I need into a travel bag. I grab my *Ouran High School Host Club* DVD set before rushing out. As I reach the driveway I hear a door suddenly slam open.

Over the rose hedge, I see Connie storming out of her house. The driveway light blinks on, outlining the shadows of her face and the unmistakable fury in her expression. Mrs. Xu calls after her. Connie freezes midstride and snaps, "He can do what he wants, and I'll do whatever I want! Now leave me alone."

I watch Connie's figure sprinting in and out of the darkness as she passes streetlight after streetlight, then focus my attention on Mrs. Xu.

This probably isn't a good time to thank her for the card.

I struggle for something to say.

Should I comfort her or pretend I didn't hear them? Family disputes are rarely simple, and I'm not exactly sure who here needs comforting. Connie isn't the dramatic type. She doesn't raise her voice like that or run out of the house without reason. Yet I can't imagine what Mrs. Xu could've done to warrant such a reaction.

"I'm sorry you had to see that," says Mrs. Xu. A tremor runs through her voice. She swallows her tears and clears her throat.

"Everything okay?" I ask, even though the answer is obvious.

Mrs. Xu manages a strained smile. "Kai's coming back."

"If this is a joke, I don't find it funny!" Ester screams as we arrive at Stephanie's.

She was in the car when Connie stormed out, but because she had to listen to Karnival, she missed the commotion. I didn't spill all the details, like the family drama I wasn't supposed to witness, but I did tell her about Kite coming back.

"Did Mrs. Xu say when and for how long? Does this mean the world tour is happening? Is Wayne going to perform in New York? Someone please tell me!" Ester squeals as we retrieve our stuff from the trunk and enter the garage.

"It's June, kind of late to announce a summer world tour," I say as we descend the basement stairs.

"Maybe they're changing it to a fall tour," Ester says.

"Doubt it. Most fans will be in school by then."

"Would it kill you to let me dream a little?"

Down in the basement, we fumble around for the light switch.

Stephanie probes the wall, accidentally groping me before she finds the switch. The ceiling lights flicker on, and immediately I notice the billiard table and grand piano in the corner draped in black velvet. They weren't there the last time I came over.

"Mom and Dad's latest hobbies," Stephanie says. She leaves to fetch us some bath towels while Ester and I rearrange the furniture to make room for the pull-out beds.

The basement is completely furnished, with a bathroom to boot. It's the Nguyens' game room. It's undergone various transformations over the years, from a workout studio to a gaming console shrine to a home theater before finally becoming a mix of all three.

A boxing bag used to hang from the ceiling. Mr. Nguyen removed it after I tackled it in midair and fractured my collarbone in eighth grade. It was Stephanie's fault. She made up a game where we were supposed to run full speed at the boxing bag to see who could leap onto it and hold on the longest. I was the first to go and the last.

"So . . . ," Ester hesitantly begins, "Mrs. Xu didn't specify when he's coming back?"

"No, she didn't. It could be tomorrow, next week, or next month." I recall Mrs. Xu's shaky smile, and a dozen questions waltz through my mind.

"What's wrong?" Stephanie asks, returning with a pile of towels. She tosses Ester a pink one and signals her to shower first.

"Mrs. Xu didn't sound exactly happy about Kite returning," I explain, trying to be vague. "She wasn't mad or upset, but something seemed off. . . ."

Stephanie scrunches her nose. "Shouldn't she be overwhelmed with joy now that she gets to see her son without having to fly to another country? Also, shouldn't *you* be overwhelmed with joy? He was your best friend before I came along."

"I don't know." The strangeness of it all lingers in my mind for another moment or two, and then I sigh.

"You didn't answer my question."

I stare at Stephanie but don't take her bait.

"I hope you brought *Ouran High School* with you, because I won't be sleeping tonight!" Ester says as she prances into the bathroom. "I almost wish you hadn't told me. Almost!"

We hear the lock click into place.

"She should seriously consider getting into theater." Shaking my head, I plop myself pretzel-style onto the rug and start unpacking my bags. "Good thing I had the foresight to—"

Stephanie and I look up as Ester tumbles out of the bathroom, half naked and screaming. I prepare myself for whatever bug's life she wants me to end. I roll up a magazine, battle ready. Then I notice that Ester isn't jumping around from foot to foot. She's tight-lipped and grim as she grips her phone with both hands.

"Kite's leaving Karnival."

WAYNE TWEETED ON JUNE 18 FROM THE OFFICIAL KARNIVAL ACCOUNT, @DREAMDROPMEDIA.

We are sad to say that Kite will be taking a break from all idol activities until further notice. He overexerted himself during practice, and his doctor recommended that he rest for a few months. The rest of Karnival will continue with our schedule, and Kite will do his best to get better and come back stronger. Fireworks, let's wish him a speedy recovery. Thank you for all your love and support!

4

A week after Karnival's announcement, the girls and I drive down to Point Pleasant for a day at the beach. I'm stretched out under the sun in a turquoise bikini, basking in the heat after a dip in the ocean, my hair drying off in the spiraling breeze.

Ester sits behind me under the beach umbrella, leafing through a magazine, while Stephanie languishes by the shore, bored out of her mind as some guy tries wooing her with talk of free booze and live music.

"Take a hint. She's not interested!" I yell over the sound of seagulls flying overhead. "Drink water if you're that thirsty!"

The guy glares at me. I point him toward the ocean, my face screaming *Any day now!* In a last-ditch effort, he asks Stephanie out to dinner, which she declines with a hard no. He trudges off but not without flipping me off first.

Stephanie joins me on our communal beach towel and takes the watermelon out from the cooler. Ester draws another line in the sand, bringing the number of guys to hit on Stephanie to five.

"I can't with these desperadoes," I grumble, crawling under the umbrella to reapply sunscreen.

Stephanie attracts attention wherever she goes. I've seen kids run up to her to ask if she's a Disney Princess (meaning Mulan).

I don't know if Stephanie should take it as a compliment or an insult, but that's not the worst of it. I'm sick of guys who approach her and the first question they hurl at her is *What kind of Asian are you?* Followed by the inevitable *Let me guess, you're Korean.*

No, you nimrod. She's Vietnamese. The last name Nguyen is the Vietnamese equivalent of Smith.

"You can't with anyone," says Stephanie. The guys around us crane their necks to steal a glance at her tiny bikini bottom. "How long have you been single again?"

"Do middle school relationships count?" I ask.

"They don't," says Ester, her eyes never leaving her magazine.

"How about when Reiko and I got together?"

"You went on three dates with her. That's not a relationship."

"Guess that means I've been forever single." I shrug as Stephanie uncaps the container of watermelon and hands me a fork.

Of the three of us, I have the least amount of dating experience. I had a crush on Irvine Hunter freshman year. I mistook the hungry gazes he used to direct at me during gym class for a sign of passion, when in reality he was simply hungry.

Then there was Reiko Harada junior year. She couldn't decide if she was as straight as an arrow or flexible like al dente pasta, and she needed to French kiss me to find out. After three dates, where we mostly traded saliva, she dropped me and started a long-distance thing with a girl she met online.

In short, my love life is nonexistent.

I wouldn't say I'm frustrated. Disappointed, yes, but not dissatisfied. If something happens, it happens, and if nothing happens, then nothing happens. But an ex or two would make it easier to relate to Stephanie and Ester and their relationship woes.

Stephanie had a history of short-term relationships before

dating Ken for two years. Last year they had an amicable breakup after he got accepted to Boston University. She's remained single since. Her prom date was some tennis player from another school. He asked to be exclusive, but she shot him down.

As for Ester, she had this on-and-off thing with Leo when she was a junior and he was a college freshman. He was the definition of an absent boyfriend, only hitting her up when he wanted something. I'm glad she ended it, and I have Karnival to thank for that.

At least Wayne doesn't treat her as a booty call.

"Do you ever think your standards are too high?" Stephanie asks.

"What do you think my standards are?" I ask in return.

Ester stops reading and trades a devious smirk with Stephanie.

"Not too long ago, when you were gaga over Karnival, Kite and Xiaoming kept popping up in your search history," Stephanie says. "You were constantly looking them up on your phone. You had Kite as your wallpaper, remember?"

"Emphasis on *had*! That was over a year ago!" I wave my phone at her so she can take a close look at my current wallpaper, of a cartoon cat in an astronaut suit.

"So you say"—Stephanie cracks open a can of iced tea—"but he was your wallpaper for months. Makes me wonder if your ideal type is a guy who looks like a bad boy but in reality is a gooey marshmallow."

"You literally just described Wayne," Ester says, her eyes glossing over. "God, what I would give to eat that spicy maple cookie."

Stephanie's referring to a photo I once set as my home screen: of Kite in a fitted black turtleneck and spiked combat boots, posing with an umbrella slung over his shoulder while standing in front of a graffitied wall. He looked smoking hot with his dark eyeliner and silver hair—except he wore the sweetest smile on his face. So sweet it would give you cavities.

I could see his middle school self peeking through that smile. There was something reassuring about it, which is why I liked it so much. Though I kept that to myself.

But that was back when I used to call myself a Firework.

"If we're talking about *ideal* types, well, why wouldn't I shoot for the stars and go for a K-pop idol?" I ask.

"You can pine after whoever you want, but Wayne is off-limits," Ester says, knowing she doesn't have any actual claim over him. "Besides, if we're seriously talking about going for K-pop idols, Kite *is* coming home this summer. Why not shoot your shot, have a summer fling?"

Like that would ever happen in this life or the next.

K-pop idols have an image to uphold. Millions of eyes are on them. Enraging fans and risking their reputation for a summer fling isn't the wisest career choice. Getting involved with an idol isn't the smartest thing to do either—unless you don't mind jealous fangirls creating a website dedicated to how much they hate you and wish to see you dead.

Just this morning, while I was changing into my bikini, Mom barged into my room and told me Kite will be flying into JFK airport. Tonight. Under no circumstances am I to tell anyone about this.

Dream Drop hasn't made any announcements about Kite returning home, only that he's on hiatus after overworking himself. If fans catch wind of this, they'll come running. No one in our neighborhood wants campers on our street, blocking driveways and scaring the stray cats that roam our backyards. Mom warned me that if word does get out, I might have to stay with a relative.

"Awfully quiet there, Lulu." Stephanie chuckles. "Thinking about that summer fling?"

"Why are you guys acting as if Kite would actually want anything to do with me?" I stuff a cube of watermelon into my mouth and chew ferociously. "For all I know, he still thinks of me as the little kid he used to swap candy with."

"Now you're just fishing for compliments."

"She'll be fishing for a lot more once Kite returns." Ester guffaws.

I lower my sunglasses and glare at them.

The late-afternoon breeze rolls in as we make our trip back to the parking lot and load everything into Stephanie's car. Our giant cooler is lighter than it was this morning and doesn't require a double set of hands. Stephanie starts the car and revs up the air conditioner. I take a seat in the front while Ester shuffles into the back, balancing a tray of waffle fries in one hand.

"According to your oh-so-thorough itinerary, Ms. Lulu Li," Stephanie begins, affecting a British accent, "we're on schedule to tour Hersheypark next week. Once we satiate your appetite for sugar and thrills, we'll then embark on a culinary adventure in Manhattan."

"Right you are," I say as she pulls out of the parking lot.

"We should stop at the Crayola Factory before Hersheypark," says Ester. No response. "What? It's on the way, might as well." Still, neither Stephanie nor I say anything. "Do you guys want me to share my fries or not? 'Cause if you do, you better answer me."

"If I say no, will you still share?" I twist my body around, and for a fraction of a second, my nose tingles with a sneeze. Ester takes the opportunity to shove a fry up my nose and cracks up like one of those hyenas from *The Lion King*. "Hot, hot, hot!"

Stephanie imitates Ester's laugh with a theatrical trill, and together they celebrate my pain. I shove a tissue up my nose to clean out the salt and grease. Sometimes I wonder how I'm friends with these girls. But then I recall my own history of dorky moments and how they've come to my rescue plenty of times— like when Ester claimed a fart that was mine during the SATs or when Stephanie gave me her Prada jacket after my tampon soaked through my shorts—and the world feels right again.

Forty minutes later, Stephanie drives up to a little blue house with a white picket fence. Ester takes her things and waves goodbye.

Next stop is my house. As we turn onto my street, we pass Connie on the sidewalk in her oversized hoodie. Her heat tolerance is astounding. Up ahead I spot Mr. and Mrs. Xu climbing into their car. They peel away from the curb right as we pull up to my house.

Stephanie pops the trunk and helps me carry some items inside. Mom and Aunt Mei aren't home, as expected. I consider lending them a hand at the bakery, but the tingling heat of the sun continues to warm my skin, and even in this quiet house, I can hear the distant call of the ocean, lulling me into a daze. Suddenly I feel light-headed.

Like this day was nothing but one big whirlwind.

"Want me to stay for a bit?" asks Stephanie.

I think back to my conversation with Mom this morning and pass on her offer. A fleeting hint of suspicion crosses Stephanie's face before she sees herself out.

I check the clock hanging above the flower vase near the door. A quarter to six. A good time for a nap.

My room is just the way I left it, except for the pile of neatly folded laundry at the end of my bed. I move the pile onto my desk and collapse into bed, staining my sheets with the smell of coconut oil and seawater.

✳

Hours have passed by the time I wake up. The sun has already set. My face feels like an oil slick, and there's a sour taste in my mouth that I can't identify. A slither of light illuminates the crack under my bedroom door, intermittently broken by someone walking by.

Mom and Aunt Mei are home.

That means I slept for a long time, longer than what constitutes a nap.

Stretching myself out with a sigh, I roll off my bed and freshen up.

Once my breath is nice and minty, I head for the living room. Mom's lounging in the recliner. Aunt Mei's on the sofa, enjoying the electric foot massager I saved up to get her for her forty-fifth birthday.

"Long day?" I peer over Aunt Mei's shoulder as she flips through a magazine.

"A customer tried scamming us into giving him change for a one-hundred-dollar bill he claimed to have paid with," Mom says pointedly.

"Did you rip him a new one?" I ask.

"That's inappropriate, but yes, I did." Mom rolls her shoulders and shuts her eyes. "Dad called me today. He wants to know when you're available to visit."

"You mean visit *his family*," I fire back, my nasty tone directed not at my mom but at the person who isn't here to receive it. "If he wants to know so badly, why didn't he call *me*?"

Back when the divorce was fresh and Dad cared about his custodial rights, I had to fly out to California the summer after freshman year to stay in his swanky mansion with his new wife, Katherine, and her son from a previous marriage.

Katherine was warm and gracious when we met, overly so, clearly trying to compensate for her role in the affair. She greeted me in Chinese, or tried to anyway.

On the first night of my stay, she cooked something that tried but failed to be beef hofan. It wouldn't have tasted half bad had she measured the soy sauce and sesame oil. The bean sprouts were cooked to mush, too. She's used to making frittatas and lasagna, she said, after everyone at the dinner table took their first bite of hofan and felt their tongue shrivel up.

I give her credit for trying. At least she's better than her son, Kyle. She had to bribe him with video games to convince him to join us for dinner each night. His presence didn't mitigate all the stilted conversations or prolonged silences.

"Dad can go suck an egg." He made no attempt to attend my graduation ceremony, so why should I visit him in California? Once I turn eighteen, in August, I won't have to see or hear from him ever again.

"At least let him know you won't be visiting. That way he'll stop pestering me," Mom says, a sharp edge lining her voice.

"Understood." I send Dad a quick text, and the deed is done. I'm about to put on a movie when headlights flood my peripheral vision. I hear the sound of crushed gravel and hastily dim the indoor lights, ignoring Aunt Mei's feeble protest as I peel back the curtains. From my angle, I can't see anything beyond the rose hedge dividing us and the Xus. I hear not one but three car doors slam shut, followed by the rumbling of luggage wheels rolling across the pavement.

"Honey, stop being a creep," Mom says. "Remember what we talked about?"

"You warned me not to tip off any fangirls. You didn't say anything—"

"—about being a fangirl?" Mom grins smugly as I scramble for a response.

"I'm not a Karnival fan anymore." Mom arches a brow. "Well, I'm not as big a fan as I *used* to be. Calling me a fan is a disservice to real Fireworks. I'm just happy that Mr. and Mrs. Xu finally get to spend time with their son."

"If you say so."

"I'm serious."

Mom simply smirks.

Dear Kai,

Congrats on signing with Dream Drop! There's no doubt in my mind you'll make it big in South Korea. I hope this is everything you thought it would be—and more! Things will be different without you. I'll miss you, but nothing should stop you from chasing your dreams. Please stay in touch!

Sending you all the best wishes,
Lulu

Unsent letter written the night before Kai left for South Korea, currently stowed away in a shoebox with other mementos.

5

Kite's return has stirred some mixed feelings in me.

He's finally back after four years.

Up until Karnival's debut, I wasn't even sure what he looked like anymore. When I saw the "Lights Fantastic" MV for the first time, I mistook Yoosung's soft features for Kai. I had to re-watch the MV three times before I recognized him—past all the makeup, the hair dye, and the screen that separated us—and when I did, I cried.

I was happy that he'd achieved his dream, but he wasn't the person I knew anymore. And with no phone calls or emails to hold on to, reality sunk in.

Kite, not Kai—that unreachable version of him—was all I had.

So I supported him from afar, as his fan. Without that, there was nothing connecting us. Calling him Kite was an adjustment, but I welcomed the distinction. I had to stop searching for the boy I used to know and see him as the idol he'd become.

Of course, Kite wasn't the only reason I became a Karnival fan. All the members are handsome, talented, and likeable in their own way, and together they have this mesmerizing presence that demands attention—but being a Firework eventually got to be too much.

I had to focus on the friends I did have, not on whatever

one-way connection I had with Karnival. I could still support Kite without following every piece of news about him.

Kite moved on, and I had to, too.

And I did . . . or so I thought.

Now that Kite's back, I can't get him out of my head. The fact that I keep checking to see if his bedroom light is on makes me feel like the world's biggest loser. Even so, the shame isn't enough to erase him from my thoughts.

Is everything in his room the way he left it? What's in his room anyway? Will sleeping in his old bed evoke memories of when he was Kai and not Kite? And, more important, why am I imagining his bed?

I want to know, but I also don't want to. I wouldn't be thinking these things at all if Kite were still eleven thousand miles away. My sanity is unraveling.

Just the thought of him has me tossing and turning in bed. My body can't decide between hot or cold. I'm readjusting my blanket and flipping my pillow every minute, like I'm anxiously awaiting a present from the tooth fairy. I try reciting the original Pokémon ending rap, hoping it'll have some hypnotic effect, but I end up driving myself nuts when I can't recall the name of that origami bird.

By the time three a.m. creeps up on me, I'm at my desk, watching the MV to "Dark Hour." The MV begins with Xiaoming wandering the dusty halls of an abandoned mansion with a candlestick raised to his face. Outside the moon is full, but its light can't penetrate the woods shrouding the mansion. Eerie harp music plays in the background, growing louder the farther Xiaoming walks. His electric-yellow hair and white suit are an anomaly against the morbid paintings and cobwebs that line the walls.

Out of nowhere, a gust of wind snuffs out the candle, plunging him into darkness, tendrils of smoke and inky shadows wrapping around him, painting his clothing black. The grandfather clock in the foyer strikes midnight. All the doors inside the mansion fling open one after another.

Cue the piano and bass synthesizer.

Souls of the dead materialize out of thin air and flood the hallways, their pearly light illuminating a path for Xiaoming. As he follows the ghostly trail, Wayne appears before him, cloaked in a similar black ensemble, and escorts him to a gilded banquet hall, where the other Karnival members await him around a long, ornate table.

Everyone's got the smoky eye shadow down to a T. Kite looks like evil royalty as he lazes in a chair while tossing an apple up and down with one hand.

Then there's a break in the story, where all members are inexplicably dancing together, alongside backup dancers dressed in butler suits. The MV is a montage of dance breaks, close-up shots of all the members looking sexy as hell, and low-effort storytelling. O-Kei gets delegated the high notes while everyone else gets a few lines here and there before the chorus takes over. Xiaoming, the rapper, has a fairly lengthy solo.

One hardcore Firework, mylightkite, who is very active on Tumblr, calculates the amount of screen time each member gets in every MV. Kite has the least amount in "Dark Hour" and also the least number of lines—ironic, considering how it's impossible to tear your eyes away from him, with his long eyelashes and lingering gaze that raises the hair on your arms. . . .

At this point, I'm too distracted to even attempt to sleep. I grab my sneakers, tiptoe into the kitchen, slide the screen door open, and exit into the backyard.

The night air is brisk. As I walk beneath the star-spangled sky, tiny bumps begin to dot my arms. Boxer shorts and a tank top aren't very insulating. A tinge of regret nips at me as my mind flashes back to the sweatshirt I elected to ignore.

But it comes as quickly as it goes as I outrun the evening chill, making laps around the neighborhood. I am breathless by the time I return to my street. Before I reach the Xus, a fluffy mass of black fur intercepts me on the sidewalk and stares up at me with round yellow eyes.

"Forgive me, Maru. I don't have any food." I turn my pockets inside out for emphasis.

Maru, the elusive stray cat that's been coming around for the last few months, narrows her eyes at me, disappointed.

"Don't judge me." I drop into a squat and clap my hands. "Will you let me pet you, my lovely queen?" Maru thinks long and hard about that. Just as I'm about to take her silence for a no, she rolls onto her back and sprawls out. "Pet, pet, pet, pet, pet," I sing as I tickle her tummy.

A velvety laugh interrupts this auspicious moment.

Maru springs up on all fours. I follow her with my eyes as she trots over to a tall figure silhouetted against the purpling sky.

Kite walks out from the shadows.

My pulse quickens. I can't hear anything beyond the pounding of my heart, now engorged with blood and memories, ready to explode from my chest like hot confetti. I hold my breath, some foolish part of me worried he might be an illusion easily taken by the wind. He stops shy of arm's length, close enough for me to see him in his entirety but not enough to graze him with my fingertips.

He is exactly as he appears in photos. His eyes are a sunny shade of brown bordering on liquid amber depending on how the

49

light hits them. They remind me of raw honey. (Is there a way to get a toothache just by looking at someone?) His lips are drawn tight and crooked at the corners as though he's on the verge of laughter. Gone are the soft edges from middle school; his cheekbones are high and pronounced, giving way to slightly sunken cheeks that melt into a sharp and sturdy jawline.

Maru breaks the silence with a *meow*.

Finally I release the breath I've been holding. My heart continues to sing, albeit with less vigor. Kite scoops Maru into his arms and cradles her like the baby she is. He blows her a kiss before his eyes flicker back to mine.

"Hey, Lovely."

See you in middle school, Lovely! I'm coming over for ice cream later. I'll bring the chocolate syrup and whipped cream. I'm counting on you to have sprinkles.

Kai's message in Lulu's fifth-grade yearbook.

6

L ulu Li.

If you say it over and over again, it sort of sounds like *lovely.*

That's how I got my nickname from Kite: when I outran all the second-grade boys in a game of tag and left them calling after me as they ate mouthfuls of dust.

Only Kite calls me Lovely. That hasn't changed, even now, as we stand here in the dead of night. Me, lost for words, feeling naked and exposed in my pajamas. Him, handsome in the moonlight, cradling a cat in his arms.

"I came out to catch some air, didn't expect to see you," Kite says as he breezes past me with a nonchalance I can't bring myself to imitate. "Do you usually go running at this hour?" He swirls around to face me with a curious tilt to his head as if to say, *Well?*

"Tonight I . . ." My voice takes on an odd pitch. I clear my throat. "No, I don't. . . . I'm surprised you're still up. Aren't you jetlagged or . . . something?"

"A fourteen-hour flight wipes you out, but I was passed out for ten of them. Sleep is the last thing I need," he says as Maru swipes at his face. "Whose cat is this?"

"No one's, she's her own cat. Her name's Maru." I speak as though I'm a proud parent.

"She's pretty round for a stray." Kite taps Maru on the nose and gives her air kisses. She returns his affection by baring her fangs, eliciting a chuckle from him.

He sets her down on the grass. Trotting around in circles, she begins to beg for treats. Her tail sways in midair, furling and unfurling as though it has a mind of its own. When no one gives in to her pleas, she quickly loses interest and disappears into the bushes.

Now it's just the two of us.

Seeing Kite here is unreal.

I didn't want to make a big commotion out of his return—though I kind of already did—but now that he's here in front of me, I have no idea what to say or how to act. I know better than to scream and wake the entire neighborhood, but knowing what *not* to do is a far cry from knowing what to do.

Kite and I aren't strangers, far from it, but going in for a hug doesn't seem right, and the urge to do so isn't coming to me as naturally as it would if Stephanie or Ester were the ones here. How familiar is too familiar? Kite's my childhood friend, but that doesn't mean he's my friend now. Can you call someone you haven't talked to, let alone seen, in four years a friend?

More important, how does he see me?

"I should get—"

"So how've you—"

A nervous chuckle escapes me. I motion for Kite to go first.

"I was going to ask how you've been," Kite says, looking me over from top to bottom. I pinch the hem of my pajama shorts and tug them farther down my thighs. "But it's late. I don't want to keep you." I stare at him, dumbfounded. "We'll talk tomorrow?"

"Y-yeah . . ." I stop gaping at him like I'm waiting for someone to feed me a hot dog. "I'm sure we have plenty to talk about."

"I'll hold you to it, then." Kite shapes his forefinger and thumb into a gun, and with a click of his tongue, he fires an invisible bullet at me. But it's not the bullet that slays me. It's the little wink he shoots me as he shuffles backward to his house. "Get some sleep, Lovely."

Dark circles underline my eyes as I go through my morning routine at eleven-thirty, after Mom woke me up by whacking me in the face with a slice of ham. A bowl of congee awaits me at the dining table, alongside an assortment of side dishes. It takes the tea to kick in before I ask Mom why she's not at the bakery helping Aunt Mei.

"Because I was waiting for you to wake up," she says, placing a second bowl of congee on the table, across from where I'm sitting.

"Did you want to talk about something?" I ask, munching on some pickled radish. "It's not about Dad, is it?" He never responded to my last text telling him I wasn't visiting.

Mom shakes her head and proceeds to the front door. I pay her no mind and stuff myself with spicy bamboo shoots and tofu skin. Then the door swings open and in walks Kite.

The food goes down my windpipe. I slam a hand over my mouth as a hideous gagging sound erupts from my throat. No way to pass that off as a cute hiccup.

I grab a tissue and wipe the gunk off my palm.

Kite raises a hand as if to say *Hope I'm not imposing,* his head dipped in an apologetic bow. He has on a baseball cap and a pair of Gucci sunglasses. Even in a plain gray V-neck and dark-wash jeans, he could pass for a model on his way to a photo shoot.

Like a mother hen gathering her chicks, Mom ushers him over and plops him down in front of the second bowl of congee—the one I wrongly assumed was for her. When Kite isn't looking, I check my sweatshirt for stains. Nope, I'm good. Thank goodness I washed my face and didn't leave any bras hanging around.

That would've been a disaster.

"I was waiting for you to wake up so Kai could come over," Mom finally tells me as she replenishes the side dishes I already demolished.

Embarrassed, Kite says, "I made the mistake of telling my parents I miss your mom's congee. My mom called your mom, and now I'm here eating breakfast at twelve."

Back in elementary school, Mom used to make congee for us almost every morning. Kite would swing by for a quick bite, and then the two of us would walk to the bus stop. Mom adds sweet potato to her congee and prefers a more souplike consistency—just how Kite and I like it.

"Thanks for having me over, Mrs. Li," Kite says.

The formality grates on my ears. (Also, it should be Ms. Li, not Mrs.)

"Is Mr. Cheng home?" he asks.

Cheng is my dad's last name. I'm a Li through and through.

"Oh, Vincent's in California now. We got divorced a few years ago," Mom says gently.

Kite instantly turns red. "S-sorry, I didn't know."

Mom reassures him with a smile. "If Vincent were here, he'd be thrilled to see you. Now then . . ." She jingles the car keys in her hand. I square my shoulders and sit higher on the edge of my chair until I'm as rigid as a plank. "I'm heading out. Kai, would you like anything from the bakery? Bread? Cake? Tea?"

"I'm good," Kite says. "Thank you."

"Are you saying that to be polite or because you mean it?"

Kite hesitates. "Do you still make that sweet-and-spicy flatbread?"

"I'll bring enough for the family." Mom nods meaningfully before pinning me with a sharp look. "Honey, stay out of trouble." Her eyes relay a telepathic message: *You know what I mean by trouble.*

"Trouble's my middle name. It's who I am." I hop out of my chair and into the kitchen with my dirty dishes in hand.

As soon as I'm alone and out of sight, I throw myself against the kitchen counter, hastily depositing the dirty dishes as they clink and clang against the sink. Cupping my face with both hands, I unleash a silent scream, my mouth a perfect O as I turn my face to the ceiling. Someone peeking in through the window might think I'm having an evil spirit exorcised from my body.

I turn on the faucet and splash cold water on my face. My heart is running a marathon. I don't know if I should be breaking out into song and dance, or if I should be hiding in my closet with a paper bag over my head, or both.

Kite is in my house.

Last night wasn't a dream.

I know that. It's not like I thought I was hallucinating, so how do I explain this disbelief? Maybe the news is finally sinking in and I can't believe it?

Oh my god. I want to tell Stephanie and Ester so badly. They know he's coming back; they just don't know when. His being here isn't that big of a secret, all things considered, but Mom was crystal clear when she warned me not to tell anyone. That includes my two favorite people, the same people I'd donate my kidneys to if we had compatible blood types. I trust that when I share a secret with Stephanie and Ester, they'll take it all the way to Pluto before they run their mouths, but my confidence in them doesn't change the fact that Kite's return is his secret to tell. Not mine.

"Need help?"

Kite lingers at the kitchen entrance, carrying a pile of empty dishes.

He has yet to remove his sunglasses.

Any Firework who catches him leaving his house is going to know it's him, with or without his disguise. It only takes one photo to light the fire. Makes me wonder how he managed to go unnoticed at the airport.

"I got it," I assure him. "You can put those dishes in the sink."

He does as he's told. "You sure there's nothing I can do?"

It would be rather awkward for him to sit around waiting. He could go home, but asking him to leave could invite misunderstandings. "Can you organize the stuff in there?" I point him to the drying rack on my right.

Pleased to be of use, Kite starts emptying the drying rack, filing the clean dishes and utensils into their respective locations without my having to direct him.

"Nothing's changed," he says, picking up on my surprise. "I see you still have that Disney mug." He holds up a coffee-stained mug with a faded image of Dumbo on it.

"I love that mug. You better not have anything bad to say about it."

"Considering I'm the one who gave it to you, I have nothing but the highest of praise," he says, beaming with self-satisfaction.

He sets the mug back into place and wets a dish towel to wipe down the dining table.

I touch a hand to my lips. Only then do I realize I'm smiling.

✳

"How does it feel to be back?"

I hand Kite a cup of tea, and we settle down on the floor in front of the TV, surrounded by throw pillows and cushions while the opening credits to *Zootopia* play across the screen.

"Foreign yet familiar," he says, bringing the cup to his lips, testing the temperature. "I almost didn't recognize you last night. Nice pajamas, by the way."

"Ha-ha," I laugh dryly. "Well, I recognized you right away." I look at him like I just one-upped him, then I realize the implication of what I said. "Wait, Kite, I—"

Kite jerks his head as if a fly flew into his ear. "Did you just call me by my stage name?"

"I did. . . . Would you prefer I didn't?"

"Doesn't make a difference to me." Kite sips his tea, then sets it down on the coffee table behind him. "I was . . . surprised, that's all. So far you're the only one who's called me Kite."

"Believe me, I had a hard time getting used to it, but when the rest of the fandom calls you Kite, it becomes a force of habit."

"You're a Karnival fan?"

My standing in the Karnival fandom seems to be a popular topic lately. "I . . . am, but more so the year Karnival debuted. My friend is a *huge* fan, though! She would have a heart attack if she knew you were here."

"What about you?" Kite rubs the back of his neck. He's still wearing his sunglasses, yet he can't look my way. "How do you feel about my being back?"

My thoughts from last night come raging back.

"It's good to see you again." I smile at him. If only he knew how much sleep I lost. "It's been a long time."

Too long.

Kite relaxes and slowly matches my smile. "So, what have you been up to?"

Kite and I spend the next hour catching up.

It takes a while for the conversation to flow, but after some rambling and awkward silences, we find our rhythm. It just so happens that, to keep the momentum going, I have to do most of the talking.

His life as a K-pop idol seems like a touchy subject, and since he has yet to volunteer any information, it's best not to ask him about it.

And so I condense the last four years of my life to the length of a short story. Because I'm a terrible storyteller, I go into painstaking detail about my high school coursework, listing every class on my transcript before segueing into college. Meanwhile, I gloss over my parents' divorce. It makes for a juicy story, but I abstain for two reasons: to spare Kite the discomfort of hearing about the affair and to spare myself the discomfort of telling him. All he needs to know is that Mom's happily single while Dad's living it up in the Bay Area with his new wife and son. I would've avoided the topic altogether if Dad's name hadn't come up earlier.

Apart from the marital drama and my nonexistent relationship with my dad, nothing much has happened. I'm just another human being who survived the tenth circle of hell (aka high school) and is on track to go to college, with the hope that I'll stick with my major.

"Why do you want to study economics?" Kite asks.

"It's a versatile field," I say contemplatively. "I'm not aiming for Wall Street or anything, but I'd like to do something finance or business related." Compared to Kite, who knew what he wanted to do since elementary school, I sound uncommitted and directionless. "Let's see how my first semester goes. Maybe I'll change my mind and switch to East Asian studies."

"I didn't know you could major in East Asian studies," Kite says. I gasp. "I'm a middle school dropout. Cut me some slack." He means it good-naturedly, but I can tell this isn't a topic he wants to pursue further.

"Remember Mr. Booker?" I wait for the name to click, for all the fond memories of our fifth-grade teacher to come flooding back to him.

Instead, he lowers his gaze to his lap.

"Vaguely," he murmurs.

"Do you remember our superhero project? We all came to school wearing costumes on presentation day. I came as Balloon Girl, and you were Unbeatable Joe. You could stop a moving train singlehandedly, communicate telepathically with snakes, and get laundry to fold itself."

The memory blooms across Kite's face, and his laughter is music to my ears. "I got a C on that," he says. "My character profile barely filled two pages, and I got points taken off for not giving my superhero real weaknesses. A shellfish allergy didn't count."

"You basically made yourself a Gary Stu." Kite tilts his head, confused. "A Gary Stu is someone who's perfect or invincible. The term originated in the fan-fiction community."

"Fan fiction . . ." Kite groans. "Don't get me started."

Quite a high number of Fireworks write Karnival fan fiction. Some stories are self-insert romances that get flamed for feeding into the writer's personal fantasy. Most are about Karnival members romancing each other despite no one being openly gay or bisexual (Kite and Xiaoming is the most popular ship while Kite and O-Kei is the least popular). I don't know how those stories differ from wish fulfillment, but I'm not going to dwell on it.

Apparently there's someone who prints popular quotes from her fan fiction onto T-shirts and sells them online. Ester considered buying one that said, YOOSUNG FELT HIMSELF FLOATING INTO OUTER SPACE AS O-KEI STARED AT HIM WITH THE INTENSITY OF A THOUSAND STARS. NO MATTER THE DISTANCE BETWEEN THEM, O-KEI WOULD ALWAYS ORBIT HIM, BE THE SUN TO HIS MOON—which makes no sense because the sun doesn't orbit the moon. Ester would've shelled out a whopping fifty dollars for that shirt if Stephanie and I hadn't staged an intervention.

"I should head back," Kite says, getting to his feet. He pats his pockets to check if he's missing anything. "Thanks for the food. Your mom needs to share the recipe with me."

"She won't. How else would she get you to come over?"

"I'd come over regardless." Kite removes his baseball cap. One moment he's combing a hand through his gorgeous mop of hair; the next he's taking off his sunglasses and holding me hostage with his eyes. "Listen, a lot has happened since we last saw each other. Are we . . . cool?"

"Why wouldn't we be?" My voice falters. "Whether you go by Kai or Kite, you're still the guy who threw up on my sneakers on the first day of fourth grade." I'm mostly joking, but I also suddenly realize it's true. I spent so long getting used to the idea that my childhood friend was gone, but maybe he isn't.

Kite drags a hand down his face. "You don't forget anything, do you?"

"No one forgets having their brand-new sneakers ruined."

"I'm very sorry about that."

"Want to make it up to me?" I walk him to the front door.

"You mean for the hundredth time?" he asks, donning his sunglasses.

"More like the fiftieth."

"So how can a guy make it up to you for the fiftieth time?"

I smile. "Just—don't be a stranger."

Dream Drop needs to be more transparent. Unlike other entertainment companies, which recruit trainees left and right, Dream Drop prides itself on maintaining a small list of artists, so that everyone receives the care and attention they need pre- and post-debut (paraphrasing from their website). Yet the only info Dream Drop has given us about Kite is that he's taking a break. How do you work yourself so hard that your doctor tells you to rest? For months? If it were as simple as being overworked, then Kite should at least be able to participate in a livestream. But he isn't even doing that. You know what? I bet he injured himself and Dream Drop doesn't want to publicize it because it'll reflect poorly on them. It wouldn't be the first time a record label exploited its stars. No one gives a damn about work-life balance or mental health.

#karnival #FireWorks #mentalhealthawareness

7

An hour later and I'm still wasting away in the living room.

This time I have *Beauty and the Beast* running in the background. With my eyes trained on my phone, I'm only half focused on the movie. My attention is split between wishing I had Emma Watson's eyebrows and wishing I could get Karnival—and all the gossip that plagues them—out of my head.

I'm such a hypocrite. I keep swearing up and down that I'm not a big Karnival fan, yet here I am, browsing their Instagram feed.

Xiaoming recently posted a selfie to Instagram: of him and Yoosung at a pizzeria, which seems perfectly innocent, because what could possibly be scandalous about two guys eating pizza?

Turns out, a lot.

Fireworks are up in arms over the selfie. I read a handful of comments to get a grasp of what all the drama is about. Kite stans are apparently appalled by the *insensitive behavior displayed by Xiaoming and Yoosung.*

HiAsAKite: "While our precious Kite is bedridden from working himself too hard for the good of Karnival, Xiaoming and Yoosung are shamelessly grabbing food instead of taking care of their maknae. They live together! They should be looking out for each other!"

WhatDoUStan4: "Kite loves pizza. Can you imagine how sad he must be that his hyungs ate without him? I at least hope they brought home a slice for him, assuming his stomach can handle it. I heard somewhere that Kite hasn't been able to eat or drink anything."

JennyKPops: "@WhatDoUStan4 It's absolutely heartbreaking to imagine! Could they at least pretend to be upset about Kite's hiatus instead of gloating on social media about how much fun they're having without him? Talk about insensitive."

With Dream Drop failing to address Kite's situation, a subset of fans (an imaginative and vocal one at that) have drawn their own conclusions. They believe that Kite sustained a major injury during dance practice and is now holed up in his room, too frail and weak to stomach water, much less food. Instead of treating him with the utmost care, his teammates are prioritizing pizza.

My eyes are about to roll into the back of my head. I've seen for myself that Kite is up and about, totally capable of ordering pizza. Even if he were as sick as fans seem to think he is, he would never blame someone for grabbing lunch without him.

Naturally, Xiaoming and Yoosung stans are outraged by those talking smack about their biases. On Xiaoming's Instagram, no less.

iSINGforMING: "@JennyKPops Let me get this straight. Because Kite's taking a break from the group, Xiaoming-oppa and Yoosung-oppa can't grab a slice of pizza? Grow up!"

MarvelousME: I hope Kite isn't sick with anything contagious. Maybe Dream Drop should rent another apartment and separate him from everyone else.

YoYoWorks: "All you Kite stans are starting shit for no reason. Kite needs a doctor if he's that sick. Xiaoming and Yoosung aren't his 24/7 caretakers! All of you need to mind your own business. Better yet, go jump off a cliff."

From there, the comments get uglier and uglier. These self-proclaimed Fireworks aren't doing their biases any favors by acting this way. Sooner or later Xiaoming will disable people from commenting on his posts. If this is the vitriol people write in a public forum, imagine what private messages are like.

I'm ready to move on to heartwarming animal-rescue videos when my eyes land on a comment in all caps:

"FIREWHORES: KITE IS USELESS. KARNIVAL WILL CONTINUE MAKING THE CHARTS WITHOUT HIM. NOW THAT HE'S GONE, HE BETTER STAY GONE. KOREA DOESN'T WANT HIM. CHINA DOESN'T WANT HIM. AND I DOUBT HIS OWN COUNTRY WANTS HIM. SAD."

A slow-burning fury churns my blood, thick and heavy like molten lava.

I close my eyes, take a deep breath, and count to ten.

Whoever wrote this is obviously a troll baiting people into an argument they'll never win. I know better than to engage, but that doesn't lessen the degree of hate I feel toward them. I am not above violent fantasies when offended, and the likelihood that

Kite has been a target of similar comments on his own Instagram curdles my stomach. His account is still private; perhaps he's edging toward deleting it altogether.

People delete and reopen social media accounts left and right, but for Kite the action carries a certain weight. If it's gone, then it's gone for good.

But I wish to remain optimistic.

Because Kite isn't gone.

He's here.

Dear Kite,

Your music is life-changing. The story about how your
parents never tried to talk you out of singing moved me
to tears. It inspired me to audition for my first musical!
My dream is to become a singer, and your support
would mean the world to me. Friend me on Instagram
@heartbeestings69!

Love,
Your Biggest, Brightest Firework!

Fan mail no. 38, received one year ago, on June 21.
Connie used it to feed a bonfire.

8

The Xus invite us over for dinner on short notice.

Mom and Aunt Mei close the bakery early—something they rarely do, even when there's a snowstorm—and now the three of us are cozied up on a love seat in the Xus' living room, where everyone's gathered. Contrary to what people assume when you have a K-pop idol in the family, the Xus lead humble lives. Their house is as minimalist as I remember, with small luxuries here and there, such as a wool carpet, a giant wall clock, and an espresso machine, but nothing gilded or swathed in crystals or diamonds.

Mrs. Xu pours us each a glass of honey kumquat tea with grass jelly. I help myself to a second glass as the adults go through their first round of idle chitchat. Connie is in the backyard helping Mr. Xu with the grill, and Kite is . . .

Kite saunters down the stairs and announces his arrival with a *hello*. He trails a hand across the back of the love seat, his fingers dancing a little too close to my neck for comfort, and plops himself down on the nearby ottoman, his too-long legs bent at an odd angle.

True to her word, Mom brought a baker's dozen of snacks, including our signature spicy brown-sugar flatbread. Kite reaches over the coffee table and breaks off a piece. Mrs. Xu spends the second round of idle chitchat trying to reimburse my mom.

"If we were at a restaurant, everyone would be fighting for the check," I whisper to Kite.

"Wrong. My dad would've slipped his credit card to the waiter before anyone got the chance to order drinks," he whispers back.

Kite ditched the disguise this evening. His hair is slicked back, damp from a shower, and his skin is so radiant and smooth, he might as well be a sparkly vampire. He smells like morning rain and freshly plucked mint. With every breath I take, it's like I'm drinking him in.

Thankfully, I had the good sense to dress for the occasion. A sleeveless black frock paired with a tassel necklace handmade by Ester should fit the bill. No need to give Kite the impression that I'm perpetually in loungewear.

Mrs. Xu pays me a motherly compliment and, in a moment of inspiration, starts talking about how she used to be a fashionista in her youth. She disappears upstairs to retrieve a photo album dedicated to her college years. She sets the album on my lap, and I flip through the pages, out of courtesy and mild interest. I see bits and pieces of her in Kite—in the bridge of the nose, the width of the lips, how they pose with their thumbs hooked to their pockets, and how their eyes curve into crescent moons as they grace the camera with a coquettish smile.

Who would have guessed Mrs. Xu was an Asian Miranda Priestly, with her fur-trimmed coats, broad-brimmed hats, and designer heels? All counterfeit, she informs me.

The biggest surprise tonight is Connie, decked out in a crop top and a whimsical rainbow skirt that cascades down to her ankles. I haven't seen her this dressed up since the time she wore glittery unicorn pumps, on a dare, to her eighth-grade graduation.

"Hi, Connie!" Aunt Mei happily waves at her as Connie

delivers a tray of barbecued ribs to the dining table without so much as a greeting.

"Food's ready!" Mr. Xu announces, scurrying in after her.

My mouth waters as I approach the table, crowded with more food than our appetites can handle: pork belly braised in garlic sauce, spare ribs coated in a five-spice rub, a whole steamed flounder, vegetable kebabs with perfect grill marks, lotus root salad tossed in a ginger vinaigrette, chilled sesame noodles, cold tofu topped with diced century eggs, and fluffy jasmine rice—and don't forget the bread.

Mr. Xu uncorks a bottle of red wine, and we dig in. Somehow I wind up between Aunt Mei and Connie. Kite sits across from me and strikes up a conversation with Aunt Mei. Mom's occupied with Mr. and Mrs. Xu, which leaves me with Connie.

"Did you grill these?" I ask, tearing into a spare rib, the meat sliding right off the bone.

"Dad did. I grilled the vegetables," Connie says.

I grab a vegetable kebab and scarf down a whole mushroom and a cube of tofu. The hot juices spill down my throat; it takes all my willpower to mask the burning pain. "Mmm."

Connie stares at me, her expression as blank as the birthday cards Dad sometimes remembers to mail each year.

"Thanks," she mumbles. "I also prepared the marinade for the pork."

"I didn't know you liked to cook."

Connie piles her plate high with sesame noodles before brandishing a pair of tongs at me, the metal ends pinching and clanking as she overenunciates her next words. "You know, I have other hobbies besides soccer, like . . . making people eat dirt, for example."

Her eyes reflect a coyness that reminds me of when we were kids, the version of her who collected stuffed animals and raised her pinkie while taking dainty sips from plastic teacups.

I gnaw at my spare rib and accidentally lock eyes with Kite—perched over the table with a curtain of noodles hanging from his mouth.

Heat surges through my face.

Suddenly I am all too aware of the grease glossing my lips. Who knows what else I have on my face? I excuse myself and head for the bathroom, where I wash my hands, wipe my lips, and floss out the shreds of meat and chili flakes between my teeth.

This is why buffalo wings are a bad idea for a first date.

Not that this is a date.

Kite rounds the corner as I exit the bathroom. I freeze, looking like a deer in headlights as I stand in his shadow with my hands suspended at chest level, prepared for the impact that doesn't come. He twiddles his sauce-coated fingers and slips around me to enter the bathroom. Scratching my jawline, I start to head back.

"You missed a spot," he says, calling me back. I stop at the doorway to find him hunched over the sink. He points to his face, then softly brushes a thumb across the apple of my cheek, taking with it a bead of soap that escaped my notice.

"Thanks . . ." The path he traced with his thumb tingles on my skin. I return to the dining room before the fangirl in me inspires a moment of instant regret.

Dinner continues late into the evening. The food is gradually depleting, but there's plenty of wine to go around. By the third bottle, people start gravitating to the living room, ready for dessert. Dessert means fresh fruit in our households.

Kite packs away the leftovers while Connie helps her mom peel what might as well be an entire fruit basket. Mr. Xu stays seated and regales Aunt Mei with stories of his overseas business trips, oblivious to the fact that she's dozing off and is about to spill wine all over his carpet. Mom rushes in to preempt the disaster.

Since everyone is busy to some extent, I clear the table, stacking empty rice bowls on top of one another. In the kitchen, Connie's standing over the sink next to her mom, both too busy skinning mangoes and pears to notice me.

"I'm heading out. Sydney's on her way to pick me up," Connie says.

"Dinner's not over yet," says Mrs. Xu. "It's been so long since we got together like this. Can't Sydney pick you up in an hour?"

"She can't. We're meeting her friends."

Mrs. Xu sighs. "Couldn't you have told me sooner?"

"How was I supposed to when you planned this dinner at the last minute?" Connie flings her knife onto the cutting board. "The Lis won't care if I leave early. Kai can entertain them—it's not like he has anywhere to go."

"Don't talk about your brother that way."

"Forgive me for speaking the truth."

I quietly retrace my steps.

I get three steps in before colliding with Kite. I shoot a hasty glance at Connie and Mrs. Xu. They're too preoccupied to notice what's going on behind them.

Kite holds a finger to his lips and coaxes me into the living room, his expression as cool as the surface of a lake in winter. Neither of us mentions what we overheard.

I relax, thinking he didn't catch what Connie said.

But as the night resumes without Connie, I notice Kite staring off into space, the carpet swallowing the sound of his restless foot. He nods along to the conversations around him, giving one-word answers as needed before his smooth expression crinkles and the *tap-tap-tap* of his foot continues.

"What airline did you fly?" Mom asks, offering him a plate of mixed fruit.

"Korean Air," he says, piercing a slice of pear with his fork.

"They're quite expensive, aren't they? How was the food?"

"Decent," he answers.

Mr. Xu laughs heartily while wrestling with a tight cork in a bottle of sparkling cider. "You pay thousands of dollars to fly business class and the food is decent?"

"Yup." Kite twirls his fork between his fingers.

His dad slips into the kitchen for a bottle opener, Mom right behind him.

Kite sets his fork down, the fruit untouched. I join him, kneeling beside the ottoman on which he's seated. "For a sec, I thought we were going to get a lecture on how to manage personal finances."

"Parents. They never change." Kite shrugs.

"Now that you've been back a whole day, is everything still 'foreign yet familiar'?" I ask.

He contemplates his answer while filling the silence with a smile that doesn't quite reach his eyes. "Yeah," he says, before his mind retreats to a place I can't reach.

Hey, Lovely,

Sorry for getting back to you so late. Things have been hectic. I can't say much, but today went better than expected. My vocal coach says I'm a natural, and I finally nailed a dance move I've been struggling with. All I need now is someone to compliment my Korean. Hope you're doing well back home, and Happy Halloween!

Last email to Lulu from Kai, sent four years ago on October 31.

9

"Can we kidnap Mother Nature and kindly persuade her to change the weather?" I say.

Ester and Stephanie look at me with varying degrees of amusement.

"Give it a try. Let me know how it goes," says Ester.

"Ask the universe to revolve around you while you're at it," quips Stephanie.

No matter how many times I refresh the weather app, this week's forecast is too stubborn to change. It's rain, rain, and more rain for the next three days, with potential flooding along the East Coast. My summer itinerary is on hold until Mother Nature graces us with clear blue skies.

Instead of hugging sweaty strangers in costume and gorging on Hershey bars, we're in Stephanie's industrial-sized kitchen, whipping up artisanal cupcakes in our *Sailor Moon* aprons. I have Mars, Stephanie has Neptune, and Ester has Venus. We spent the late morning prepping our ingredients while waiting for the butter to reach room temperature. Only now, at noon, are we getting our batters started.

All three of them.

We don't do boxed cake mix, not after Ester made us take an online cupcake personality quiz during a fire drill junior year.

She's since moved on from Funfetti and now swears by triple-salted caramel. Sweet, sticky, and devilishly good—like her.

Stephanie has always loved lemon cupcakes with lavender-vanilla frosting, and lo and behold, that's what she is. According to the quiz, she's elegant, divine, and perfect for teatime—which is vague enough to be true (although I heard she picked her nose in public as a kid).

I'm a pineapple-coconut cupcake: zesty, vibrant, and packed with flavor in every bite. Bad news for me, because making these cupcakes is a pain in the butt. I don't *have* to make them, but Ester gets so passionate about our signature cupcakes, I can't help but play along.

"Let's play Monopoly after everything's in the oven," Ester says as she scoops her brown sugar cake batter into a lined cupcake tin.

"We still have to do our frostings," Stephanie reminds us as she rinses her mixing bowl. "We can play after we figure out lunch."

"I'm not really hungry." Ester shrugs.

"My dad made samosas the other day. They're in the freezer," Stephanie says.

"I love his cooking!" Ester suddenly musters up an appetite. "My dad can't cook to save his life. If Mom could leave her office at a reasonable hour, I wouldn't have to eat cardboard and charcoal for dinner!"

"Your mom's working overtime again?" Stephanie asks.

"With pleasure. She's such a workaholic. I see Lu's mom more than I see mine—which is telling, because, in my opinion, running a business is more demanding than what is supposed to be a nine-to-five job."

While it's likely that Ester does see my mom more often these days, Mom used to be like Mrs. Tan, back when Dāngrán Bakery was nothing but a bank loan and a deserted piece of real estate. The first two years after opening were also rough. Mom worked long hours and never had time to sit down for breakfast (yet she went out of her way to make congee for me). Fifty percent of small businesses fail in their fifth year; Mom was determined to be in the other fifty percent. Dad was around to make up for her absence, but Kite played a bigger role in curbing the loneliness.

The oven beeps at 350 degrees. My cupcakes go in with Stephanie's. Ester needs the oven to be 325 degrees, so hers will go last. We set the timer and get to work on our toppings.

Ester connects her phone to a Bluetooth speaker before heating up a saucepan for her candied-caramel swirls. Red Velvet's "Russian Roulette" begins blaring from the speaker. We sing along, having memorized the lyrics but not their meaning.

Up next is "Meteor Shower" by Karnival, one of their jazzier numbers, which opens with the popping of a cork, followed by the bubbling hiss of champagne being poured over ice. Ester can be so hardcore when singing along that she imitates the sound effects, too. The music overtakes her. I snap my fingers, drawing her attention back to the sugar and butter crystalizing in her pan. Her caramel is ruined, and she starts over.

"Any word on Kite? Is he coming home soon?"

For once it's not Ester but Stephanie who asks.

"Haven't heard anything," I lie.

Kite's been back for about three days now, which means I've been quiet about it for three days. I didn't see or hear from him yesterday, and today might not be any different.

An episode of *Celebrity Circus,* a variety show featuring musicians, singers, and actors, aired in South Korea last night with

Karnival as this week's guest. I watched the unsubbed version on YouTube this morning. Kite appears in the episode; evidently it was prerecorded. People were bickering about him in the comments section, about how he's not going to make a comeback and that his medical leave is a guise and that he's faking an injury to fade out of Karnival and quit the music industry.

Fireworks also criticized the show's host for being rude, specifically referring to the segment where the host roasts Kite on how fans consistently rank him the weakest dancer in the group. I thought the comments were speculations at best and exaggerations at worst, but then I watched the segment myself. You don't need subtitles to read Kite's body language. His downcast eyes, slumped stance, and evasive answers said everything. Yet the host goads him into a dance-off with Yoosung (ranked the second-worst dancer) and then relentlessly teases Kite for recycling the choreography in their MVs instead of improvising his own moves.

Kite was being such a good sport, doing something he didn't want to do, and the host still made fun of him!

"Your cupcakes are done," Stephanie says, interrupting my secondhand rage.

I silence the timer and pull my cupcakes out of the oven to cool.

My frosting is nowhere near finished.

I leave Stephanie's house with a box of all three cupcakes.

Ester burned her caramel again, and rather than start over for a third time, she made a caramel sauce. Her cupcakes are dee-li-cious. For some reason, mine came out close-textured, but I don't think anyone will complain about the flavor.

I pull up to my house and find Maru napping on the porch, her body curled into a cocoon as she takes shelter from the rain. I manage to reach the steps before Maru awakens and stares at me with those mesmerizing golden orbs that I envy so much. She strolls over and rubs her head against my leg before rising on her hind legs to inspect the box in my hands.

"Not yours," I chastise her.

She looks at me as if to say, *Everything's mine, foolish human.*

I stroke her behind the ears. She leans into my hand, savoring my scratches. For a second, I believe she's chosen me as her number-one human, but then I hear footsteps, and suddenly I am nothing more than chewed-up gum under a desk. Maru pads down the steps, oblivious to how she hurts me when her butthole is pointed in my direction.

Kite stands before me. In one hand, he holds a black umbrella with a Vincent van Gogh painting printed on the underside. In the other, he holds a plastic bag that swings absently in his grip. Today he's sporting a pair of orange-tinted glasses with large circular lenses and a navy-blue rain jacket zipped halfway up his chest, revealing a faded graphic T-shirt underneath.

I've seen this outfit on Instagram.

"Let's get out of the rain," he says, coaxing Maru back onto the porch. I make room for him as he shakes the raindrops off his umbrella, folds it, and then opens a can of cat food. Maru watches curiously as he scoops out a chunk of food with his fingers and smears it onto the back of his hand. She inches forward, her little nose twitching as she sniffs the food and, without further hesitation, laps it up.

"Are you a cat whisperer?" I ask, amazed and jealous.

"More like irresistible," he says.

He doesn't seem as withdrawn as he was the other night; at least he can joke around. But there's no humor in his body: no smile, no sparkle in his eyes, no wolfish lilt to his voice, nothing. Gone is the playfulness he had during our first interaction.

"Maru's been on your porch for almost the entire day," he continues. "I figured I'd stock up on cat food, make myself feel less guilty when I see her."

"You walked?" It's a twenty-minute walk to the nearest store from here.

"Kind of have to, not like I have a driver's license."

"If you ever need a ride, let me know." I watch as Maru licks Kite's hand clean. Her content expression is too adorable for this world. "I don't remember you liking cats this much. Aren't you more of a dog person?"

"I used to be." Kite serves Maru the remaining can of food. "Wayne's a big cat lover. I went to a lot of cat cafés with him in Korea, and he's infected me with his obsession."

My heart flutters. This is his first time sharing something genuine about his life in South Korea. The fangirl in me feels like it's a privilege, but the old friend in me also feels reassured that, despite his on-and-off behavior, I'm someone Kite can talk to.

Trying not to sound overeager, I ask him if the cat cafés were in Hongdae.

"Yeah," he says somewhat distractedly. "How'd you know?"

"Remember how I told you I'm planning to minor in Korean?"

"You did tell me that." Kite stands to his full height, seemingly attentive to what I'm about to say, although his tone leaves much to be desired in the way of interest.

"Rutgers has a study-abroad program. I want to spend a semester in South Korea, so I've researched all the touristy spots, and Hongdae kept coming up." I wait for Kite to respond, but he gives no indication of wanting to. The mood between us is suddenly as gloomy as the weather. To lighten it up, I jokingly add, "Maybe one day I can listen to your songs without relying on translations."

"Right. *My* songs, the ones I don't get to write," he mutters under his breath.

"Huh?" I gawk at him.

His shoulders deflate, and suddenly he seems smaller. Behind his tinted glasses, I can see his face crumbling with confusion and perhaps remorse. "S-sorry . . ."

He rushes back to his house.

I don't give myself a chance to think. If I did, I wouldn't be chasing after him right now.

Rounding the hedge, I cut through a puddle, and my feet slide out from under me. I catch hold of Kite's jacket to keep myself upright, nearly bringing him down with me. As he turns around— probably to yell at me for almost dragging him into the mud— I thrust the cupcakes into his chest and blurt out whatever comes to mind first.

"These are for you!"

Like an idiot, I let go of the box before Kite can take it. We scramble to catch it before it lands in a puddle. We succeed, but not without crushing some of the cupcakes.

"Never mind, then." I pull the box toward me, expecting him to let go.

He doesn't. "You made these?" he asks. His glasses sit crooked on his face, knocked askew when we both reached for the box.

"I did, well, I didn't make all of—"

"Thanks." He swipes the box out of my hands and darts for his house. Along the way, he scuffs his sneakers against the stairs, nearly sending the cupcakes sailing through the air and his head through the door.

I race back to my own house and trip over Maru lazing on the porch. She bares her fangs at me. *How dare you! Watch where you're going,* she hisses.

Sorry, Maru. Please forgive this stupid human.

The producers of *Celebrity Circus* better fire that douchebag host or else there's going to be World War III. Karnival took time out of their schedule to go on the show, and how do they get treated? With complete and utter disrespect. I'm willing to acknowledge that Kite isn't the best dancer, but that doesn't make him any less talented. Everyone has their strengths and weaknesses (and water is wet). The fact that *Celebrity Circus* chose to prey on Kite's weakness speaks volumes to the kind of people they have working on the show.

#boycott #karnivalstan #kiteismybias #respectidols #shameoncelebritycircus

10

Don't be a stranger.

I must've been overconfident when I said that.

Kite and I haven't seen each other in years, yet he seems to have very little to say to me. We had a good reunion when he came over for breakfast; since then, something's been off.

He's hot one moment, cold the next, and I don't know why.

Whatever, I'm not going to cry about it. I'm not going to be one of those girls who mope around like a sad puppy because of a boy. I'm going to take the leftover ingredients from our baking spree and surprise Mom and Aunt Mei with homemade pineapple-coconut cupcakes, so they get the zesty and vibrant Lulu Li.

Hi, Kai,

So glad your training's coming together! I'm sure you'll be fluent in Korean by the end of this year. Exactly how long do you have to train for? Do you get time off for holidays or vacation? I'm guessing you won't be back for Thanksgiving, since they don't celebrate that in South Korea, but what about Christmas? I'll be on winter break in December. It would be the perfect time to get together, and if we can't do it in person, I can stay up late for a phone call.

Last email to Kai from Lulu, sent four years ago on November 1. No response from Kai.

11

I can't believe it's July. Summer might as well be over.

Today's forecast is cloudy with a chance of sunshine in the afternoon. The humidity is through the roof. Still no Hersheypark or New York City. Ester is in Hoboken for her cousin's Sweet Sixteen. Stephanie's out shopping for dorm supplies.

As for me, I'm staying indoors with the air-conditioning on, binge-watching *The Great British Bake Off* while completing as many Chinese lessons on Duolingo as I can. I considered helping out at the bakery, but it gets too stuffy when you're boiling boba and constantly going in and out of the kitchen to stock the shelves with fresh bread.

I left a bowl of water outside for Maru in case she comes around, though I doubt she'll drink it. She only cares about food. I've never seen her take a sip of water. Maybe Kite can convince her to drink. For some reason, she prefers him over me.

Ugh, sadness.

Suddenly there's a knock at the door.

I'm not expecting any guests or deliveries. Either I have missionaries at my door, it's a shady salesperson, or Maru has learned to knock.

I open the door, prepared to tell them I'm not interested in whatever they're selling, and come face-to-face with Connie.

"Here." She hands me a tray covered in aluminum foil. "From Kai, a thank-you for the cupcakes."

I lift the aluminum cover to see chocolate-chip cookies underneath. Some are dark brown around the edges, bordering on black.

"About that . . ." Connie reads my mind. "He didn't want me to give you the burned ones, but I'm the one going out of my way to deliver them"—I crane my neck to measure the distance between her house and mine—"so beggars can't be choosers."

"Well, thanks for the trouble." I start to close the door until Connie steps one foot into the house. I immediately back up, keeping the tray between us.

"Did something happen between you guys?" she asks.

"Uh, no, why would something happen?" My eyes flit back and forth. She's staring intensely at me; it's scaring me.

"My brother doesn't bake."

"You said it yourself. He's thanking me for the cupcakes I gave him."

Connie makes a noncommittal sound, grabs a cookie that isn't burnt, and takes off. Once she vanishes behind the rose hedge, I step onto the porch and look up at Kite's window on the second floor. As soon as I do, the curtains flutter back into place.

She came crashing in like a meteor
With her starlight hair
Her half-moon eyes
And her larger-than-life mind
Girl, you're too bright for this world

Unused chorus for "Meteor Shower" written by Kite, translated from Korean.

12

Of course the weather is the picture of perfection on the Fourth of July. The clouds have gone from dark gray smudges to wispy white paint strokes on a blue canvas.

Mother Nature is such a tease, and I am a mortal creature subject to her whims.

I can't complain. How can I when Stephanie's family is throwing a backyard pool party? If an ice cream bar with ten different flavors and limitless toppings doesn't impress, behold the pizza truck. You can build your own pie and have it baked on the spot. Ester's demolishing her second one while chilling in a hammock skirting the woods that run behind the neighborhood.

Stephanie and I have more of an appetite for adrenaline. We're jumping off the diving board and plunging cannonball-style into the pool, competing for the biggest splash.

"Guess who I saw the other day," Stephanie says as I break through the surface of the water and come up for air. There's a split second of panic where I think she means Kite, but then, "Kellie. I bumped into her at the bookstore and we chatted for a bit."

"Okay . . . and?"

"You two would've made a cute couple."

"Last I checked, you were surprised she even asked me out," I say, climbing out to sit on the concrete edge of the pool and soak in the afternoon sun. "Even if Kellie and I had started dating, she's bound for Amherst in the fall—in Massachusetts."

"May I remind you that long-distance relationships are a thing?" Stephanie joins me on the edge and dries herself off with a towel.

"And long distance isn't *my* thing," I retort, swinging my legs and drawing circles in the pool with my feet. "I'm sure Kellie will have no problems finding herself a girlfriend at Amherst, one who deserves her."

"And who will you find?" Stephanie asks coyly.

"Myself. Duh? Isn't that what college is all about?" I'm joking, but instead of playing along, Stephanie drapes her arms around me and rocks me back and forth. I find her sudden affection suspicious. "What is it?"

"Just thought you needed a hug."

"Everyone could use a hug." My eyes dart across the lawn and land on Ester napping in the hammock. "Shall we surprise dear Ester with our love?"

Stifling our giggles, we each grab a water gun and slip barefoot onto the grass, entering stealth mode as we advance on our target. Ester is sound asleep with her earbuds in, unaware of the water gun I have positioned a centimeter from her nostrils. I pull the trigger.

Ester's eyes fly open. She flings forward and blows her nose, grimacing at what I assume is the stinging sensation of water trickling down the back of her throat. Then Stephanie shoots her in the forehead, then two more times in the chest.

"Steph! Seriously?"

Ester lunges at us, reaching for our guns. The hammock lurches under her, threatening to spit her onto the ground. She stops to steady herself, and by the time she gets to her feet, steam spewing from her ears, Stephanie and I are rolling on the grass, laughing so hard our sides are splitting. It hurts to breathe, and it is the best kind of pain the world has to give.

By eight o'clock, the sky has transformed into a riot of hot pinks and oranges, the chaotic blend reminiscent of an airbrushed shirt I once commissioned from an artist who misspelled my last name as Lee. The smoky apple scent of the barbecue pervades the air and teases my brain into thinking I'm on the brink of starvation. This summer has been feast after feast. I'm torn on whether or not I want it to stop.

"What's taking so long?" Ester grumbles under her breath.

She and I are on the front lawn, waiting on Stephanie to join us so that we can go to my house, where we can get a better view of the fireworks.

Ester impatiently swings an enormous key ring around her forefinger. It's loaded with all sorts of knickknacks: a bunny tail, a tin whistle, a mini photo card of Wayne, and a key chain of the Karnival logo, to list a few.

Xiaoming designed the logo. Every member came up with a design, and their entire team of managers and assistants voted for their favorite one. The winning logo consists of a white rectangle with a black perimeter. Within the perimeter is a black half-moon that connects with the frame at three points, loosely rendering the negative space into a curved "K."

"Ready to go?" Stephanie asks, skipping over.

"Ready when you are," Ester says, unlocking her car.

Stephanie takes the front passenger seat while I take the back and make friends with a pile of clothes Ester picked up from the dry cleaners earlier today.

Seconds later we're careening through the backstreets, avoiding holiday traffic while keeping an eye out for children playing. I text Mom to let her know we're on our way in case Kite happens to be over. She responds with a thumbs-up.

Ester slows the car to a crawl as we enter a street made infamous by an old man who lives in a brick house with a rooster weathervane. He's known for sheltering stray cats, and as commendable as that is, he lets them roam freely. The last thing I need to see is a cat whose death could've easily been prevented. Ester comes to a complete stop when she spots a white cat up ahead, chilling in the middle of the road like a handsome turkey.

Not wanting to frighten the cat with the horn, Stephanie takes it upon herself to get out of the car and bring him to safety. We watch as he turns his nose up at her, raises a leg, and licks his nether region. At least the cat is neutered.

Stephanie looks back at us helplessly. I fetch a towel from the trunk and drape it over the cat. He starts thrashing as I wrap him up as best as I can. With Stephanie's help, I carry him to a nearby house and release him on the grass. He dashes into the driveway, jumps onto the hood of a car, and makes himself comfy. Mission accomplished, we return to the car and continue on our merry way.

"Cats." Ester shakes her head. "You love 'em and you hate 'em."

"That's what unconditional love is," I say as we pull onto my street.

Then several things happen at once.

A firework explodes in the sky, unannounced, casting a blinding white light over us. As the brilliance recedes and prickles our vision, I catch sight of Maru as she scurries out from nowhere and crosses the street.

In front of our car.

Ester's too distracted to notice. As I'm shouting for her to stop, Kite comes running after Maru, the headlights washing over him as Ester screams at the top of her lungs and slams on the brakes. The car jolts to a halt, our bodies jerking forward then backward into our seats as stray items fly onto the floor and off the dashboard.

The car is less than a foot away from Kite.

His expression mirrors our own.

We all stare at each other for what feels like an eternity, numb with shock. Kite is the first to snap out of it. He reorients himself and stumbles backward onto the curb with Maru safe in his arms. Ester parks her car at the side of the road, and the three of us sit in silence as the gravity of what we narrowly avoided sinks in.

Ester grips the steering wheel tightly and screws her eyes shut. A screech escapes the thin crack between her lips, the sound undulating from high to low, reminiscent of a deflating balloon.

She spins around to face me. Her eyes are feral, her cheeks streaked with mascara.

"Oh. My. God. Did I just almost kill *Kite*?"

"We chose Fireworks as the name of our fandom, because without the support of our fans, we wouldn't be here today. The music industry is competitive and sometimes lonely. Our fans keep us going. They're the light at every crossroad of a decision, and without them we'd be lost."

O-Kei, in an interview with K Sound magazine after Karnival's debut.

13

We scramble out of the car to check on Kite.

He's sitting on the edge of the grass, wide-eyed and alert, with Maru cradled over his shoulder. Ester and Stephanie hang back as I rush over and ask if he needs medical attention. He shakes his head no, and although I know the car never hit him, I look him over just in case.

"I'm fine, really," he says after a shaky breath. "Are your friends okay?" He casts an uneasy glance in their direction.

"We're fine, just a little shaken up," I assure him.

Is now an appropriate time to introduce him to Ester and Stephanie? Mom said not to tell anyone about him, but the truth is out. Even if I don't say anything—

"Holy crap! It's really him!" Ester's bouncing up and down with both hands clapped over her mouth to stop herself from screaming.

Even Stephanie is slack-jawed next to her.

The door to my house swings open. Mom appears on the porch. Her eyes go from me to Kite, then to Ester and Stephanie, before landing back on me.

"All of you come inside," she says. "Now."

Kite follows us inside with Maru clinging to him, unwilling to let go even as he tries to pry her off. We take off our shoes and line them neatly by the door. Mom points a commanding finger at the dining room. We seat ourselves around the table while she slips into the kitchen to phone Mrs. Xu.

The Xus are away at the moment.

Only Kite stayed home.

Bits and pieces of the phone call float into the dining room, but no one else says a word. I cross my arms, uncross them, and cross them again. I keep my eyes trained on my lap and listen to the ticking of the clock, every second slow and grueling. Next to me, Stephanie suppresses a sneeze, and I hear the sound of a tissue box being pushed across the table.

Does Kite regret leaving his house? I know Ester doesn't, even though she almost ran him over. She must be a bundle of happy nerves right now, and judging by her leg jiggling under the table, she won't be able to stay in the same room as Kite for much longer, not without going all fangirl on him. I try to catch her eye, but she's too busy examining her cuticles to look up—no doubt fighting the urge to stare at Kite.

Mom returns and does a triple take when she sees Kite and Maru. "Sorry, Kai. When I said 'all of you,' I didn't mean you. You can go home."

Mortified, Kite gets up and leaves without a word.

I could die right now.

Mom clears her throat. "Ester. Stephanie. I'm sure you know who Kai is. It should go without saying, but I'll say it anyway." She stares them down with a look of warning, one she reserves for customers who try to scam her with a fake coupon. "While it's not my place to decide what you can and can't talk about, I hope you'll respect Kai's privacy and give him the space he needs while he's here visiting family."

"I would never tell a soul!" Ester blurts. "I swear on my grandmother's grave. May I swallow a thousand needles if I go back on my word."

"Ester, I appreciate your enthusiasm, but please hold off on the theatrics," Mom says, the hard lines of her expression smoothing over. "I assume I can trust you ladies?" We all nod in unison. "Good. Now, can someone tell me what exactly happened?"

The fireworks are in full bloom, exploding with a deafening bang before joining the stars in the sky. Stephanie, Ester, and I are sprawled out on a picnic blanket in my backyard, gnawing away on ice cream sandwiches as the sky erupts in rainbow colors. I know what's on their minds. I'm counting down the seconds to when one of them breaks their silence.

"I can't believe he's back." Of course, it's Ester. "I mean, I believe it, since I saw Kite with my own eyes, but at the same time, I can't believe it, you know?"

"I know." I recall my own cycle of disbelief, however brief.

"This is going to sound horrible—don't judge me—but I'm kind of glad I almost ran Kite over with my car. I wouldn't have met him otherwise. Of course, I'm also grateful that I didn't." Ester sighs, all hot and bothered. "Thank you, Lady Luck, for preventing a tragedy! Imagine me, responsible for the death of such a sexy beast. Wayne's forever my bias, but I appreciate a handsome guy when I see one. I don't discriminate."

"Cool it down and eat your ice cream." I guess Ester's ignoring how Kite looked more like a deer in headlights than whatever sexy beast she's imagining.

"I totally get why you didn't tell us," she continues. "People just recently stopped making up stupid theories about Kite's hiatus. Hopefully things stay quiet, long enough for Kite to spend quality time with his family."

Finishing my ice cream sandwich, I wipe my fingers on the blanket and nudge Ester with my elbow. "But?"

"But it was risky of him to fly out here after the address leak, you know. If my doctor told me to rest because I've been overworking myself, I'd be chilling at home with enough chocolate to last me through another ice age—not taking a fourteen-hour flight."

"You're overthinking it," Stephanie says. "Kite hasn't been home in years. Why confine himself to an apartment he shares with four other guys when he could be with his family?"

"It feels like there's something else going on. . . . I don't know, maybe I'm spending too much time in the rumor mill," Ester says, her confidence waning. "What do you think, Lu?"

I'm not sure what to think.

There are many things I want to say to Kite, things I can't begin to articulate. I want to fill the void carved by his absence, to bridge the gap between the lives we've been leading, but when I recall the distant look in his eyes that night at dinner and his attitude the afternoon we stood in the rain, I can't picture us talking anytime soon.

But he did bake me cookies.

A firework soars into the sky and blooms hundreds of glimmering red petals, followed by gold and sapphire showers. I shift my gaze to Ester, and as I watch the glow of the fireworks fade in and out of her eyes, a thought occurs to me.

Is this what it feels like to be starstruck? To have the one you adore appear before you, and all you see are lights parading across your vision, burning impressions into your mind while gunshot sounds go off around you?

"Whatever the truth is," I say finally, "I hope Kite's back because he wants to be."

✳

After pestering me for Kite's autograph, Ester ropes me in for a hug, nearly cracking my rib cage, and departs with Stephanie in a plume of car fumes.

Backyard fire pits continue to blaze vibrant shades of orange. Judging from the sporadic bursts of laughter echoing from every direction, bedtime is still a long way off.

The night is young, but I'm eager to wash the barbecue smoke from my hair and fall into a world of soft cotton sheets. I need as much sleep as I can get, because Hersheypark is finally happening tomorrow. Bright and early, at Ester's suggestion. I suspect she has a ton of pent-up emotions roiling inside her; screaming her head off on a roller coaster is the release she needs.

We could all use a good scream.

As I'm tidying up the backyard, Kite's voice ripples over me like cool silk.

"Lovely," he says, like it's a question.

I follow his voice and spot him along the fence. "Yes?"

"Do you mind coming . . . closer?"

I fold the picnic blanket over my arm and answer him with my feet, stopping once I'm close enough to make out the lines of his face. "What's up?"

Kite scratches his head and shifts his weight from one foot

to the other before settling on his right. "I was letting Maru out when I overheard your friends. . . ."

Oh no, he overheard us talking about him. Kill me now.

"Kite, I am so sorry. We didn't—"

"Can I come with you to Hersheypark?"

I blink once, then twice.

Several houses down, someone ignites a bouquet of sparklers. They burst to life in a cacophony of crackling flares. For once I'm glad to have unruly neighbors who'll fill what would otherwise have been an uncomfortable silence.

With a hand to the back of his neck, Kite holds my gaze for a few seconds longer before his eyes sweep the grass. "I know I'm inviting myself on your trip. Please don't feel like you have to be nice and say yes."

Now I'm scratching my head. I'm relieved to know he didn't overhear what Ester said, so relieved that I want to tell him yes, of course he can come. But I do have some concerns.

"Aren't you worried people will recognize you?"

Kite does his best imitation of a shrug; even then, everything about it feels forced. He knows it. I know it, and he knows I know. "I'll be fine as long as I take some precautions. Don't sweat it."

"Aren't you on medical leave?" There, I said it. "Your doctor said you needed rest."

"That doesn't mean I'm sick. I just need to"—he tousles his hair—"get away for a bit. My doctor's not going to freak out if I hop on a roller coaster."

"But your fans will if they find out."

"Lovely." Kite pierces me with a look that is honest and pleading. "You don't need to protect me. That's what bodyguards are for. I just need you to be you."

For someone who said I didn't have to say yes, he sure is adamant about coming on this trip, and damn, can he be persuasive.

"If you're not worried, I don't see why you can't come. Stephanie and Ester would love to have you." Without meaning to, I overenunciate "love" as if I'm tasting and savoring every letter. I clear my throat. "I'll let them know. Be ready to leave at seven-thirty."

"Got it!" Kite immediately brightens. "See you in the morning."

"See you . . ." I turn my back to him, eager to hide my face even though he can't possibly see me blushing in the dark, and head inside. That's when I remember. I never thanked him for the cookies.

"Hey—" I look back, only to find him gone from his spot.

Then I hear incoherent grumbling, followed by a thud and a *meow*.

"I love amusement parks. The only time I got sick from a ride was during a school trip. Seventh grade, I think? My friend begged me to ride the teacups with her. So I did. There was a contest to see which group could spin the fastest, and let me tell you, she went wild. She put everything she had into her arms and spun our teacup until we were almost flying out of it—but we didn't win. It was after we got in line to buy churros that my lunch came back to say hello."

Kite in an interview with JK Pop News at Tokyo Disneyland, after Karnival's spring concerts in Osaka and Tokyo.

14

Stephanie's car smells like a sugar factory.

The drive to Hersheypark is long, but not so long that we need a dozen donuts and a large coffee each—in addition to the mini pandan waffles Ester prepared. I have a hunch my friends are out to impress Kite. The way to a man's heart is through his stomach, so they say.

"These are tasty," Kite says, devouring a waffle in one bite.

"She'll share the recipe if you give her your autograph," I say.

Ester whips around the front seat, almost splashing her coffee on us. "No can do. It's a family recipe. I am sworn to secrecy, but I do want your autograph—and Wayne's."

"I can make it happen." Kite laughs lightheartedly.

Ester shoves a permanent marker into his face. "Please sign my shirt and let me die a happy woman." Unfazed by her (sudden) request, Kite signs his name on her shirtsleeve. "Thank you! I am never washing this shirt again!"

Stephanie and Ester were immediately on board with Kite joining us when I texted them last night, as I predicted. But much to my surprise, Ester isn't as tongue-tied as I'd expected. The less silence the better. The four of us are going to be confined in a car for the next two hours, and nothing spoils a road trip more than boredom.

"How long have you all known each other?" Kite asks.

"Too long," answers Stephanie. "I've known Lulu since eighth grade, Ester since ninth."

"I didn't become friends with them until eleventh grade," Ester clarifies. "The same year Lu introduced me to Karnival."

Kite gives me a sidelong look. As soon as I catch his eyes on me, he averts his gaze to examine a piece of lint on his shirt before staring out at the dense forest lining the roadway for miles on end.

"I heard you and Lulu grew up together," Stephanie says, sipping her coffee with one hand while gripping the steering wheel with the other. "Got any embarrassing stories of her?"

"Uh, objection! I—"

Kite cuts me off. "Did she tell you about our third-grade invention project?" Stephanie and Ester answer him with a simultaneous no and sit a little higher in their seats. Meanwhile, I sink a little lower in mine. "We had a unit dedicated to American inventors, and our teacher assigned a project where we had to create something from scratch."

I remember this too well. Our "invention" had to include a minimum of three different materials. It also had to be functioning. I loathe Ms. Velez to this day for assigning what was basically a project meant for parents to complete for their kids.

Mom and Dad were too busy having marital disputes to help, so I went ahead and made my own pinball machine—out of a shallow rectangular box I dug out of the recycling bin. I glued plastic party favors onto the surface to form the playfield. For the flippers, I drilled two holes into the base of the box to fit a pair of chopsticks. I had to use a scissoring motion with the chopsticks to propel the pinball (a mini bouncy ball). Since I didn't know how to create a ramp or launcher, I had to toss the ball into the box to start the game.

Overall, the mechanisms were clumsy, and the ball often froze in place, since the box had no elevation and therefore not a whole lot of gravity.

I cried a liter of tears the morning Kite and I walked to the bus stop carrying our projects. He had constructed a working claw machine out of cardboard, rubber bands, pencils, pompoms, and a Poké Ball. Another classmate built a remote-controlled tank out of cardboard and toy wheels, which his parents obviously did for him.

Things got worse once we got to school. Everyone's invention put mine to shame, and the fact that we had to present our projects to the other third-grade classes had me bawling before the bell rang. I wanted to destroy my lame pinball machine, toss it in the garbage, and take an F.

"Why can't I make an invention?" I sobbed after Kite asked me why I was leaking like a burst pipe in the middle of the hallway.

Kite remembers this exact line. He recites it for Stephanie and Ester, albeit with fewer theatrics, and they laugh uncontrollably.

"That's so sad but funny." Ester guffaws. "I can't see you acting like that."

Ester has never seen me cry. I don't plan for that to change unless Mom and Aunt Mei get eaten by cannibals or something.

One thought that forever warms me is remembering Kite's enthusiasm. Everyone knew my project was the bottom of the barrel, but when it came time for presentations, Kite kept oohing and aahing as I explained the various parts of my pinball machine. During my demonstration, the ball bounced around for five seconds before it was game over. Still, Kite awarded me a standing ovation and got his friends to join him. In hindsight, the enthusiasm was over the top and fake, but it did give me the confidence boost I needed.

Kite and I keep this memory to ourselves. As Stephanie and Ester gather their wits, the two of us exchange half smiles. Combined, they make a whole.

Hersheypark is teeming with people who don't understand the concept of a single-file line.

To avoid recognition and a possible stampede, Kite has plastered washable tattoos all over his neck and arms. Covering your body in tattoos seems like a sure way to attract attention, but the tattoos are convincing. I doubt anyone would suspect a guy that inked up to be Kite.

He also has on a wide-brimmed fisherman's hat and black aviators. His disguise has transformed him into someone who likes to wrestle alligators and go camping on the weekend. As a final precaution, from here on out, Kite will be known as James. We got used to calling him James during our drive while Kite learned to respond to his new name.

"James, is there anything you want to ride?" I ask after we go through the bag check and officially enter the park grounds.

"I'm up for anything," he says.

"Then we'll let Ester lead the way."

And lead the way she does, to the tallest and fastest roller coaster in the park. Ester shoots for the frontmost cart, and the rest of us board without question. As the attendants go up and down the platform, making sure everyone is securely fastened, my nerves begin to tingle with anticipation. The tingling intensifies during the crawling ascent.

To my right, Kite flashes me a smile, and I return it, all teeth and instant regret. We all unleash a collective scream as we plummet. My heart drops to the pit of my stomach before bouncing up to my throat as if tethered to a bungee cord. The track dips and rises again. I squint against the wind as it whips through my hair and dries out my eyes. Amidst the screaming and the thunderous roar of the roller coaster, I hear Kite hooting and laughing into the wind. My heart leaps, even as the tracks flatten and the wind fades to nothing.

After hot dogs and curly fries, we agree to hit the arcade to let our stomachs settle, trading the overhead sound of rumbling steel and hoarse screams for laser guns and air hockey. We've been baking under the morning sun, and the indoor air-conditioning is an overdue but welcome reprieve.

I try my hand at pinball after losing a round of air hockey to Ester.

"Testing out your latest invention?" Kite says, sidling up to me.

"Don't you dare." I try to be firm but can't help laughing. "I can't believe I still cringe at something that happened in third grade."

Our last few one-on-ones haven't been promising, but right now we laugh easily.

"Your project wasn't bad for something made by a third grader." Kite pauses at his own words. "That must sound like a backhanded compliment. I didn't mean it that way."

"Sure you didn't . . ." Even with his sunglasses on, I can see panic beginning to set in his eyes. "I'm kidding, but since you had to go and bring up the past, it's only fair you win me something from the claw machine."

"Sounds simple enough."

Kite exhausts all his arcade tokens to try to win me the latest iPhone. When he goes to restock his tokens for the third time, I drag him away. The claw machine's rigged, and the physics aren't on our side, but I appreciate his perseverance. Maybe it's just my imagination, but it feels like he's trying to make up for something.

I didn't think it could get any hotter, but the afternoon sun proves me wrong as the temperature soars to almost 100 degrees.

It's high time we got wet and wild at the waterpark.

By some miracle, Stephanie manages to rent us a locker. It seems everyone got the idea to hit the waterpark at the exact same time.

The girls and I wore our swimsuits underneath our clothes to save ourselves a trip to the changing room. We strip on the spot. Kite releases a strangled noise. Curious, we all turn to look at him. He claps a hand over his mouth, and his face reddens.

"Never seen a girl in a bikini?" Stephanie teases, shaking a canister of sunscreen.

"I have, but they're not . . . common in Korea," Kite says, missing the fact that her question was meant to be rhetorical.

"Are they that conservative over there?" she asks, spraying sunscreen over her arms and legs before passing the canister to Ester, who helps her with her back.

"Depends on where you are." Kite hasn't shown any signs of removing his clothes. As if reading my mind, he says, "I'm going to pass on the waterpark." He circles a hand over his tattoos. "Better to be safe than sorry. You guys can go without me."

"Are you sure?" I ask. There's a long line for the lazy river, and Ester wants to do at least five laps. Kite would be waiting at least two hours for us to finish with the waterpark.

"Don't sweat it. I'll find something else to do," Kite assures me.

Without warning, Ester throws my clothes back to me—*at me* is more like it. I scramble to catch them before they scatter across the wet concrete. My hands are full by the time she tosses my drawstring backpack. Kite grabs it out of the air—before it hits me square in the face—and slings it over his shoulder.

"Lu will keep you company," says Ester.

"It would be her pleasure," adds Stephanie.

After much convincing, Kite relents, allowing me to accompany him for the next couple of hours while Stephanie and Ester go wild in the water. The two of us go back and forth on what to do. Neither of us wants to make an executive decision, so we wind up strolling through the park, stopping now and then to check out whatever kiosk attracts our attention.

"Your friends seem chill," he says as we queue for ice cream.

"Stephanie is. Ester? Not so much."

"You met Stephanie in eighth grade?"

"Yeah, she transferred to our school at the beginning of the year. You've probably seen her before. We started hanging out around the time you got scouted." I step up to the register and order two vanilla soft serves. Kite taps me on the shoulder, gently sweeps me aside, and hands the cashier some cash before I can object.

"If I knew you were paying, I would've ordered something expensive," I tell him.

"Did you want something else? Order whatever you want."

"I'm joking!" I assure him as the cashier hands me two soft serves. Part of me feels flattered by his generosity while another part feels flustered.

Why am I getting worked up over ice cream?

We find a bench under the shade. The ice cream is already dripping down the cone and onto my fingers.

"How are your friends over in South Korea?" I ask.

"You mean Wayne and them? They're . . . cool. Stephanie reminds me of Yoosung." Kite trains his eyes on the steady stream of people passing by and taps his foot. I count six taps before he says, "We're like family, but we're colleagues as much as we are friends. Sometimes we don't agree with each other."

He finishes his ice cream so fast I wonder if he even enjoyed it.

"I get along with—" He cuts himself off as a girl our age stops near the bench to tie her shoes. Once she's out of earshot, he continues. "I get along with Wayne and Xiaoming the best. They're the jokesters of the group, and there's less of a language barrier between us. Xiaoming says my Chinese is impressive for someone who can't shake off an American accent."

"Aren't you fluent in Korean? You've been learning for years."

"Conversationally I am."

"Don't you co-write some of your songs?"

Kite leans forward, props his elbows on his knees, and clasps his hands together. "Co-writing isn't always evenly split, and songwriting isn't the same as writing, let's say, an essay. My vocabulary is limited. I recognize words more than I can recall them from memory."

"Could've fooled me." I drink whatever is left of my ice cream and gobble up the soggy cone. "Is that why . . . you were upset the other day, when I said 'your songs'?"

Kite's foot freezes mid-tap. "Sorry. I was in a bad mood and took it out on you. I have . . . a lot on my mind lately."

"Do you want to talk about it?"

"Where do I even begin?"

"What's it like in South Korea?" seems like a good place to start.

"It's . . . different. I wouldn't say my experience is the norm." Fully aware that he isn't giving a concrete answer, he starts listing things rapidly. "Summers are hot; winters are cold. Public transportation is top-notch, at least in the cities I've been to. I see a lot of businessmen in blue shirts and navy suits, guess that's the trend. Bubble tea is hard to find, and it's not cheap like in Taiwan, and . . . I'll never get used to squatting toilets."

"That's a lot of words"—I hesitate for effect—"to say nothing."

He laughs briefly. As soon as the joyless sound recedes, his expression turns serious.

"If you want an honest review, life there is"—his gaze sweeps to the sky, at the roller coaster track cresting the other structures in the park—"crazy and repetitive. Between workouts, vocal lessons, choreography lessons, language lessons, and practice, there's always something else demanding my attention. The hecticness triples whenever there's a live performance; you run on fewer calories and less sleep . . . but all that work isn't for nothing."

A smile chips away at the corner of his lips. "The release you feel when you nail the last notes of a song, and the fans won't stop cheering after you've exited the stage . . . . It's why I chose K-pop in the first place."

I lean in, eager to hear more, but like the glory of a memory, this moment has peaked, and Kite and I are left with the present. This bright and scorching here and now.

"Sorry, I got carried away. Didn't mean to unload all that on you."

"Don't be sorry! I wanted an honest review, and I got one."

"Since we're being honest, can I ask you something?"

His request for permission puts me on edge, but this is the first time in a while that he's openly talked about himself. How can I deny him this one question?

"Sure, what's up?" I keep my tone light and encouraging.

"A while back, you said you wanted to study abroad in Korea. . . . Why do you want to learn Korean so much?"

I'm more than happy to answer, but as soon as I open my mouth, the words are lodged in my throat. Suddenly my body feels heavy. Inside me something hot and sticky threatens to ooze out, as if my blood has thickened into molten chocolate.

Kite sits up and patiently waits for an answer.

I wet my lips, close my eyes, and in the momentary darkness, all I see is Kite.

"Because of Karnival," I finally say. "You guys got me excited about South Korea—the music, the fashion, the food. I want to see what life is like over there, and . . ." Now that I hear myself, I realize there might be another reason. "I guess, seeing you there would've been a plus."

Kite's sunglasses slip down the crook of his nose. His gaze is studious and pins me to the spot. Face flushed red, I'm an easy read.

"Don't get me wrong," I hastily add. "It's not like I'd go to another country just to find you. That would be weird."

"But if you did happen to find me, by coincidence"—Kite playfully stresses the last word—"seeing me would be a plus."

He's teasing me.

I use my forefinger to push his sunglasses up his nose, hiding his gaze and eliciting an amused chuckle.

"I'm going to wash my hands." I scurry off in search of the nearest bathroom. Once again, the sun is beaming down at me, but the intensity is nowhere near as consuming as Kite's eyes burning holes into my back.

"That guy is so creepy-looking."

Firework on spotting (but not recognizing) Kite on a bench at Hersheypark.

15

Stephanie's car still smells like a sugar factory.

The taste of peanut butter lingers in my mouth, and I'm still finding patches of confectioners' sugar on my clothes from the gooey funnel cake we all shared. We swore not to overspend at Hershey's Chocolate World, yet here we are, with a year's supply of candy.

Barely an hour into our ride home and already we're dipping into our stash. Ester is in beast mode, tearing into a jumbo packet of Twizzlers with the voraciousness of a starved wolf.

The world around us descends into darkness as we careen onto the interstate.

Kite tosses his hat onto the rear dash and starts texting someone, his phone reflecting light boxes in his eyes, casting deep shadows against the profile of his face. Maybe he's sharing photos with Wayne and the others of all the giant chocolate bars we saw.

Back when we were shopping, Ester in all her bravery asked Kite what Wayne's favorite chocolate is. Unsurprisingly, she bought him a giant Kit Kat, which Kite promised to mail over (along with a letter Ester had the foresight to write). He offered to do the same for Stephanie and me, but neither of us wants to impose.

All the things I want to say to Karnival I'd rather say to Kite, and if I can't tell Kite, then what's the point?

This is what I tell myself as I fall asleep in the backseat, wrapped in the soothing aroma of chocolate, its pervasiveness a bold reminder that today wasn't a dream.

I wake up to the sound of my own snoring. My eyes flutter open. Then I realize I'm leaning against something warm and sturdy, not too hard and not too soft.

That something is Kite.

I fling myself away from him, igniting the tense muscles in the crook of my neck. A string of drool extends from my mouth, connecting to the wet blotch on his shoulder. I hastily wipe my mouth with the back of my hand and whip my head in Stephanie's direction. She's doubled over, her shoulders shaking with barely contained laughter. Ester is fast asleep with her head against the window while Kite dabs the spot of drool I so generously left him with a napkin.

"You were sleeping so soundly, we didn't want to disturb you," Stephanie says, her voice straining.

"I am so sorry," I sputter, combing a hand through my hair, grimacing when I realize it's the same hand I used to wipe my drool.

"It's been a long day," Kite says, offering me a sympathetic smile.

"We're all ugly sleepers," Stephanie chimes in.

"That is not true and you know it," I grumble, crossing my arms.

We hit a bump in the road, and the car jolts. Ester bangs her head against the window with a nasty crack. She sleeps through it, sighing blissfully as she adjusts her position.

Later, as we pull into my neighborhood, Ester wakes up with a throbbing headache. I rush inside to fetch an aspirin to quell her moaning while Kite unloads our things from the trunk.

Stephanie suggestively wiggles her brows at me. The trunk slams shut, and she evens out her expression before Kite catches her. She wishes us good night and drives off, leaving Kite and me alone on the side of the road.

The temperature has significantly cooled, the dramatic contrast revivifying the events of today—the dizzying heat, the clinging flavors of everything I ate, the spike of adrenaline, and my time with Kite. My day was full, but my heart is fuller.

Once again I apologize to Kite for snoring into his face and drooling on him.

"I'll stop apologizing for throwing up on your sneakers if you stop apologizing for borrowing my shoulder without asking. Deal?" He offers me an outstretched hand.

"Deal." We shake on it. His grip is strong, and I find myself lacing my fingers with his as he starts to pull away. I realize my mistake and drop my hand. "Hanging out with us wasn't so bad, was it?"

"Not at all," Kite says.

"Your disguise worked. That badass forest ranger look is growing on me."

"Now I get to have the fun of scrubbing these off." Kite holds out his tattooed arms for emphasis. The door to his house swings open, although no one steps out to greet us. "I better head in. Thanks for letting me come. I . . . needed this."

"Anytime. I'm glad you had a good time."

"Too bad we didn't ride the teacups. They probably went too slow for you anyway."

Before I can ask him what he means, we hear his mom call to him from inside the house.

Kite takes me by my upper arm, his grip firm and reassuring. "Let's do this again," he says.

His mom calls again, her words unintelligible but insistent. The worry in her voice reminds me that even though today felt so normal, for Kite a day out isn't just a day out—it's so much more complicated.

Kite doesn't quite let go of my arm. Instead, he weakens his grip and lets gravity drop his hand back to his side before he turns and walks away.

CELEBRITY CIRCUS TWEETED ON JULY 5.

We apologize to Karnival for how they were treated on *Celebrity Circus*. It was not our intention to disrespect our guests. However, actions speak louder than words, and everyone on the staff will work hard to do better.

16

Fresh out of the shower, I'm in the living room with an aloe mask on my face, singing along to "Dark Hour" while painting my toenails turquoise.

Kite brought back a ton of skin care products from South Korea. Mrs. Xu dropped some off, and by "some" I mean enough to last a zombie apocalypse: toners, serums, exfoliators, moisturizers, spot correctors, and face masks for skin tightening, minimizing pores, and deep hydration. Mom and Aunt Mei follow a strict skin care regimen and only use Korean brands, but they'll never use all this, so I helped myself to the lot, setting aside a few items Stephanie and Ester will appreciate.

All's quiet at home. Mom and Aunt Mei will be back shortly. I have a pot of water on the stove waiting to boil, so that I can have two bowls of instant ramen ready for them.

Just as I finish painting my toes, the house phone blares to life. I ignore it, chalking it up as a robocall. No one I know—at least, no one I want to talk to—uses my house number. After several rings, the phone goes to voice mail.

My dad starts speaking.

"It's me, Vincent. Hope everyone's having a great summer. Kath and I will be flying into New York City the first Sunday of August. Kyle's coming, too. Let me know if you'd all like to get dinner together while we're there."

The message concludes with a beep.

I cross my arms, kick my feet up, and fall into the soft cushion of the recliner.

Should I delete the message?

Mom wouldn't force me to have dinner with them, especially not after Dad skipped my graduation. And I'm the only one who's met his new family! Mom would never agree to meet Katherine and Kyle, and if any of them disrespects her in front of me, things will get ugly.

I'm floored that Dad even suggested this. I told him I wasn't visiting him in California. Why does he think I'd want to see him here? Does he expect us to all sit around a campfire and sing kumbaya until dawn with his former mistress? Then again, Dad's not the most considerate person. That much he's proven.

A car pulls into the driveway, and suddenly I remember the pot of water, which reached its boiling point long ago. On my way to the kitchen, I erase Dad's message.

"Did you get my voice mail?"

Unanswered text message from Lulu's dad on July 6.

17

"We should go to a Michelin-starred restaurant. How can we go on a foodie adventure in New York without splurging on some fancy dish with flecks of gold sprinkled on top?"

My phone has been attached to my ear for the last hour. Stephanie and I can't agree on what to eat tomorrow. We agreed on waffle sandwiches for breakfast, cheesecake for our afternoon snack, but we can't come to a consensus on lunch. Ester wants ramen, Stephanie wants soul food, and I want handmade pasta drizzled with truffle oil and Parmesan shavings.

"Let's have Kite pick," I suggest, pacing back and forth in my living room.

"We need an *impartial* judge," Stephanie says pointedly. "He'll choose what you want. A Michelin-starred restaurant is spare change to him. That's how rich people think."

"Aren't you rich, Stephanie?"

"I'm not *filthy* rich. Kite is. Did you not notice him decked out in Supreme the night Ester almost sent him to the ER?"

"Um, no? I was more concerned about his safety?"

Stephanie sighs. "Text Kite the three restaurants. Don't tell him who picked what, just tell him to choose one."

"But I don't have his number."

"Good thing you have legs." Stephanie hangs up.

Clicking my teeth, I pocket my phone and slink out to the backyard, wincing against the sun. Immediately my ears are assaulted by the whirring buzz of cicadas. Half blind and fully committed, I dash over to Kite's house.

After a rhythmic knock matching the ending chords to "Dark Hour," I hear the rattling of the chain lock on the other side of the door and come face-to-face with Connie. If she's surprised to see me, she doesn't show it. We trade hellos, and she lets me in.

"Kai's in his room," she says before gliding up the stairs.

I linger in the foyer, expecting Connie to return with Kite. After several beats of silence where I idly swing my arms, waiting, I realize I'm on my own.

I take off my shoes and let my memories lead the way—up the stairs to the last room at the end of the hall, where the sound of a piano emanates from behind a closed door. I shake away my nerves before knocking. A single rap is all it takes for the music to stop; the swiftness of it makes me feel like someone intruding on a private conversation.

The door opens wide enough for Kite to poke his head out.

"Hey, what are you doing here?" he says, his voice one decibel shy of a whisper, as he steps into the hallway and leaves his bedroom door cracked open behind him.

"I have a question, nothing terribly important. I can come back later if now's not a good time." Upon further reflection, interrupting his day for the sole purpose of asking him to choose a restaurant for a lunch he isn't invited to is a bad idea.

"I got time. Want to sit?"

"Sure." I step back and plop onto the floor, pretzel-style, as I've done many times at Ester's and Stephanie's—except I'm not at Ester's or Stephanie's.

Kite coughs into his elbow. "We can talk in my room."

I try not to scramble too quickly to my feet.

His room is different from what I remember. Gone are the 2PM and SHINee posters. The off-white walls are devoid of decorations, and the blue carpeting has been stripped away, replaced with hardwood floors. His bed has been upgraded from a twin to a queen; it's so well-made, it doesn't look like anyone sleeps in it. I do a double take when I spot the collection of luxury skin care products neatly arranged on top of his dresser. Hard to believe he used to wash his face with hand soap.

More important, his digital keyboard—the one he bought with his own money after shoveling people's driveways for an entire winter—is nowhere to be seen.

Kite catches me staring at the empty corner by his closet. "My dad moved the keyboard into the basement." I hear the lie in his voice, that wobbly hesitation. His lips curl into a guilty smile. "I'm not convincing, am I? Truth is . . . Connie sold it."

He sees the alarm in my face, and in a hushed voice, he says, "I don't blame her. No one was using it after I left, and . . . she needed new soccer cleats. This was when I was still a trainee, so we didn't have much money. . . . Anyway, what did you want to ask?"

He wheels a chair out from his desk and motions for me to sit while he takes the bed. I explain the restaurant situation to him, and he takes the question more seriously than I thought he would. Despite my impassioned stance on haute cuisine, he chooses soul food.

"Why?" I have to ask.

"Fried chicken is where it's at. It's one of the most popular foods in Korea. Pair it with yellow pickles, and boom, you're in heaven."

"I doubt the restaurant is going to have yellow pickles. That's an Asian thing."

"Yellow pickles go with almost anything, even pizza. Once I go back, the first thing I'm ordering is a prawn-and-sweet-potato pizza."

His words hover in the air, precariously suspended by my own denial, and like a storm cloud overtaking the sky, the mood shifts as I'm reminded of his inevitable departure.

"When are you going back?" I ask, not sure if I want an answer.

"Maybe late August?" he muses, toying with a loose thread on his shirt. "As you already know, I came home because my doctor told me to rest. I didn't physically injure myself, but the . . . stress was getting to me. He said to take at least a month off."

The K-pop industry is notorious for its intense and sometimes inhumane treatment of idols. Burnout is common. While Dream Drop isn't like other entertainment companies, which churn out K-pop idols like a factory, that doesn't mean their artists don't work as hard or that they don't face the same pressures as everyone else.

Even so, it feels like Kite is holding back, like there's more to the story than he's willing to say.

"Is the stress usually *this* bad?" I ask.

Kite continues fiddling with his shirt, twining the thread around his finger before unraveling it again and again and again. "Usually? No. I can be busy without being stressed. But there's another kind of busy, the kind where your mind won't turn off. You forget to stop, and when you can, you don't want to. . . . You ignore the stress, let it build for too long, and next thing you know, you've worked yourself down to the bone and you're not acting like yourself."

"How are you feeling now?" I ask, emboldened by his honesty.

"Better. It took some getting used to, but . . . it's good to be back." He smiles. "Who knew roller coasters and chocolate had medicinal properties?"

The dark cloud hanging over us disperses, and I inwardly breathe a sigh of relief. "Well, I'm happy to have you back despite the reasons that brought you here. Take all the medicine you need and rest up."

"Will do, Doctor."

"I heard piano music earlier. Were you playing it from your phone?"

Kite slides an iPad out from under his pillow. "I was fooling around with this music-making app," he says, as though it's the most trivial thing in the world.

"It sounded nice." I could've used a more descriptive adjective, but *nice* was the first word that jumped to mind. At least I didn't use *interesting*, which almost always carries a negative connotation.

"It's nothing worth listening to." He slides the iPad back under the pillow, out of sight and out of mind. "You said you're going to New York this Saturday?"

"Yeah, want to come?" The words slip out before I can give them a second thought.

"Believe me, I do, but I might be pushing it."

Someone's bound to recognize him in the city. The risk is greater in K Town. Unless he dons a fake beard, someone with a sharp eye will spot him.

"Say no more." I touch my feet to the floor. "I should get going."

Kite sees me to the front door, seemingly distracted as I slip into my shoes. Suddenly his eyes find their way over to me. "Can I see your phone?"

I hand it over without question. By the time I ask myself why, he's passing my phone back to me. I look down at the screen: he added himself to my contacts.

"Feel free to text me," he says with a parting wink, "and tell Ester I mailed her letter and Kit Kat. She can expect Wayne's autograph sometime soon."

Happiness does not begin to describe what I'm feeling right now. To say I'm on cloud nine or on top of the world doesn't cut it either. I feel like I've been entrusted with a devastating secret— a thrilling burden, like I'm flirting with danger.

Kite's phone number is one of the most coveted things in Karnival fandom. It's also one of the most private things he can share. Rumor has it a sasaeng acquired O-Kei's number by bribing his cell phone provider and then bragged about it on social media.

There's something scandalous yet flattering about possessing something so personal. Kite put himself down as James, and behind that fake name is a story only I have heard. I repeat his number over and over again as if it's a spell that will bind me to him. But the spell is as weak as a spool of thread, fraying as soon as I'm aware of the thoughts I shouldn't be having.

Red Alert: O-Kei and Yoosung sighted at a 7-Eleven! DM me
for details!

18

Later that day, Stephanie calls to tell me that AP exam scores are available. We promise to meet at Pho King Delight to discuss.

After pulling into the parking lot, I check the College Board website. My fingers tremble as I type in my account information, and a knot forms in my chest as I wait for the page to load. Every second of waiting is a second too long, and doubt begins to creep in—a complete contrast to how I felt on the final day of exams.

Finally, after a decade, I pull up my exam scores: a five in comparative government and in language and composition. Relief floods over me. I lean back and close my eyes. When I reopen them, Stephanie's in the parking spot next to me. She waves at me, her lips stretched into a wide grin.

Looks like we both have good news.

Inside Pho King Delight, Jason greets us with a sweaty high five before seating us at a table against the wall, near the windows. We order straightaway.

"Who wants to brag first?" Stephanie asks, tying her hair back into a ponytail.

"You're the genius who took five exams. The honor is yours."

"I got a five in calculus and lang comp, a four in world history and statistics, and a three in biology," she says, conceding her one bad score.

"You'll have a semester's worth of college credit before you start at Barnard. You should be proud." I offer her an extra dose of enthusiasm in case she's feeling down about biology.

"I know, but for something I thought was a breeze, a three feels like a slap in the face," she says, pouting. "How'd you do?"

"Scored two fives. That's two fewer college classes to worry about."

"All you have to worry about now is romancing Ki—James." Stephanie corrects herself as Jason delivers two bowls of pho and a plate of garnishes.

Just as I snatch up a pair of chopsticks, Connie and her soccer friends, Maggie and Lola, sweep through the front door, a blast of hot air chasing after them.

"Why are we coming to a sandwich shop for smoothies?" Maggie grumbles.

"Because I said so," Connie mutters, picking a table as far from us as possible.

Maggie and Lola trade exasperated glances. Right before they sit down, they catch me staring at them. I look away quickly.

Too late. I hear footsteps heading my way. Stephanie widens her eyes, intrigued as to where this is going. Jason steps aside, making room for Lola and Maggie as they stop at our table.

Lola speaks first. "You live next door to Connie, right?"

I nod. Lola and I once bonded over Karnival, at homecoming junior year.

"You know about Kite's hiatus?" Again I nod. "Have you heard anything about him coming home?"

"We asked Connie," Maggie adds, "but she won't tell us any-thing . . . or let us come over."

"I haven't heard anything." Through the sliver of space between Lola and Maggie, I catch a glimpse of Connie, arms crossed and scowling.

"You haven't heard *anything*?" Lola insists.

"I haven't, and even if I did, it's none of your business."

Lola flushes with indignation.

Maggie speaks up: "We're asking as one worried fan to another. No need to act high and mighty."

"As one high-and-mighty fan to another, why don't you order a smoothie and chill out?" I retort before noisily slurping my noodles, ending the conversation.

"Ladies, I make a mean mango smoothie," Jason says, escorting the girls back to their table, "and our shaved ice is almost award-winning."

Stephanie raps her knuckles against the table. I lift my eyes to see her smirking through the flimsy screen of steam rising from her pho.

"You sure put them in their place," she says, amused.

Plenty of strangers and acquaintances have approached me to strike up a conversation—only to look past me as if I were a glass door that would lead them to Kite. If it's like that for me, I can't imagine what Connie goes through. Ester, as big a Firework as she is, has never made me feel invisible or used. I'm not sure I could say the same for Connie's friends. . . .

I dip my head to take another bite of noodles, then my phone vibrates in my pocket.

Ester texted me a video.

"I heard what happened. How are O-Kei and
Yoosung doing?"

Text message from Kite to Wayne on July 7.

19

"Are you watching that again?" I groan, digging my heels into the floor as the train departs from Newark airport. Today we're finally going into the city.

"I can't help it," Ester says, eyes glued to her phone.

Fireworks are in an uproar after a fan recognized O-Kei and Yoosung at a 7-Eleven and leaked their location. A horde of girls (who happened to be nearby, I guess) flocked to the store and had them surrounded. The incident was caught on camera.

In the video Ester first sent me, you see Yoosung in the center of a crowd, pleading with his fans, asking them to make way and let him leave—to no avail. His voice is drowned out by screaming fans shoving their phones in his face. At the nine-minute mark, you see O-Kei with one hand over his mouth while holding his phone to his ear.

In another video, taken from outside 7-Eleven, Karnival's manager arrives with a troop of bodyguards, and they elbow their way into the store. Seconds later a police car pulls up and fans disperse, the cameraman fleeing with them.

Since the incident went viral, Fireworks are working overtime to identify the fans in the videos in hopes of banning them from the fandom. Dream Drop also released a statement about idol harassment and public disturbances.

"Some people have zero respect for others." Ester sighs, shaking her head. "I will never understand sasaengs. They put Fireworks to shame. How can you call yourself a fan when the idol you worship is begging you to move out of the way?"

"You answered your own question," Stephanie says, primping her hair while admiring her reflection in the window. "Anyone who worships another human isn't necessarily thinking clearly."

"And you guys think *I'm* intense!" Ester flings her arms above her head and collapses backward into her seat. "Did Ki—I mean James—say anything about the video?"

"He hasn't . . ."

"What happened to O-Kei and Yoosung is exactly what'll happen to James if people find out he's here," Ester says, cautiously looking around for eavesdroppers. "I can't believe word hasn't already got out. Seems the stalkers aren't very good at stalking."

"Ester," I chastise her. "You make it sound like that's a bad thing."

Stephanie gets her soul food, but not at the restaurant she intended.

Our growling stomachs couldn't handle the long wait at Heartful Kitchen, so we opted for HK Seoul, a hole-in-the-wall in the East Village, owned by a Hawaiian Korean couple. Tucked between a craft store and a Laundromat, the restaurant is narrow and cracking at the tiles, the inside sweltering thanks to the open kitchen. By chance or destiny, fried chicken with yellow pickled radishes is on the menu.

I send Kite a selfie of us eating. He surprises me with an immediate response: *"Jealous."* He texts me a photo of his lunch:

limp glass noodles sautéed with onions and carrots. *"I was hungry, and this is all I had to work with."*

"How does it taste?" I write back.

"I'd rate it a five."

"That's not too bad."

"On a scale of one to a hundred it is."

I laugh out loud, spitting half-chewed chicken into Stephanie's face. "Oops."

Ester snorts into her drink.

Stephanie grabs a napkin and dabs her face. "Talking to James?"

"How'd you know?" I tuck my phone away before she can peek at the screen.

"A hunch." Stephanie tips her chin and bites off the end of a sweet-potato fry. "So, are you two in love yet?"

"Are *you* in love with me?" I quip, eliciting another snort from Ester.

"Just answer the question."

I click my teeth. "I don't love him, he doesn't love me, and that's that."

"You get the same look on your face when you deny being a Karnival fan. You're a bad liar." Stephanie rolls her eyes. "Ester and I think you're missing out on a once-in-a-lifetime opportunity."

"If you mean a once-in-a-lifetime opportunity to ruin my friendship with Ki—James, then I'm happy to miss out."

"Lu, we're not blind," Ester chimes in. "It's obvious you like him."

"Of course, I like him! We grew up together, *and* he's a K-pop idol."

"Stop deflecting," Stephanie says flippantly. "You know exactly what she means by 'like.' You're not fooling anyone but yourself."

"I'm not deflecting! You guys are—" I don't know what to say or what I want to say, and the frustration of it burns through me, stinging my cheeks. "Shut up and eat your pickles!" I throw my hands in the air.

My arm makes contact with something solid. I swivel around to find a girl behind me. She staggers back, hands held up to her chest, palms out to brace herself. I don't know how I didn't see her.

"Sorry," I stammer. She places a piece of paper on the table before mumbling something and hurrying away.

Stephanie leans over to read the paper, which turns out to be a napkin. "She left you her number," Stephanie explains, amusement tugging at her lips as I stare at her, perplexed.

"What?" I ask.

Stephanie hands me the napkin, the girl's phone number scrawled across in red lipstick.

I read the numbers once, twice, and then a third time. "Is that a three or a five?" I tilt the napkin at a forty-degree angle. "That one at the end looks like a seven."

"Forget her. She could be a serial killer out to harvest your organs for all we know," Ester says, her tone ironically casual. "Don't let anyone steal your heart but James."

"Oh, shut up."

Back home, after I've had time to decompress and shake myself out of my sun-induced stupor, Kite surprises me again by asking to come over. Having spent all day indoors, he's aching for a distraction.

Making sure the coast is clear, I sneak him in through the back door, and then we're side by side on the living room floor. He's all ears as I recount the events of today.

"Fate wanted you to appreciate the culinary genius of fried chicken and yellow pickles," he says with an easy smile.

I bump shoulders with him. "I would've appreciated it more if a certain someone was there to savor such culinary genius with me."

Even though I'm teasing, the words leave a bittersweet aftertaste in my mouth, and the longer it lingers, the more my chest tightens. If I had insisted, would Kite have tagged along?

Then I remember the incident at 7-Eleven.

Hope and reality are at odds with each other. All the hope in the world won't change the fact that every outing comes with a risk. The last thing I want is to make Kite feel bad for doing what's best for him.

"Not that I blame you," I amend. "We don't want a repeat of what happened to O-Kei and—" I realize my mistake and cut myself short.

Why did I have to bring up that video?

Before I can fix my blunder, Kite says, "The video's unfortunate, but it's nothing the guys and I aren't used to. It's the price we pay for fame."

I want to argue that no one should lose their right to privacy because they're famous, but right now it's Kite's turn to speak.

"Having people recognize you in public used to be an ego boost. It was . . . almost insulting when people didn't," Kite continues. "Then one time at the airport, after our first concert in Taiwan, a girl followed me into the restroom."

"What?" I exclaim.

"I locked myself in one of the stalls until security dragged her out. She had a camera on her, and my manager threatened to press charges." Kite rolls his head from one side to another, his Adam's apple bobbing as he swallows. "That was . . . a bad day. I avoided public restrooms for a while after that."

He sounds detached from his own experience, but his clenched fists and downcast eyes tell a different story.

It's no secret sasaengs can be obsessive to the detriment of others, but hearing it from Kite and watching him pretend to be unfazed makes it all the more appalling.

"I'm sorry you had to go through that. What that girl did was absolutely wrong." I have some colorful choice words for her, but what's the use in ranting?

For all I know, it could make Kite feel worse about a situation neither of us has the power to change. You can't control other people's actions, but at least I can control my own. I want Kite to know that his thoughts are worth sharing.

"Thanks for telling me," I say. "I appreciate it."

"I didn't make this sentimental, did I?" he says, his tone self-admonishing.

"Seriously, Kite, I appreciate it." I offer him a smile, and his expression softens into a tender gaze, one that makes me warm and fuzzy inside.

We sit in silence for a moment, the two of us reflected in the TV screen, and then I notice how small the gap is between us. Suddenly I'm self-conscious of where my hands are and keep them in my lap.

Kite bumps his knee against my leg, startling me. "About that girl who gave you her number . . . you never told me you're bi."

"The opportunity never presented itself, and it's not something

I constantly think about. Straight people don't go around telling everyone they're straight."

"True." Kite strokes his chin and nods. "So . . ."

"So?"

"Are you going to call her?"

"Nah." I shake my head and twiddle my thumbs. "Her handwriting is a mess. You could read her phone number five different ways."

Kite breathes a sigh of relief. "That's good."

I snap to attention. "What did you say?"

"N-nothing." Kite squares his shoulders. Every inch of his skin deepens to a vibrant shade of crimson that crawls up his neck and to his jawline before blossoming into his cheeks.

I scoot forward, twisting my body so that I'm more or less sitting in front of him. "I heard you. What do you mean, 'That's good'?"

He averts his eyes and looks everywhere but at me. "Because . . . she could've been a serial killer or a cultist or a recruiter for a multilevel marketing scheme."

"Are you listing those in any particular order? One of them seems a bit inconsequential compared to the others," I say, bursting into giggles as the blushing intensifies. Any darker and his skin will be stained red. "Thanks for the concern." I pat him on the shoulder. "I'm in the mood to bake cupcakes. Want to help?"

"I'm game." Kite follows me into the kitchen. "What kind are we making?"

"Something Kite-inspired? I'll need you to take this personality quiz first."

I slide my phone out from my pocket and accidentally drop the napkin with the girl's phone number written on it. I pick it up and read it over again.

"That is some sloppy handwriting," Kite says, peering over my shoulder. "If her threes didn't look so much like fives, she might've had a chance." His tone isn't exactly sympathetic.

"Or maybe her fives look too much like threes." I crumple the napkin into a ball and shoot it into the garbage bin.

If I didn't know any better, I might think Kite is jealous.

POSTED BY MYLIGHTKITE ON JULY 7.

Shame on JennyKPops for leaking Yoosung and O-Kei's location. True Fireworks love and admire their idols from a safe and healthy distance. We don't F.A.P. (Fans Attacking Privacy) or F.U.K. (Fans Upsetting Karnival). We support privacy and respect Karnival. We S.P.A.R.K.

#7-11-Gate #KeepCalmSPARKOn

20

"You and Kite baked key lime coconut cupcakes?"

Stephanie skeptically eyes the tray of sweets I just delivered to her doorstep.

It's nearing midnight, a few hours after Kite and I finished baking cupcakes worthy of a French patisserie. Our buttermilk frosting was whipped and piped to perfection, and we sprinkled toasted coconut flakes and lime zest on top, arranging the pieces to resemble fireworks.

"Are these not to your liking, princess?" I wave the tray under her nose, hoping the sweet aroma will tickle her appetite.

"Can't say, haven't eaten one," she says, taking the tray before welcoming me into her house. She puts on a kettle as I boost myself up onto the kitchen island. "Did he take the cupcake personality quiz?"

"Yeah, he got key lime: sweet, tart, and unsuspecting." I compare the kind and sunny image of Kite from my childhood to the one acting cool and intense for the camera, and the results seem fitting.

"Where did the coconut come from?" Stephanie peels back the paper lining to a cupcake, surveys it like it's a rare specimen, and bites into it. I watch as her eyebrows lift in pleasant surprise. "These are dangerous," she murmurs to herself.

"As you know, I'm pineapple coconut. Kite and I thought it would be fun to mix the flavors," I respond, not thinking much of it.

Stephanie bites her knuckles, a low effort attempt to conceal the smirk on her face. "I call these cupcakes a marriage of two flavors, a delectable union joining Kite and Lulu." She holds the half-eaten cupcake to my lips and makes a kissy face.

I groan. "Kite and I are just friends. How many times do I have to repeat myself?"

"As many times as it takes for you to stop lying to yourself." Stephanie finishes her cupcake before grabbing two clean mugs from the dishwasher as the kettle begins to whistle. "Are you sure Kite didn't have a crush on you in middle school?"

I shake my head, an adamant no.

"Elementary?"

"Seriously, Stephanie?"

"Kids mature fast these days."

I hop down from the kitchen island, loop my arm through my purse straps, and make my way to the front door.

Stephanie hurries after me. "You're leaving? I just made tea, decaffeinated too!"

I throw my arms into the air and gasp. "Oh, no! What are we going to do now?"

"Sit your butt down and have tea with your best friend. How often will we get to do this once September comes?"

I lower my arms and frown. I haven't put much thought into college lately. Stephanie will be moving into the dorms come August.

Quietly though not reluctantly, I return to the kitchen, and she pours me a cup of tea in my favorite mug, the one that changes colors when heated.

"You're lucky I love you," I tell her, helping myself to a cupcake.

"I'll drink to that. Bottoms up!" Stephanie bumps cupcakes with me, and we tilt our heads back, devouring the union between Kite and Lulu in two sweet bites.

✳

Despite my late bedtime—fueled by what I suspect wasn't decaffeinated tea—I'm up by sunrise, refreshed and renewed, ready to sell bread and bubble tea.

I've been neglecting the bakery, and all this unspent energy could be put to use.

Mom woke up with an earsplitting headache, so Aunt Mei and I convinced her to take a half-day. The plan is for me to work until noon, check on Mom, and depending on how she's feeling, I'll either work the afternoon or let Mom relieve me of my daughterly duties.

Business is mildly slow, with most people ordering drinks and hanging around to use the Wi-Fi. I languish behind the counter after fifteen minutes go by without anything to do.

Then Ester barrels into the store. She cuts a sharp path through a cluster of dillydallying customers before slapping a flyer onto the counter. I read it. Tonight, Roller Rave, an indoor skating rink on the west side of town, is hosting a costume night. There's a discounted entry fee for those who come dressed.

"We're going," she says, pointing. "You, me, and Steph."

"I don't know if I'm—"

Aunt Mei slides up to the counter to stand beside me. "Lulu would love to go." She turns and winks at me. "Your mom's feeling better. She'll be in after lunch."

Ester raises a brow at me. "You were saying?"

✳

It's a quarter after seven when I'm putting the finishing touches on my outfit—gold and silver stars that line the right side of my face, starting from my brow and ending at my jawline.

Ester wants us all in costume and warned us not to come as a schoolgirl or teacher because "a skirt and blouse doesn't count." So I dug up the figure skating dress I wore last Halloween. Its dramatic midnight blue dye job and spangled bodice should fit the bill.

I trace over the last star with a final coat of glitter and examine myself in my vanity mirror. Perfect. My phone vibrates from somewhere among the mess of makeup brushes, paint bottles, and tissues.

"*Here,*" Ester texted me.

There's someone already in the backseat when I climb into Ester's car. They're outfitted in black from head to toe, a motorcycle helmet hiding their face. I look at Ester, the dead bride having a bad hair day in the driver's seat, and then at Stephanie in the front passenger seat, with her Burberry trench coat and steampunk goggles.

"That's my cousin," Ester explains, backing out of the driveway, "from Hoboken."

I stare at Ester. She throws a backward glance at me, then another, and when I don't stop staring, her neutral expression crumbles. She starts laughing.

The mystery person lifts back their face shield, and I immediately recognize the pair of striking eyes behind them.

"Kite!" I balk. "What are you doing here?"

"Drag racing, obviously," answers Stephanie.

147

Kite speaks up before the sarcasm war can begin. "Ester dropped a flyer off at my house, inviting me to join you tonight. I've been wanting to go out again and—"

"—since we're all in costume, no one will recognize him," Ester adds. "No worries, Lu."

"I'm not worried, I'm just . . . surprised." Surprised that Kite wants to hang out with us despite the 7-Eleven incident, but also, overjoyed that he's here.

✳

Walking into Roller Rave is like traveling forward in time to October.

All the employees are luminescent in their orange polos and visors, their necks and arms ringed by countless glow sticks. Ninjas, pirates, witches, and vampires swarm the main entrance. Beyond them is the arcade, taking up an entire corner of the building before extending outward into a narrow alley along the back wall of the skating rink.

After we grab our rental skates, Ester and Stephanie merge onto the rink without so much as a goodbye. I take a moment to adjust to my skates and find my balance while Kite makes laps through the snack bar, weaving in and out of the tables while seamlessly changing directions—forward and backward, then forward again—before he finds his way back to me.

"Ready?" he asks as we approach the nearest entrance to the rink.

"Yeah, I got it." I'm not a newbie at this, but I'm not as graceful as Kite either.

"Which look do you like better? Forest ranger or biker?" Kite leans in so he can be heard above the music. His face shield is pulled down but not all the way.

I laugh. "Hard to say. I do miss those tattoos."

A steady flow of traffic moves through the rink, and when I find an opening in the crowd, Kite whisks me off the carpeted floor and onto the hardwood. We speed up, matching the pace of the skaters around us, and the world blurs. Disco lights flash above us—a prism of colors reflecting off Kite's helmet—as we circle our way around the room.

"How often do you do this kind of stuff?" I ask. "Go out with friends, do what normal people do for fun?"

"Free time is rare. Back when I was a trainee, I could go out on weekends and not worry about crowds. Now, not so much. If the guys want to do something together, we need to reserve private accommodations and bring our entourage. We try to do things individually or with one other person—easier to keep a low profile. Face masks are common in Korea; it's not hard to make yourself unrecognizable unless you encounter a very . . . perceptive fan."

"I have another word for perceptive."

He throws up his hands to say *What can you do?*

"Who's your go-to partner when you go out?" I ask.

"Wayne," he answers immediately. "He likes to go with the flow and is genuinely fun to be around. He once reserved an entire cat café for the two of us. Well . . . he originally did it for O-Kei's birthday, but that was before O-Kei said he didn't like cats."

I gasp.

"I know, right? O-Kei's a workaholic anyway." Kite moves away from the center of the rink, closer to the wall, where the pace is more relaxed. "He's the type who gets annoyed if we're not spending every hour practicing like him."

"Last I checked, humans require sleep."

"He wants Karnival to be the next international sensation. According to him, no one who gets four hours of sleep each day reaches BTS's level of fame."

"Don't you guys have fans all over the world though?"

"We do, but we don't consistently top music charts. Coming from a small label like Dream Drop, Karnival's doing well, don't get me wrong, but there are always greater heights to strive for. There were talks about doing a world tour, but that didn't pan out. . . ."

"How does O-Kei feel about you being away for the summer?"

Kite places a hand over his helmet, as if to make sure I can't see him. "We're not exactly on—"

I trip before he can finish. He wraps an arm around my waist, keeping me upright as we slow to a stop. There's a banana peel in the spot where I tripped. I don't have time to question it before the music cuts abruptly, the disco lights freeze, and a security guard enters the rink.

People make way, clearing a path that leads straight to a person in a gorilla suit flinging banana peels everywhere.

"Were you guys targeted?" Stephanie glides over to us, Ester not far behind. "A guy next to me took a banana in the face, almost crashed into him when he fell."

"Something's about to go down," Ester says, a little too excited as we watch the gorilla dart for the nearest exit. What the gorilla doesn't know is that another security guard is already waiting there.

"Okay then . . ." Before I can head for the snack bar, the

ceiling lights dim and the music comes back louder than before, this time with an R&B remix of "Lights Fantastic."

Ester screams, Kite raises his face shield, and I have no idea what Stephanie's doing because I'm looking at Kite and he's looking at me. The mood shifts, the excitement lost to the lush and hard-hitting notes of a song that has brought so many new beginnings.

Kite holds his hands out. "Can I have this dance?"

"I'm not much of a dancer," I say, and yet, I'm reaching for him. Our fingers connect.

I hook onto him, just enough for me to go where he goes as he drifts backward. He sways to the left, then after a moment, to the right. I follow his feet with my eyes, trying to match my movements with his without disturbing the rhythm we have.

"Relax," he says, "I got you."

I stop staring at the floor and focus on him. I can sense the beginnings of a smile as the corners of his eyes lift. He picks up the pace a little, testing my comfort, and soon my hand is in his and he spins me around, maneuvering himself in front of me so now I'm skating backward. I feel as light as a feather despite these heavy skates weighing me down.

I have no idea what's going on around us or who may be watching. Kite is all I can see right now, and I have to trust that my feet know what they're doing.

Because I certainly don't.

21

Around noon the next day, Dad calls again. I stand within arm's reach of the phone, smoldering at the sound of his voice as he leaves a voice mail reiterating his vacation plans, as if anyone in this house wants to see him.

I'm tempted to cut his message short until he says, "Lulu, let's get together for your birthday. Kath would love to see a Broadway show with you. She also has a coupon for a spa in Tribeca. You two can have a girl's day. Think about it. Miss you, bye."

I delete the message as soon as it's done recording.

Nothing he said sounded sincere. Is the spa supposed to be a birthday present or a matter of convenience since Katherine has a coupon? Does Dad actually want to celebrate my birthday? He forgot the last two, what makes this one special? Turning eighteen is a milestone, but so is graduating high school, and Dad couldn't bother to attend the ceremony. And nowhere in his message did *he* mention wanting to do anything with me.

The afternoon finds me in a better mood but not by much.

I spend the early half of it at Stephanie's, browsing Pinterest and Etsy. She plans to spruce up her college dorm with string lights, wall decals, and fake succulents to transform her drab prison cell into a luxurious micro-apartment. After debating over which bedspread to buy, I hightail it home and spend the rest of the afternoon weeding the backyard. Holding the Asian squat for an hour is a workout in and of itself, never mind wrestling with stubborn roots. By the time I'm done, I'm itchy and sore all over.

Wiggling out of my garden gloves, I collapse into a lawn chair and wipe the sweat off my forehead. Kite appears at the fence. I wave him over. He hops the fence, and I lead him inside, staying a few paces ahead so he can't smell the sweat and dirt on me. He waits in the kitchen while I wash up and change into a clean shirt.

"You were out there for a while," he says, handing me a cold water bottle.

"Were you watching me?" I ask, flushing at the thought.

"Maybe . . ." He shrugs. "Don't you hate yardwork?"

"Does anyone enjoy it?" I press the water bottle to my neck, savoring the sensation.

"No other fourth grader I know called yardwork illegal child labor."

It takes a moment for the memory to surface, and when it does, I only recall bits and pieces, something about a fourth-grade writing assignment.

"For Mother's Day, Ms. Katz had our class discuss all the hard work our moms do. You said your mom wakes up at dawn every day to cook breakfast even though she's busy running a bakery. You also said yardwork felt like illegal child labor, but you did it anyway, so your mom had one less thing to do."

That is something fourth grader me would've said.

A metaphorical lightbulb suddenly turns on. "Remember the fifth-grade talent show?"

Kite's pinched expression gives him away.

"I'm talking about fourth grade," he says, a pout in his voice. "Why are you bringing up the talent show?"

"Because fifth grade comes after fourth grade?" I counter.

"Third grade comes before fourth. Does that mean your pinball project is fair game?"

"Don't you dare!" I jab a finger into his chest, but my indignation soon dissolves into giggles. "I'll drop it if you really don't want to talk about it, but that performance was epic."

Kite discovered his love for K-pop in fifth grade.

He also discovered his passion for music.

SHINee was one of many boy groups to inspire Kite, and wanting to emulate them, Kite corralled a couple of his friends to do a dance cover of one of their songs for the school talent show. No one in the group knew a lick of Korean, and of the five of them, only one person knew how to dance—and that wasn't Kite.

I learned from Connie that Kite and his friends trained in the garage for two weeks. She helped with their costumes: black pants, charcoal gray T-shirts with spike-studded shoulder pads, and matching boots. To distinguish himself, Kite wore winged eyeliner and a shredded red scarf that resembled a feather boa (but most definitely wasn't a feather boa). He kept the performance a secret, said he wanted to surprise me.

On the day of the talent show, Kite's group was the closing act. The stage lights dimmed as the curtains were drawn, and after a pause, disco lights started flashing in tandem with the music. Kite stood center stage with his friends behind him, their movements perfectly synchronized as they danced to the beat and lip-synched their hearts out.

Midway into the performance, Principal Donnelly rushed onto the stage and ordered the stage crew to cut the disco lights and music. Apparently, the disco lights hadn't been screened by the talent show committee. Kite and his friends were given in-school suspension for breaking the rules and endangering members of the audience who could've suffered an epileptic seizure.

Before that day, I never would have thought I'd see Kite in makeup or spiky shoulder pads.

Now it's commonplace.

"Hey, Lovely, are you there?"

I'm grinning ear-to-ear when Kite pinches my cheek.

"Ow!" I swat his hand away. "I'm reminiscing here."

"That performance was cringe. I don't get why you're impressed by it."

"Because you were amazing and it technically counts as your first K-pop performance."

"We weren't even singing," Kite says sheepishly, "and the choreography was basic. It's not like we were moonwalking or doing backflips."

I'm about to argue with him until I remember the drama with *Celebrity Circus* and how fans ranked Kite as the weakest dancer in Karnival.

"You could do the hokey pokey, and I'd still think you're the coolest thing since avocado toast," I tell him. When he doesn't argue or deny it, I inwardly relax; then I realize how I just admitted to Kite that I think he's cool.

Not cool but the coolest.

I sneak a peek at him. He's fighting back a smile.

"Is that supposed to be a compliment?" he says, flicking the tip of my nose. "When have I ever seen you eat avocado toast?"

"I used to eat it every day until avocado prices went up." Impassioned by the incredulous look on his face, I keep going, against my better judgment. "Don't believe me? Ask my mom, or Ester, or better yet, Stephanie!" Kite is now on the verge of laughter. "Why are we talking about this again? Weren't we—"

"Talking about how cool I am?"

"Yes! Wait, no! Forget I said that."

"Why? Because you didn't mean it?"

"Of course I meant it. Why would—I'm done. Let's change the subject."

"You started it, now you have to finish it." Kite pinches my cheek. I scowl. "Okay, okay. Moving on . . . I have a song I want you to listen to. Can I send it to you later?"

"Can't you show me now?" I ask.

"I haven't recorded it yet," he says, piquing my curiosity. "Consider it a surprise."

Kite doesn't give me a time frame for when to expect this surprise.

Since I'm in a sentimental mood, I flip through my yearbooks, cooing at kindergartener Kite with his toothy grin that progressively develops into a smirk with each passing year.

Shortly after Karnival's debut, someone scanned every yearbook photo of Kite onto the internet. People have been using them to sell Karnival merchandise. Connie's friend Lola used to wear a pendant with Kite's seventh grade portrait encased inside.

Connie caught her kissing it once and then the pendant mysteriously went missing from Lola's gym locker.

Over the years, former classmates of mine (people I used to call friends) have uploaded their own photos of Kite—at birthday parties, school trips, family events, and the like. Luckily for Kite, his talent show performance never made it into the yearbook or onto social media.

None of these photos have been damaging to his career, but I can't imagine being in his position, having people share photos of me without my permission, especially snippets of my life prior to all the fame and glory. I bet it never crossed Kite's mind that the group photo he took at Ben's tenth birthday would wind up on Instagram with thousands of likes, all because Ben's sister, a Firework, recognized him from their family photo album.

It's as if your past and present are no longer your own.

Miraculously, I've managed to evade public notice. People approach me now and then, but no one has ever posted a photo of me and Kite together, not unless you count class pictures. Even during the address leak, no one posted a photo of me stepping outside my house or fixing a wedgie. Fans were probably too busy harassing Connie to pay attention to me.

Photos of Connie did spread online at that time: of her playing at a soccer game, yawning into a book at the library, and sticking up the middle finger when she spotted the creep with the camera. The photos have since been reported and removed, due in part to a campaign led by mylightkite, urging Fireworks to respect Karnival and their families.

Scrolling through mylightkite's account, I see that her latest posts have all been about the 7-Eleven fiasco and denouncing JennyKPops for her "treasonous breach of trust in the fandom."

A notification box dings into view on my phone. Kite sent me a large video file.

I immediately press Play.

At first all I see is his bedroom wall. Seconds later Kite slips into view and takes a seat on a stool. He's wearing a violet button-up patterned with tiger butterflies, half tucked into a pair of black pants. As if he's performing for a crowd, he also has on a full face of makeup.

My heart seizes.

"Hi, Lovely." Kite waves at the camera. "This is my third time recording this . . . Don't judge me too harshly." His attention seems to wander for a moment before he looks back at the camera. "Anyway, this is for you."

Closing his eyes, he taps the rounded edge of the stool and begins to sing.

His voice is soft with a breathy timbre that reminds me of a summer breeze. Without the background track, it takes me a minute or so to realize he's singing "Marvel," a jazzy ballad that was released with Karnival's second mini album. The official album track is sung by Kite and O-Kei. I've only heard them perform it twice at fan meets.

This is the first time I've heard Kite sing it alone. The song is a bit jarring without the instrumental and supporting vocals, but that makes the experience all the more intimate, not to mention surreal: Kite is singing *for me*.

I'm barely keeping it together as Kite's falsetto fades away. After a beat of silence, he looks at the camera with a shy smile and shoots air bullets my way.

I feel each and every one.

"Thanks for listening," he says before the video ends.

Pressing my phone to my chest, I screw my eyes shut and swallow the lump in my throat. My heart feels so full, yet so empty, plunging me deeper into confusion. How can something feel good and bad at the same time? Every part of me tingles, and I don't understand why.

My body is singing its own song, one I don't know the lyrics to.

Every shade, every hue, every shadow finds you
Black and blue, our future burns a single flame
You and I are right where we should be
In the city that never sleeps, you tell me you love me

Second verse to "Marvel," written by O-Kei, translated
from Korean.

22

Midweek, my chest still feels tense.

I ride my bike to the park to clear my head. The trip proves treacherous. Six blocks in, I'm breathless and halfway through my water bottle. Bypassing the sidewalk, I cut through a neighborhood of condominiums to take an unpaved path through the woods that spits me out on the eastern side of the park, by the soccer field.

After completing a lap through the park, I return to my starting point and notice that the soccer field is teeming with orange cones and girls in scrimmage jerseys. I pedal closer and recognize Connie, with her neon-yellow cleats. Even when school's out, she never stops thinking about soccer.

Before I head home to take a much-needed shower, I get a drink from the water fountain. As I'm refilling my bottle, I hear footsteps coming up from behind me. I don't think much of it until . . .

"Can I talk to you for a minute?"

Connie stands a few feet away with her hands on her hips. There's a tick to her brow, a pensive look on her face bordering on a scowl.

I reflect back on my recent encounters with Connie—her storming out of her house, Mrs. Xu hot on her heels; the conversation I walked in on when I came over for dinner; and finally, my tense run-in with her friends. The source of Connie's irritation is easy to trace.

"Sure," I say.

"I assume you saw the video?"

"If you mean the 7-Eleven video, yes, I saw it."

Connie and I were at Pho King Delight when the video leaked. She knows I saw it.

"Since you've seen it, do you think it was smart to bring Kai to Hersheypark? Or Roller Rave?" Her tone is patronizing. I used to play teatime with this girl, and here she is, reprimanding me as if I were a clumsy teddy bear that spilled tea all over her imaginary white tablecloth.

Still, she has a point. Bringing Kite out wasn't wise, but I don't regret it, and that's exactly what I tell her.

Connie's quiet afterward. I can almost hear the cogs shifting in her head. The silence expands between us, and in this heat I'm so desperate to flee, I'm tempted to leave her with her thoughts. She's undoubtedly angry about Kite being home. But it never occurred to me that she might be angry with me.

Finally Connie asks, "Are you in love with my brother?"

"Of course not!"

For the briefest moment, she seems taken aback, her stony expression faltering at what sounds like a blatant lie even to my ears. The shock passes, and she steels herself.

"You're an awful liar." Connie pauses long enough to welcome a response.

"Think whatever you want." I try to be the picture of apathy, but I don't need a mirror to show me I'm failing. My inflamed cheeks aren't sunburned, and the rasp in my voice isn't from dehydration.

"Do you want a repeat of last year? Because I don't. I don't want those crazy fans coming near me again. I don't want them mailing letters to my house, I don't want them ringing the doorbell every day and night, and I don't want them zooming in on my bedroom with their damn cameras. Whatever it is you're thinking of starting—don't."

"I'm not in love with Kite" is all I can manage before my voice cracks. I clench my jaw and squeeze my water bottle to keep the maelstrom of emotions at bay.

"Good. I'll hold you to that, then." Connie fixes me with a final look of warning before rejoining her friends on the field.

Dear Kite,

I hope this letter finds you well and that you take what I say to heart. There have been ongoing debates in the fandom about who the best singer and dancer is in Karnival. I'd hate for anyone to be ranked the worst in anything, but I will say this: you're not a strong dancer. It's impossible to live up to everyone's ideals, but as an idol, you should at least try. This isn't to say you aren't trying, but I know you can do better. I believe in you!

Sincerely,
Anonymous Firework

Fan mail no. 145, received one year ago on July 2.
Connie used it to fold an origami frog.

23

I'm in love with Kite.

There, I said it.

I'm in love with my childhood friend who happens to be a popstar in a country that's an ocean away, with fans scattered across several continents who would give an arm and a leg to romance him. If that isn't a recipe for disastrous clichés, I don't know what is.

Riding my bike at the speed of light won't chase my feelings away, and yelling at the top of my lungs brings only temporary reprieve. The more I tell myself not to think about Kite, the more I think about him; the more I think about him, the more intrusive the thoughts. His distractingly handsome smile, the crisp edge of his voice that embraces you like a cozy campfire, the phantom touch of his fingers that leave you yearning for more, and the penetrating glint in his eyes as he lights up your world—here I am waxing poetic, and I don't even like writing!

With a guttural scream that rattles the neighborhood dogs, I pedal harder, zipping around a corner two blocks from home. My calves are throbbing, but the muscle aches are nothing compared to my burning thoughts. I open my water bottle and empty it over my head. Almost immediately, the cool relief evaporates, and with a disapproving grunt, I shake out my hair and cut across the street.

"Lovely, look out!"

I slam on the brakes, oblivious that I'm stopped in the middle of the road. Kite stands on the sidewalk, frantically pointing at something.

I hear the car before I see it, tires screeching, horn blaring.

Everything after that is a whirl of colors and tangled limbs as I'm thrown off my bike and onto the asphalt. Something cushions my fall, and with my eyes screwed shut, I tumble into the curb. I lay there, waiting for the pain to hit me, but it never comes.

My face is pressed against something soft, a stark contrast to the loose gravel digging into my legs. I feel arms tightening around me, and a familiar voice stirs me.

Slowly I open my eyes, and the first thing I see is Kite.

His arms are around me, one hand squeezing my shoulder, the other cradling the back of my head. My own hands are pressed against his chest, and I feel the rhythm of his heart, how it matches the pulse beating in my ears.

Kite pushed me out of the way.

Not just pushed but protected me.

Kite releases a shaky breath before drawing me into a sitting position. He looks me over, gingerly tipping my face left to right, up and down.

"Does it hurt anywhere?" he asks.

Swallowing hard, I shake my head. Before I can find my voice, I hear a car door open, followed by another familiar voice.

"Oh my god! I am so sorry!" Abandoning her car in the middle of the road, Ester comes racing over, her face sleek with inky tears. "Is anyone hurt? Should I call 911? Please tell me no one's dying! First it was Ki—I mean James—and now this! I should have my license revoked!"

"We're okay," Kite says, his voice pouring over us like cold water onto a flame. "Let's take this inside."

"R-right." Wiping at her never-ending tears, mascara smearing everywhere, Ester returns to her car.

Kite takes me by the arm and coaxes me into the backseat. Since there isn't enough space to fit my bike, he rides it back to my place.

During the five-second trip to my house, I try to get my breathing under control. My legs are wobbly, and I still can't muster a single word.

Inside, Ester fetches the first-aid kit. Apart from the nicks and scratches on my legs, I'm relatively unharmed. Kite bore the brunt of the fall. His knees and shoulders are already bruising, and his elbows and knuckles are bleeding—nothing that won't heal on its own, but still, he's hurt because of me. I can't believe I was careless enough to cross the street without looking. What if he scarred his face or sustained a major injury? How detrimental would that be to his career and everything he's worked for?

"Lovely." Kite lightly shakes me by the shoulder. He's stooped at eye level. "Are you sure you're okay? You haven't said anything. . . ."

His voice is so kind and tender, I could cry.

If I speak now, the floodgates will open.

"I think the shock hasn't worn off yet," Ester cuts in, redirecting Kite as his eyes wander away from my face.

I take the opportunity to blink and shed a few tears. Quickly and discreetly, I wipe them away. "Sorry, I'm trying to process what happened. Could you guys . . . leave me alone?"

"Anything you want!" Ester says, too eagerly.

"Let me know if you need anything," Kite says as Ester

beckons him out of the house. "Tell us right away if you start feeling dizzy."

I offer him a small smile. "I will. Thanks."

Once I'm alone under the covers of my bed, I replay the video Kite sent me, and his voice is all it takes to launch me into outer space and fly me to the moon.

But Connie's words knock me down from the clouds, grounding me with the simple fact that being in love with Kite can only end badly.

"I checked my dash cam and I was nowhere close to running you over. There was at least two yards between us. I kind of did you a favor if you think about it. Now you know Kite would throw himself in front of a car for you. Anyway, I'm in your driveway. Can I come back in?"

Text message from Ester to Lulu, sent twelve minutes after she left.

24

I watch Stephanie and Ester through my vanity mirror as I hold the curling iron in place, counting the seconds before unclamping the bundle of hair looped around the heated metal.

Only once in a blue moon do I make the effort to curl my hair.

The blind date Ester arranged for me better be worth it.

Wes, the guy I'm meeting today, is an incoming freshman at NYU and a friend of Ester's cousin. That's all I know about him. Although Ester's judgment can be questionable, she knows better than to set me up with a weirdo. On any other occasion, she might do it for shits and giggles, but I was crystal clear when I told her to find me someone who could take my mind off Kite, which means I need to date someone I'd genuinely want to meet a second time.

Hanging upside down from my bed with her hair fanned out on the floor, Stephanie pushes her lollipop aside to say, "I think you should cancel this silly date. You're head over heels for Kite. No one can measure up to him. Why waste your time?"

"I'm not replacing him," I snap, bending over to unplug the curling iron. "I just . . . need a distraction."

Stephanie makes a popping sound with her lips and points

her lollipop at me. "You like Kite, and Kite likes you back. Anyone with a quarter of a brain can see that."

"Then you need glasses." Kite can't possibly reciprocate my feelings.

I close my eyes and douse myself with body spray. Blinking against the cloying aroma, I catch Stephanie shaking her head. I spin around to face her, my expression cross.

"Kite spent the last four years in South Korea surrounded by gorgeous women who share the same passion as him. Why would he want me, some forgotten childhood friend, when he could date some smoking-hot model or another singer from a girl group?"

Stephanie sighs. "Who are you trying to convince here? Me or you?"

"You are impossible." Now I'm the one shaking my head.

"Lu." This time Ester chimes in from her seat at my desk. "Has it ever crossed your mind that Kite might've been in love with you *before* he moved to Korea and that maybe he's still in love with you now?"

I scoff. "Enough. My date starts in an hour." I do a little twirl in my forest-green skirt. "How do I look?"

"As sweet as pie," Stephanie says plainly.

"That apple blouse is cute but not really you," Ester adds.

"I'm going to ignore that comment and say I look absolutely fetching." I blow a kiss at myself in the mirror before taking a quick inventory of my purse.

"Can't wait to hear about your date," Ester squeals, clapping like a seal. "My cousin says Wes is a nice guy. I hope he's everything you could ask for."

"Everything except Kite," Stephanie says, rolling away before I can smother her with my pillow.

*

Wes and I agreed to grab lunch at Sushi Pagoda, two towns over. I arrive five minutes early and wait outside by the double doors flanked by potted bamboo plants.

Seconds slide into minutes, and after smoothing out my skirt for the sixth time, a flashy blue car careens into the parking lot and screeches to a halt. Out walks a guy with chiseled arms and legs for days. A few strides later, he stops in front of me and takes off his sunglasses, tucking them into the front pocket of his polo.

"Lulu?" he says, his brown eyes fixed on me.

"That's me. You must be Wes. Nice to meet you."

Apart from the seven-minute delay, my first impression of him is positive. He has a nice tan and an even nicer pair of arms. I keep my own arms at my side. A hug seems too intimate, but a handshake seems too formal. I settle for option three and open the door for him. "It's crazy hot out here. Let's go—"

He reaches over my head and pushes the door farther back, out from under my hand. I stumble and catch myself on the doorframe.

"I got it," he says. "Ladies first."

"Thanks . . ." I manage a half smile before entering the restaurant.

We're seated quickly, at a corner booth away from the other guests.

"Do you come here often?" I ask Wes. Sushi Pagoda was his idea.

"I come here a lot with my friends," he says as the waitress brings us tea.

"Anything you'd recommend?" There are over a hundred items on the menu.

"The spider roll, the green dragon . . . Are you a picky eater?"

"Nah, I'll pretty much try anything."

"Cool. My ex was picky, only ate pizza, string cheese, and fries."

We end up ordering miso soup and three specialty rolls to share. While we're waiting for our food, we exchange basic information: what high school we attended, what we're planning to study in college, what we like to do on the weekends. I don't get very far into my self-introduction before Wes interrupts me, so I let him do the talking.

Turns out, Wes wants to work on Wall Street and one day become a portfolio manager for a hedge fund. He hopes to retire early so he can travel the world. He's an avid weight lifter who loves rock climbing, escape rooms, and EDM. He also has a pet bearded dragon.

"What music do you listen to?" he asks once our soup arrives.

I eat a spoonful before answering. "A bit of everything. Right now I'm mostly into K-pop."

"My ex was big on K-pop. Last year I took her to KCON to see her favorite boy group. I don't get the hype. K-pop sounds all the same to me." Wes flicks a stray piece of green onion off the table. It lands on my shirt. "You're planning to study Chinese and Korean?"

"Yeah, that's what I said earlier." I brush the green onion off.

He leans forward to inspect my face. "Are you Korean?"

"I'm Chinese."

"Me too." Wes leans back, inexplicably pleased. "Where are your parents from?"

173

"Taiwan, but they moved here when they were young."

"How come you're not already fluent in Chinese? Your parents didn't teach you?"

"Like I said, they moved here when they were young. They mostly speak English now." I mindlessly twirl my spoon, scraping it against the bottom of the bowl.

"*Nǐ míngbái ma?*"

I freeze. Is this guy seriously testing me?

"Yes, I understand," I grouse. "It's not like I don't know any Chinese."

"Most of my Chinese friends know more Spanish and French than Mandarin or Canto. It's sad how so many people are out of touch with their roots."

I look at him, unmoving, unblinking, and unimpressed.

Down the aisle, I spot our waitress with our food. I raise a hand to get her attention. "I'm sorry. Can you please split our order in half and put them in to-go boxes?"

"Sure . . ." The waitress looks back and forth between Wes and me. "I'll be back with the check," she says.

Wes stares at me, dumbfounded. "Is something wrong?"

"I made a mistake. Like, gargantuan."

Our waitress returns with two boxes. I thank her, slip her my portion of the bill, and hightail it out of there.

On the drive home, I call Ester and put her on loudspeaker. She and Stephanie are back at my place, waiting to hear about my date. As soon as Ester picks up, I let her have it.

"Tell your cousin that Wes is a pretentious jerk who's still hung up on his ex and that he should take a college course on tact."

Ester is silent for a moment, and not-so-apologetically she says, "She did mention that he can be condescending. His ex broke up with him because he used to mock her for having the diet of a third grader."

"When did they break up?"

"Last week? Before you chew me out for not telling you sooner, I found out after you left. My cousin texted me and was like, *by the way* . . ."

"I hate to tell you I told you so, but I told you so," I hear Stephanie shout in the background. "No one can measure up to Kite!"

"It was one date! This guy doesn't represent all of human-kind!" I shout back.

"Who cares when the one you want is Kite."

"Stephanie, where are you right now?"

"At your house, remember?"

"Do me a favor and stay where you are. I am going to end you."

"I appreciate the advance notice."

Ready to unleash my fury, I thunder up the porch and burst through the front door, screaming, "Heeeeeeeere's Johnny!"

Like a pair of curious gophers emerging from the ground, Stephanie and Ester pop up from behind the sofa. Seconds later they're joined by Kite.

The room freezes over.

"*The Shining* is an awesome movie," Kite says encouragingly. "A classic . . ."

I want to crawl into a hole and die there.

After I kill Stephanie and Ester.

"Quit standing there like an axe murderer." Stephanie makes

a come-hither motion, and I reluctantly oblige. Fanned out across the coffee table are my family photo albums.

I balk at the sight of them. "What the hell are you doing?"

"Taking a trip down memory lane," says Stephanie. "Relax, there aren't any naked bath photos. I checked."

Mom was an active photographer when I was a baby. We have a small library of photo albums documenting my infant, toddler, and preteen years.

Kite bookmarks the album in his lap before closing it. "Sorry for coming over unannounced. I thought I'd surprise you."

"I was surprised, all right. I bet you were, too."

We laugh. All the fire and ice from before melts into an afternoon of nostalgia, poring over forgotten memories.

My middle school days are my ultimate source of shame. I was the living definition of an awkward girl, who thought that pigtails were stylish and you could never use too much lip gloss or blush. Kite wasn't always the handsome prince he is now. I forgot he wore braces in sixth grade and had a late growth spurt, but that's nothing compared to caking your face with orange blush.

"Ugh!" I slam a hand over a close-up shot of me taken on our sixth-grade field trip to Medieval Times. "Don't look at my pizza face."

"You have nothing to be ashamed of!" Ester exclaims. "Puberty is natural. Embrace it. Wear your acne scars like battle scars."

My skin improved drastically over the years, but still . . .

Kite brushes my hand away, his touch feather-light yet insistent. "You look fine," he says, eyeing the photo with an endearing look that spreads into an even lovelier smile.

I don't know what he sees in that photo. All I see is a girl with a sweaty forehead and a land mine of pimples waiting to explode and shift the earth's axis.

Turning the page, Kite flips to a group photo taken in front of the faux-chateau exterior of Medieval Times. He and I stand on opposite sides, me carrying a bouquet of battery-charged roses while he wields a foam sword—both purchased from the gift shop.

"One thing I absolutely hate about Medieval Times is when the knights give roses out to the audience," Ester says. Forgetting herself in front of Kite, she adds, "I've been there three times, and not once did I receive a rose. It's worse when the knight on your team is hot! My mom would buy me those fake light-up roses to cheer me up."

Stephanie taps a finger to the photo, at the fake bouquet in my arms. "You're not alone, Ester. Looks like Lulu got snubbed by her knight in shining armor."

"I bought them because they glowed in the dark, unlike real flowers," I snap.

From the corner of my eye, I catch a glimpse of Kite as he leans in to say something but stops short. I don't think much about it.

We continue reminiscing for the next hour until Stephanie and Ester have to head out, the energy in the house departing with them. As I'm tidying up, Kite's attention remains glued to the photo album on his lap.

"Can I keep this?" he suddenly asks.

He's pointing at a photo of us at Six Flags, posing in front of the spinning-teacup ride. He's hunched over, gripping his knees, while I stand triumphantly beside him.

"Why? Are you embarrassed by it?" I laugh.

"Believe it or not, I like this photo," he says. "So . . . can I?"

"Sure, I won't miss it." As soon as I say that, curiosity grips me, and I begin to question the photo's significance. I remember our seventh-grade trip to Six Flags, but not this ride.

"You wanted to be the fastest teacup," he says, reading my expression, "and I was your unfortunate but willing partner."

"I can't believe I don't remember this."

Memories are elusive. As a former Karnival fanatic, every moment I ever shared with Kite should be engraved in my hippocampus. I suppose I took some for granted, back when I thought Kite and I would always have each other. Now, when I stare at the photo, there's this hollow feeling that wasn't there before.

"I mentioned this in an interview when I was in Japan," Kite continues.

"Really?" This is my first time hearing about it.

"The interview was published in a magazine. You wouldn't have heard about it unless someone translated the article." Worry flickers across his face. "I didn't mention your name or anything."

"Because living next door to you isn't enough to rile up your fans?" I casually reference last year's address leak.

"I'm really sorry that happened."

"It's not your fault someone invaded your privacy like that." I slip the teacup photo out from the album and hand it to Kite. "It's all yours. Frame it, tuck it under your pillow, do whatever you want with it."

"Thanks." Kite shuts the photo album and sets it on top of the stack I have going on the coffee table. "I better head out. Mom wants me to cook dinner tonight."

Slipping into his sneakers, he reaches for the doorknob, then stops mid-motion. He rubs his neck and shoots me a timid look. "Did you get a chance to watch the video I sent you?"

"I did!" I completely forgot to talk to him about it. "Would you call me a creep if I told you I replayed it ten times?"

"Hmm . . ." Kite brushes my bangs back and briefly studies my face before mussing my hair. "You're too cute to be creepy, even when you're channeling Jack Nicholson."

"Lulu went on a date today. She already has a second one scheduled. If this bothers you, you might want to do something about it."

Note from Stephanie that Kite discovered in his pocket when he got home.

25

Restlessness finds me by nightfall.

Revisiting my middle school days has spurred countless thoughts in me. Time flies, and as cliché as it is, it'll never stop being true. I'm already struggling to recall names and faces. It's funny yet sobering how quickly people enter and leave your life. To think Stephanie and Kite are the only people from middle school I'm still friends with . . .

"Guess who called me today," Mom says when I step out of the bathroom in a plume of shower steam, my hair twisted up in a towel. She's at the dining table, nursing a cup of tea while reading the newspaper.

"He Who Must Not Be Named." I unwind my hair and sling the towel over the back of a chair. "Did he call about New York?" Mom nods. "Ugh, how dense can he be? It's like he can't believe someone would ignore him."

"Your dad is stubborn." Mom rubs her eyes and yawns into her elbow. "He wants to celebrate your birthday."

"And what did you tell him?"

"I told him you aren't interested. Then he hung up on me."

"Joke's on him. The conversation was over before it began."

I'm done with him, and he made it loud and clear he was done with me when he left to be with Katherine and Kyle. So why care now? Why the persistence? Why do people abandon their families and then act surprised when their actions have consequences?

"I'm going for a walk." I throw on a sheer jacket over my pajamas, slip into a pair of flats, and leave the door unlocked behind me.

My hair is damp, but the warm air dries it in no time. I make it to the end of the street before Maru scurries out from under a tree. She leaps into my arms, and I make kissy noises at her. Her affection doesn't come without conditions. I know she wants food, and once she realizes I don't have any, she swipes at my face. I instinctively let go of her.

"Let me love you!" I trail after her, all the way to a playground near the park.

Several feet away, I hear the eerie squeak of metal, the sound amplifying as Maru leads me to a silhouetted figure on the swings.

"Look what the cat dragged in," Kite says, his profile thrown into sharp relief against the lamppost behind him.

"Ha-ha." I claim the swing next to him while Maru lounges by my feet.

Kite isn't wearing any disguise. It's late; no one's going to see us.

"Did you go running?" I ask, eyeing his track pants and sneakers.

"Yeah, have to stay fit or my manager's going to get on my case. Staying indoors all day isn't doing me any favors . . . and running helps me think."

"Is something on your mind?"

"There is." Kite side-eyes me. "Are you seeing someone?"

"What do you mean?"

"Are you . . . dating someone?"

"Oh my god, Stephanie said something to you, didn't she?" I kick the air, tilt my head back, and sigh. "I don't know what she told you, but, yes, I did meet someone today. It was a first date, and Ester set me up with a total dud."

"Is that why you came storming into your house like that?"

"Like an axe murderer? I swear, my friends are a piece of work."

"Same. Wayne is the biggest schemer I know. Fans don't call him a spicy maple cookie just because he's Canadian. He and Stephanie would get along."

"Don't let Ester hear you say that." I laugh. "Have you been in touch with Wayne and them? Must be difficult with the different time zones."

"That doesn't stop Wayne and Xiaoming from spamming me with selfies. They say it's to keep me company, but I know that's not true. They're just narcissists," he says, cracking a smile that conveys a brotherly fondness. "They've been keeping me in the loop with stuff back home. Everyone's busy planning our next mini album."

"Are you writing any of the songs?" I ask in earnest.

"As of now, no, but things can change. Better that Wayne and Xiaoming get a chance. They don't co-write often. O-Kei has a habit of steamrolling anyone he works with."

"Didn't you co-write some songs with him?" I ask carefully.

"Yeah, and it wasn't easy. He can be overbearing. I don't think I'm the best songwriter or anything. I'm grateful to have any creative input, but . . . when people keep shooting down your ideas, you start to feel underappreciated. Maybe that's the nature of O-Kei being the group leader and me being the *baby* of the group. The seniority culture can be toxic."

"That's rough. They shouldn't take you less seriously just because of your age."

"Tell me about it. I don't hate O-Kei or anything. . . . He's just too much sometimes."

It doesn't escape me that this isn't the first time Kite's complained about O-Kei.

"Venting's good for the soul," I say.

Kite readjusts his position on the swing, straddling the seat without bumping his head against the metal beam weighing the swing set in place. "Want to get on?"

I fit myself between his feet, like I used to when we were kids and there weren't enough swings at the playground. It's a bit cramped with the two of us but also strangely comforting. Shifting his weight, he pushes the swing forward, and after a few tries, we get a rhythm going, the swaying motion calm and meditative. My mind feels lighter than when I left the house.

A strong breeze rolls in, and I sneeze.

"Are you cold?" Kite slows the swing down and steps off. Standing behind me, he holds the swing in place while I secure my jacket.

"I'm good." I look back over my shoulder, my eyes inadvertently focusing on his lips, and I realize how close we are. My breath catches in my throat, and within the span of a silent gasp, the world around me falls away, and I see and feel nothing but Kite.

My back is flush against his chest, his body heat seeping through my clothes, warming me from head to toe. I'm all too aware of his cologne—citrusy and woodsy, reminiscent of sage and orange sunshine. If you could get drunk off someone, Kite would have me intoxicated after just one breath, which means I'm already gone.

His own breath is hot against my ear, tickling my neck. I can't help but wonder what it would be like to feel his breath in my lungs.

I don't have to wonder for long.

He tips my head back and closes the distance between us in one fluid motion. His lips meet mine, and everything stops. My neurons misfire, my muscles seize, and the roaring in my ears dulls to an instant quiet, like the calm before the storm.

. . . .
. . . .
. . . .
. . . .
. . . .
. . . .

Neurons misfiring in Lulu's brain.

26

I spend the next three days in a walking daydream.

My body feels impossibly light. The gentlest of winds could sweep me off my feet and carry me into the clouds. I don't want to fly too high, though.

The higher you fly, the harder you fall, and I'm not ready to fall.

Kite's away visiting his aunt and uncle in the Connecticut countryside. I'm glad he's out and about. He could use a breath of fresh country air.

What I'm not so happy about is how he left me with a million questions.

That night I couldn't form words, not when our lips touched or when he pulled away—or when he walked me home and wished me good night. My brain couldn't function. I'm not sure if it's even functioning now.

How do you measure the gravity behind a kiss?

At such a sensitive point in his career, Kite wouldn't kiss me out of sheer impulse. No one kisses their neighbor without considering the consequences. He must've put a lot of thought into it . . . at least that's what I'm hoping, but there's no use agonizing over it. I need to ask Kite what that kiss meant to him.

I need to ask him face-to-face, so there can be no misunderstanding.

I nearly lasted a full day without telling Stephanie and Ester what happened. I did have reservations at first. It felt wrong to share such an intimate moment with someone else, as if the magic of the moment would vanish the second I spoke of it, but all the uncertainty, excitement, and joy swelling inside me became too much, and I caved.

No surprise, Stephanie gave me the I-told-you-so talk before Ester asked if I'll be taking her wedding-dress shopping with me (what a comedian). They're as hungry for answers as I am, but until Kite returns, I'll have to keep myself occupied.

Which is how the girls and I end up at a house party.

Our former classmate Gwen's house is palatial, with a circular driveway and a fountain at its center. Cars are parked along the perimeter without an inch to spare. After Stephanie finds a parking spot at the very end of the street, we walk to the house, going straight to the backyard, where we find Gwen chilling with her friends on the trampoline.

"Yoo-hoo!" Gwen bounces over and draws Stephanie into a hug while Ester and I wave hello. "So glad you all made it! Ping-pong and foosball are in the basement, and there's a movie playing in the living room."

"Thanks. So, what's the word with you and Aline?" Stephanie asks, absently waving at some guys sipping beers on the patio.

"Someone means business." Gwen fakes a hurt look before flipping her hair. "We broke up; it was mutual. Everyone saw it coming as soon as she got into the University of Hawaii, but I don't need an oceanography degree to know there are plenty of fish in the sea," Gwen says, with a hint of bitterness that leads me to believe the breakup wasn't as mutual as she claims. She then sets her eyes on me. "Too bad you and Kellie never became a thing. You two would've been great together."

Gwen was student council vice president and worked closely with Kellie for four years. She also helped Kellie with her promposal. . . .

Stephanie smacks Gwen on the arm. "I'm thirsty. What's the selection?"

"Food and drinks are inside. Cheers!" With that, Gwen sashays off.

In the kitchen, there's beer pong and an impromptu contest of *let's see who gets brain damage as we scarf down a gallon of ice cream*. Stephanie riffles through the wine coolers and tosses a few hard lemonades my way, picking up a water for herself. We find a spot on the wraparound sofa in the darkened living room as Spiderman swings across the TV screen and flashes his crotch. Everyone's too engrossed with side conversations to pay attention to the movie.

It doesn't take long for the three of us to start our own.

"Has James texted you at all?" asks Stephanie.

"Nope, I haven't heard a peep from him," I say, tipping back my lemonade.

"He wouldn't have kissed you if he wasn't serious," Ester chimes in. "If this gets out, you will be public enemy numero uno! Fireworks will hate you, wish you dead, and drag your name across the World Wide Web."

"Jeez, Ester, don't fret on my behalf." I've been floating around in a bubble these last few days, and the reality of what it means to involve myself romantically with Kite is a reminder of how thin that bubble is. The dullest needle could pop it.

"It's not too late to start that summer fling," Stephanie adds, clinking drinks with Ester.

"I could never treat James as a fling!" I exclaim.

"So you prefer a serious relationship, then?" Stephanie raises a brow, feigning innocence when I know she's trying to provoke me.

People come and go, like the people at this party I never planned on seeing again after graduation. Kite means more to me than that, but I've said goodbye to him before, and eventually I'll have to say it again.

"I . . . I don't know what I want."

By the end of the night, I'm sprawled across Stephanie's backseat, drowsy and disoriented.

I thought my alcohol tolerance was higher than this, but physiology doesn't lie. Six bottles of hard lemonade were a few too many.

"Can you hold still? We're not leaving until your seat belt is on." Stephanie has her hands full trying to strap Ester into the front passenger seat.

"I can't. The human body is sixty percent water. I am water and water is me. You can't contain me, but if you ever need me to put out a fire, I can do that."

Ester's one of those loud, nonsensical drunks.

I tune her out as best as I can, and gradually sleep takes me.

After an indeterminate amount of time, I become semiconscious to something poking me in the cheek. My eyelids are heavy, I can't lift them, but I notice the car isn't moving. The poking stops and is replaced with something silky smooth. I lean into it and fall back to sleep.

27

I t's ten in the morning when I wake up.

My legs ache, my tongue is drier than sandpaper, and my phone has a dozen unread messages. Shaking out of my stupor, I roll onto my stomach and stretch like a cat.

Ester sent me a dark, grainy video. I tap the screen, and the video begins to play.

Then I scream.

Kite returned home from Connecticut sometime last night. I know because in the video I'm passed out in the backseat of Stephanie's car while Kite's trying to poke me awake. He taps me on the cheek with the palm of his hand, and drunk-me interprets it as an invitation to use him as a pillow. I can hear Ester cracking up in the background while the camera shakes.

After some indecipherable footage, the camera refocuses to capture the moment when Stephanie and Kite carry me to the porch and into the house. Stephanie has me by my armpits, Kite has me by my ankles, and I'm like a pig on a spit between the two of them. The video ends with Ester zooming in on my greasy face and chapped lips as Kite lays me down on the sofa.

My phone dings with a new message from Kite: *"How are you feeling? Got a nasty hangover?"*

I feel like strapping myself to a ton of TNT and blowing myself up.

Grabbing my pillow out from under me, I smother myself with it and scream until I'm blue in the face.

✳

The time has come for me and Kite to talk.

As much as I want answers, I'm a little embarrassed. "One-percent alcohol" labels have betrayed me, and so have my friends.

"Want to meet me at the park?" Kite asks when I call him. He's in the middle of a jog. I can hear squawking in the background. "It's pretty lonely over here, just me and the geese. Fresh air will help your hangover."

"I'm not hungover," I argue, despite swallowing an aspirin earlier. "I woke up dehydrated, and that's about it." Memories of the video flash before me, then, after a moment's pause, "I'm heading out now. See you on the soccer field?"

"Sounds good. I'll be waiting."

I don't leave him waiting for long.

A short drive later, I find Kite in the middle of the soccer field, not another soul in sight. If Connie knew I was meeting him out here like this, I'd be ancient history.

When he sees me, he smiles and pats the spot next to him on the grass.

We sit side by side under a rolling procession of clouds, the sky a perfect blue.

"How was your trip?" I ask, hugging my knees to my chest.

"Eventful," he says. "My aunt taught me how to make apple cider and spotted dick, then we all went hiking in the woods. Connie wrestled a mountain lion, and I caught a wild salmon with my bare hands."

I laugh. "I wouldn't be surprised if Connie did wrestle a mountain lion."

"I have pictures to prove it."

"Wait, seriously?"

"Kidding." Kite bumps shoulders with me. His musical laughter fills the air before it's swept away by a blast of wind. "Are we glossing over the fact that someone on this planet thought *spotted dick* was an appropriate name for a dessert?"

"Who do you think I am?" I scoff. "I watch British baking shows. I'm too worldly to be amused by toilet humor."

"Then can we talk about how I kissed you and left you speechless?"

The wind ceases, and within the span of a heartbeat, the grass becomes a bed of hot lava. I release the breath I didn't realize I was holding and fan myself with my baseball cap.

Kite looks on, amused. Curse that smooth devil.

"It must've seemed random," he says. "Sorry for surprising you."

"You don't sound very sorry."

"That's because I intentionally kissed you when you least expected it."

"Does that mean you kissed me for the shock value?" I ask, averting my eyes in case his answer is one I'd rather not hear.

His silence unnerves me, and I start fussing with my hair, chewing on my ponytail before undoing it altogether. I brave a glance in his direction and find him looking at me, his expression somber yet tender.

"No," he finally says. "Never."

"Isn't it dangerous? If someone had seen us . . ." The thought dies in my throat, but the unspoken words reach him.

"I thought about it a lot, so much I was losing my mind,

but . . ." He sighs. "We lost so much time together. I'd rather regret having done *something* instead of nothing." Realizing the implication of his words, he says, "Just so you know, I don't regret the kiss."

"I don't regret it either." I train my eyes on my lap and let my hair cascade down the side of my face, hiding my cheeks. Knowing I wasn't the only one going crazy delights me.

"Glad to know the feeling's mutual."

"When . . ." I bite my lip, sampling my own words and the courage to voice them. My hands are back in my hair, sorting through the unruly strands as if they'll disentangle the bundle of thoughts crowding my mind. "When did you start to . . . like me?"

"I've always liked you."

"More than a friend is what I meant."

Kite inches closer, his head bent conspiratorially as if he's about to whisper a secret, but then his voice rings out, sure and clear. "I've liked you since we were kids."

It takes every muscle and sinew in my body not to snatch my baseball cap off the ground and scream into it. Am I dreaming, or have I been unwittingly cast in a K-drama? Kite, the same person who started distancing himself from me once we entered middle school, had a crush on me the entire time?

This moment feels so much bigger than me. It's grand and unexpected, but most of all, it's real.

Before this summer, meeting Kite again after all these years seemed impossible, yet here I am. And the best part is, it's not Kite, the international K-pop star, but Kai, my childhood friend, who's changing my reality.

"I wanted to tell you sooner, but"—Kite leans back on his hands, his legs splayed out in front of him as he angles his face toward the clouds—"I didn't want to ruin things if you didn't feel the same."

"You wouldn't have ruined anything!"

Kite straightens his back, surprised by my outburst.

I don't know how far back my own feelings go, or whether Kite and I would've dated in middle school had he confessed his feelings sooner. What I do know is that it wouldn't have ended things between us. It was his leaving for South Korea and ghosting me that almost ended things. . . .

"Why didn't you write me all these years?" I try to keep the hurt from my voice, but the disappointment still seeps through. I understand that he was extremely busy, but he could've found the time, even if it was only one email a year.

"Because it would've only made me miss you more." Kite blinks a few times and then scratches his nose. "My first year as a trainee was . . . rough. I knew it would be. I read about the strict diets and how I'd be up before dawn every day, but living it was . . . a big adjustment. I thought if I didn't message you, I wouldn't think about home so much, and then I could focus on my training."

It's not that he wasn't thinking of me, but it was better for him not to. It's unfortunate, but I understand why he had that mindset.

Kite's waiting for me to say something, but I'm still processing everything he said and everything that went unsaid.

Finally I ask him the one question that's been lurking in the back of my mind since that night on the swing.

"So what happens now?"

One kiss doesn't make us girlfriend and boyfriend, does it? Everything that's been said in these last, I don't know, achingly long five minutes doesn't have to lead to anything . . .

Unless we want it to.

As this uncertainty looms over us and muddies the rational part of my brain, Kite firmly takes my hand in his and says, "Go out with me."

A sweet surge rushes through me, and I lock eyes with him. That coy smile of his is my undoing, and I speak before thinking: "We can't be seen outside together, so *going out* is a misnomer, don't you—"

Kite shushes me with a swift kiss. He pulls back, enough to register the shock on my face before delivering another kiss, one to my left cheek then another to my right.

My mind is blank, my hands are stiff, and soon the heat creeps in, my skin glowing like a red-hot poker.

Just when I think he's finished, he swoops in once more for a longer, deeper kiss, one that has me melting into him. He gives me time to catch my breath, his lips hovering temptingly over mine, and once I do, our bodies reconnect, and my hand is in his hair as he lowers me onto the grass.

POSTED BY MYLIGHTKITE TWO YEARS AGO, AFTER KARNIVAL'S DEBUT.

Dream Drop Media has a two-year dating ban in its idol contracts. Mark your calendars, Fireworks.

#helovesmehelovesmenot #takeanumber #curbthethirst #KarnivalKoolaid

28

K ite and I are officially dating.

Only Stephanie and Ester know. This time I asked Kite for permission before sharing the news. They couldn't be happier for me. Although Kite and I can't be open about our relationship, I can't stop feeling like I'm the luckiest girl in the world.

He's been coming over the past couple of nights to cook dinner with me. Since we can't go out to eat, to replicate the restaurant experience, we occasionally dine by candlelight while playing atmospheric music interspersed with ASMR (the sound of clinking glasses and bubbling champagne can be very relaxing). Ester offered to role-play as a waitress to make the experience more authentic, but I declined. I know she just wants to eavesdrop on us.

Kite surprised me yesterday by having flowers delivered to my door. The cosmos and daisies are perched by my bedroom window in a mason jar we painted earlier this week while he taught me conversational phrases in Korean. Whenever I catch a glimpse of the flowers, I can't help but break into a smile too big for my face.

We might be limited in what we can do, but that hasn't dimmed my affection for him.

It's startling how a kiss can change everything. Ever since

our rendezvous on the soccer field, every time I lay eyes on him, stars are shooting across my vision, flowers are blossoming in my chest, and butterflies are dancing in my stomach. The world is brimming with renewed sights and sounds, yet Kite remains the brightest of them all.

"You gotta visit Jeju," Kite tells me while cleaning my kitchen. There's more strawberry smoothie on the ceiling than in the blender he forgot to cap. "It's an amazing place for sightseeing. The Manjanggul Cave and Hamdeok Beach are must-sees."

"Are you offering to be my personal guide?" I ask, raising a mop over my head to wipe away the gunk splattered across the ceiling.

"I would if I could," he says, wringing out a rag in the sink. "Depending on when you visit Korea, I might be able to arrange something."

"I'll probably study abroad the summer after sophomore year. Assuming I get into the Rutgers program, I won't be standing on South Korean soil for another two years." I sigh. "I can't wait that long. There's a box of fried chicken and yellow pickles over there with my name on it."

"I'll save you a piece," Kite says, wrapping a comforting arm around me in jest, "but it might be moldy by the time you get there."

"So thoughtful."

Although we haven't had a serious discussion about it, Kite and I know we'll eventually part ways, but for the sake of enjoying what precious time we have left together, I want to delay the conversation as long as I can. Worrying about the future takes away from the present, and the future will come whether or not I'm ready for it.

Once the kitchen is immaculate, Kite and I have a second go at the smoothies.

We draw the curtains, put on a movie, and cuddle on the sofa. We're diligent for the first half of the movie, but then Kite starts tracing spirals on my skin with his fingertips.

Soon my eyes don't know where to look.

Interlacing my fingers with his, I press my back against his chest, and kiss his chin. When I go in for a second kiss, he tilts his head, and our lips connect once, twice, and by the third time, the movie is long forgotten. All I can think about is the sweet buzz in my head and how natural this moment feels.

Then Stephanie calls me. I ignore my phone and sink into the cushions with Kite. When she calls again, I reluctantly detach myself and pick up.

"Took you long enough to answer. Were you in the bathroom? Anyway, how do you feel about an emergency sleepover at my place tonight?"

"Why the emergency?" I ask.

"Because it's already late July and our last sleepover was on graduation night," Stephanie says, appalled at the question. "Kite can come, too. We'll have the house to ourselves."

"Just so you know, Kite's sitting next to me," I tell her, in case she doesn't want him overhearing the rest of our conversation.

"Perfect, the two of you can give me your answer now. What will it be?"

I look at Kite. He has no objections.

"What time should we come over?" I ask Stephanie.

"There's no time like the present."

Under the cover of night, Kite and I set out for Stephanie's.

The drive over unfolds without incident. We slip into the garage, drop our things in the basement, and find Stephanie and Ester in the kitchen, prepping their signature cupcakes. "Lights Fantastic" is blaring throughout the house, and Ester's singing along without a care in the world. She bounces over with cupcake batter on her cheeks and flour in her hair.

"About time you got here! These cupcakes aren't going to bake themselves!" Ester tosses me my Sailor Mars apron.

"Are sleepovers usually like this?" Kite asks me, donning a Sailor Saturn apron.

"To a degree." I watch as Stephanie takes out a bag of limes from the fridge and sets it on the kitchen island, next to a package of dried coconut.

She shoots me an insinuating look.

Key lime coconut cupcakes are just what I'm in the mood for, and judging by the smirk on Kite's face, he is, too.

"When can I expect Wayne's autograph in my mailbox?" Ester asks, doing her best impression of Leatherface with her Korean snail face mask.

The four of us are in the basement, laying out futons, blankets, and enough pillows to supply a pillow-fight flash mob (which is a thing, believe it or not).

"It's on its way," Kite assures her, smoothing out his blanket. "He's mailing it to my address. I'll let Lovely know when it gets here."

"This is the best news I've heard all day!" Ester pumps the air with her fists before whipping her hair back and forth, her face mask sailing into the air and hitting the wall with a splat. "I'm going to have his autograph cremated with me when I die."

"That's pretty morbid, but you do you." Kite sneaks a smile my way, eyes squinting as he suppresses a laugh.

I did have a few concerns about Kite tagging along. Amusement parks and skating rinks are one thing; sleepovers are another. I worried that his presence would change the group dynamic, but so far everyone's proven me wrong. Ester's not afraid to be weird, Stephanie's not afraid to go barefaced, and Kite's not afraid to join in on our ridiculous conversations.

"If you're all finished, I'd like to get this game going," Stephanie says, unboxing a board game no one here has played before. It has a haunted house on the cover. "Don't take it personally when you lose."

"This game is meant to be cooperative," I tell her, paging through the instruction manual.

"Then you better pray we're on the same team."

"Playing Mario Party with her is such a pain," I whisper to Kite. "Joke's on her: Ester and I let her win."

Hours later I'm stirred awake by a strange sensation.

Eyes adjusting to the dark, I sit up and look around. Ester and Stephanie are sound asleep on the sofa beds. The spot next to me on the floor, however, is empty. I touch the pillow where Kite's head was and feel its fading warmth.

I venture upstairs and find Kite seated at the kitchen island with his iPad and earbuds in. I glance at the clock above the stove. It's one a.m.

"Couldn't sleep?" I ask, pulling up a stool.

Kite takes out one earbud. "All that sugar is getting to me."

"We went overboard, didn't we?" I laugh. "I'm not interrupting anything, am I?"

"Actually . . . you're just the person I wanted to see." He swipes a finger across his iPad and pulls up a music app. "There's a song I want you to listen to."

"Is it the piano song I heard the other day?" The one he didn't think was worth listening to?

"Yeah, I've tweaked it since then." He extends his right earbud to me, and I gladly take it.

The song opens with a playful and uplifting melody; the image of a ballerina skipping across a lake springs to mind, her slippers barely grazing the water as she glides through the air one step after the other. Then the song transitions into something that is still playful but grand—a full-bodied experience, as if the ballerina has touched the ground and is now twirling and leaping through a field of flowers.

"It reminds me of spring," I tell Kite as we sit shoulder to shoulder, the ending notes petering into silence.

"That's the mood I was aiming for," he says with a slight smile.

"I bet this would sound more beautiful if you played it on the piano downstairs."

"Probably, but . . . I wanted to share it with you first."

I kiss his cheek. "And I'd love to hear it again."

"Your wish is my command."

The song begins once more.

This time I close my eyes and lean into the music. It's no longer the ballerina I see but Kite and me, standing ankle-deep in a bed of pink and yellow tulips with the sun shining over our heads, lost in our own little world.

"Call me. It's important."

Kite's inbox: voice mail from Wayne on July 26.

29

"Why are you cutting so much fruit?"

Aunt Mei walks in on me at lunchtime and sees me slicing and dicing up a fruit salad.

"Kite and I are going out for a picnic," I explain. Indoor dates are getting a bit old. We can at least keep a safe distance from others while at the park. "I'm driving us down to Mercer County Park." I wrap up the fruit salad, store it in the fridge, and start on the sandwiches.

Kite's bringing kimbap and homemade apple cider.

"Just the two of you? Are his parents okay with him going out?" she asks.

"I think so. I mean, this isn't his first outing, and he'll be covered up." And if Kite thought the picnic wasn't a good idea, he'd tell me. "Anyway, what brings you home this early?" I hold my breath, hoping she won't call me out for changing the subject.

"Bakery's unusually slow. Thought I'd stop home for lunch." Aunt Mei grabs a plate of leftovers from the fridge and heats it in the microwave. "Connie dropped by before I left. She asked about you."

My ears perk up. "And?"

"I told her you're doing fine." Aunt Mei gives me a puzzled look. "Should I have answered differently?"

"Nope, not at all. I am in fact doing fine."

*

I load up the car, then drive two streets over, where Kite's waiting in a shaded area under a tree. He wanted me to pick him up somewhere away from his house. A safety measure, he said.

Back in his sunglasses and baseball cap, he greets me with a faint smile, drops his bag in the backseat, and climbs in next to me. He swiftly pecks me on the cheek before settling in, leaving me no time to deliver a kiss of my own.

I bury my disappointment and put the car into drive.

"Everything okay?" I ask as the trees and houses slip past us.

"Everything's cool," he says distractedly, "a little sleepy is all."

"Oh, you didn't sleep well last night?"

After a pause, "Something like that."

I wait for him to elaborate. The traffic light in front of us blinks green. The explanation never comes.

"We can postpone if you're tired," I tell him, ready to make a U-turn.

"No, don't, it's fine." Kite reaches under his sunglasses to rub his eyes. "I'll just . . . take a nap, if you don't mind."

"Go ahead. Let me know if you want to stop for coffee."

"Thanks." Kite tugs his baseball cap over his eyes, and the remainder of the drive is quiet. He doesn't wake up until we arrive at the park.

Part of me wonders if he actually slept. His shoulders were stiff throughout the trip, I could hardly hear him breathing, and he woke up a little too quickly as I pulled into the parking lot.

Kite hauls his backpack over his shoulders and volunteers to carry the cooler, leaving me empty-handed. "You did the driving. Now I'm doing my part," he says, grabbing my sun hat from the backseat and patting it down onto my head.

The park is teeming with activity. Beach towels pave the grassy terrain, and the sky is a map of vapor trails and sailing kites, their long, colorful tails rippling in the wind like ribbons.

Standing under the sun, Kite soaks in the scenery, and a smile finally graces his face. His smile makes me smile, and, with a glistening view of the lake to accompany us on our walk, we arrive at the picnic area and find a spot on the grass to lay out the gingham.

"This is the best kimbap I've ever had." I shove a roll of seaweed-wrapped rice into my mouth and nearly bite the inside of my cheek. Who knew kimchi, ham, and fish cakes could taste so divine? "Is this your own recipe?"

"O-Kei taught me how to make them," Kite says.

"Is he the chef in the group?" I ask, and after swallowing a mouthful, "I read somewhere that he's a connoisseur of food. Is that true?"

"Don't believe everything you read," Kite says. His tone isn't harsh, but I can't help feeling a little chastised—like for a second I'm just another fan spreading internet rumors. Then, more playfully, he adds, "He thinks he makes the best fried rice. Xiaoming's is way better, hands down."

"Does he also think fried chicken and yellow pickles go together like bread and butter?"

Kite chuckles into his water bottle. "That's one thing we agree on."

"You once mentioned that you get along with Xiaoming and Wayne the best. Does that mean you're not close with O-Kei or Yoosung?" It's a bold question, but I'm willing to take my chances.

A contemplative look crosses his face.

"We're a different kind of close," Kite begins, uncapping and recapping his water bottle. "We do everything friends do. That

207

includes butting heads . . . more often than I do with Wayne or Xiaoming. If there's one person I argue with the most, it's O-Kei. Yoosung and O-Kei are tight; he usually takes O-Kei's side over mine."

"How bad do your arguments get?"

The worst fight I ever had with Stephanie happened sophomore year, after she shot down my idea to do a *Battle Royale* hall-decorating contest in favor of Gwen's idea. I argued that high school was a metaphorical bloodbath and that a *Battle Royale* contest would be a productive outlet for promoting true school spirit. At first she thought I was kidding, but once she realized I wasn't, she told me I was out of my mind.

We got into a shouting match over it in the girls' bathroom.

In hindsight, it *was* a bad idea. Blood splatters and papier-mâché weapons would've gotten us into hot water with the school board.

"How bad did our arguments get?" Kite repeats the question, thinking. "Not bad enough to disband the group."

After lunch we follow a bike trail that leads us westward through the park. The canopy of leaves looming over us mitigates the afternoon haze, and we take our time on the trail, walking hand in hand, pointing out the little things that fascinate us, like the wild berries that neither of us dares to eat and the unfamiliar species of birds observing us from low-hanging branches.

"Would your manager ever enroll you in a survival show?" I ask out of curiosity.

"Probably not. Xiaoming's allergic to nature, Yoosung can't

read a map to save his life, and Wayne would start a forest fire."
Kite smiles at the thought—not at the idea of decimated wildlife
but at the idiosyncrasies of his friends. "What about Stephanie
and Ester? Could the three of you survive the wilderness?"

"Stephanie's a princess. She'd be useless." And I mean that
in an endearing way. "Ester has an uncle in the Philippines who
runs a YouTube channel dedicated to primitive technology. He's
taught her how to hunt for edible insects. Fried crickets are delicious, I hear."

Kite grimaces. "Now I'm imagining the taste. Thanks for
that." He flicks the brim of my hat. "How are you going to make
the taste go away?"

"I have a few ideas."

Taking off my hat, I get up on my tippy-toes and meet Kite
halfway. His hands find their way around my wrists, his thumb
brushing across my palm in one hot stroke before he laces his
fingers through mine. I gaze into his eyes with all the love I can
convey through a single look, and when I see my own feelings
reflected back at me, my knees go weak.

We share a kiss under the cover of my hat, the sensation lingering on my lips for the remainder of our walk.

Back at the parking lot, as if on cue, Kite's phone begins to
rumble in his pocket.

I can hear the deluge of messages, one text dinging after the
other, unrelenting as Kite's eyes flicker back and forth across
the screen.

All the color drains from his face.

Against the blue backdrop that is the sky and the rolling green
landscape around us, he's paper white. His phone slips from his
hands and lands at his feet with a resounding crack.

"What's wrong?" I ask, unable to hide the worry in my voice.

He flounders for a moment, his mouth opening and closing as words evade him. I place a hand on his arm, and he crumples, folding in on himself like a thin sheet of paper. I wrap my arms around him and feel him burrow his face into the crook of my neck.

"It's all over."

Trigger warning: violence. This video is gut-wrenching. Watch at your own discretion. For those who don't want to, the video was taken this past May at Karnival's apartment. It starts with Kite and O-Kei shouting at each other and ends with Kite punching O-Kei in the face.

POSTED BY MYLIGHTKITE ON JULY 27.

No one's life should be ruined over a thirty-second video. Anything can be taken out of context. Did Kite punch O-Kei? Yes, there's no doubt about it, but we don't know all the events that led to it or what happened after. This argument was meant to be between O-Kei and Kite—only. They're the ones who have the whole story. Instead of sending Kite to the guillotine, we should be outraged that someone leaked this video with malicious intent, but no, all you sanctimonious haters want to do is attack Kite.

#FireWorks #FlyHighKite #hatersgonnahate #stanwithkite

ENLIGHTENFANTASTIC COMMENTED ON MYLIGHTKITE'S POST.

Dream Drop hasn't been honest. I suspect that this whole "Kite taking a break from idol activities as advised by his doctor" thing is a lie and that Dream Drop put him on leave because he's a menace to the group. He might look like an angel, but plenty of sociopaths hide behind innocent facades. Who knows if he's been violent with other members? Whoever leaked the video did everyone a favor!

30

The higher you fly, the harder you fall.

It happens without warning, a crash landing.

But Kite is still falling.

"Any word from James?" Stephanie slides into the seat across from me with an iced coffee in hand. The two of us are at a café in Lower Manhattan famous for its shortbread ice cream sandwiches. Despite my summer-long cravings, I can stomach only a few bites.

I shake my head. The video leaked three days ago, and I haven't seen or heard from Kite since.

People online are calling Kite every name in the book, including a "two-faced sociopath." Anti-fans are dissecting every interaction between him and O-Kei to prove that Kite secretly despises O-Kei and wishes he could be Karnival's leader. A PhD student wrote a blog post on how to distinguish a genuine smile from a fake one, using Kite's photos for comparison, and now a bunch of internet strangers are convinced that if he squints and smiles with his lips closed, he's faking it for the camera. (I hope that PhD pot-stirrer gets expelled for her bogus analysis.)

Fireworks are also calling out Dream Drop for overworking their artists to the point of destroying their mental health, Kite being a prime example. Anonymous armchair psychologists are diagnosing him as emotionally unstable, "someone who's developed violent tendencies as a mechanism for coping with the harsh realities of an exploitive entertainment industry." Fans are starting petitions demanding a criminal investigation into Dream Drop, which will most likely accomplish nothing.

The video doesn't capture the events leading up to the argument. What you do see is Kite and O-Kei standing in what is presumably the living room, arguing over a mistake Kite made during dance practice earlier that day. Kite tells him to shut up, O-Kei keeps hounding him, Kite threatens to hit him if he doesn't back off, O-Kei doesn't listen, and then Kite punches him in the face, hard enough to cause a nosebleed. A third voice cuts in, and the video ends.

"There's a buzz going around about people sending James hate mail," Stephanie says with downcast eyes.

"You mean *here*?" I balk, eyes wide. "Why would people send hate mail to his house?" His return should still be a secret. If it weren't, my neighborhood would be mobbed by now.

"Maybe to shame his family? People are hateful busybodies."

I throw my head back and chug my iced tea. "Why can't people mind their own business? They act like they're morally superior to James, but in the same breath, they're slandering him and harassing his family."

"It's the entertainment industry. People thrive on drama."

"If only I could do something," I grumble, holding my face in my hand. "I wish I was a genius hacker. I'd wipe the internet clean of that video, but no, I'm just—"

"—Lulu Li," Stephanie finishes for me before sipping her coffee. "Give it time. A new scandal will break, and everyone will stop talking about James like he's the worst thing since squiggle brows."

✳

I knock on Kite's bedroom door.

The house seems to shake from the impact, or maybe I'm the one shaking. I'm alone in the hallway, standing in this suffocating silence, my shoulders heavy, as if my body is struggling under the weight of a thousand pairs of eyes. The same eyes confining Kite to his room.

I wait for the sound of life behind the door—the swivel of a chair, a squeak of the mattress spring, the shuffling of clothes—but I hear nothing.

After another knock, "Hey, it's me . . . I brought some congee."

I tried replicating Mom's. The consistency isn't the same, and neither is the taste, but it's delicious in its own right. I heard from Mrs. Xu that Kite hasn't been eating much and, if left to his own devices, probably wouldn't consume anything.

Still, all I get is silence.

Down in the kitchen, I store the food in the fridge, making sure to put Kite's name on it. Connie enters, sorting through the day's mail with mechanical speed. She didn't say a word to me when she let me in earlier. I'm surprised she opened the door, considering I haven't exactly been her favorite person (not that I should be).

Scowling, Connie rips up a dozen or so envelopes. At first I assume it's junk mail, but then I notice a pink envelope stamped with heart stickers.

"Are those letters addressed to Kite?" I ask, pointing to the bundle in her hands.

"Yeah, what of it?"

"Shouldn't you let Kite read them?"

"You know he's getting death threats and psychotic love confessions, right?"

"Not every letter is like that." There must be some fans out there who mean well and want to show their support without professing their undying love for him.

"You think Kai has time to filter his mail? If there's one thing I learned from last year, it's that you should expect the worst of people." Connie tears into another envelope, a thick one. She tosses the torn halves onto the countertop.

Something falls out, landing in the space between us.

We recognize it at the same time: a pair of women's underwear.

Connie groans before launching daggers at me. "*Now* do you want Kai to read everything he's sent?" I open my mouth. "That was a rhetorical question!"

Gritting her teeth, Connie grabs a paper towel, picks up the underwear (which we can only hope came unworn), and whips it into the trash. While she aggressively scrubs her hands in the sink, I see myself out.

As uncaring as Connie might seem, she has her own way of protecting Kite. When she confronted me at the park, I thought she was simply being Connie. Looking back, I was too quick to dismiss her feelings and the effort it took for her to admit how vulnerable last year's incident left her.

Now I feel guilty for dating her brother. I invested a lot of thought in my decision, but maybe it wasn't enough, because if it had been enough, my choice should've been different.

But guilt and regret aren't the same.

That's what my heart is telling me, for now.

This is Kite. In light of recent events, I want to apologize to my family, to Dream Drop Media, to Karnival, and to all the Fireworks I have deeply hurt through my shameful, childish, and reckless display of violence against a fellow teammate. On the day the video was taken, I was stressed and frustrated with myself for making mistakes throughout dance practice, and I lashed out in the worst way possible. Our manager immediately intervened, and although O-Kei and I have since reconciled, I will continue to reflect on my actions during my medical leave. I promise to work hard to regain the trust of our community.

Apology letter written by Dream Drop Media's PR team, released on July 29.

31

The last day of July is marred by rain clouds.

Kite and I haven't spoken. I reached out a few more times since showing up at his house but was met with silence. Hard to believe that, within only a week, we went from talking like best friends to *this*.

The scandal hasn't escalated, but the outrage is very much alive. To curb the hate mail and love letters, the Xus have directed the post office to hold their mail and a patrol car has been cruising through the neighborhood. Mr. Xu also installed an outdoor camera to discourage fans from hand-delivering letters, and judging by the numbers, it's working.

Last year's address leak seemed more chaotic for the Xus. They're managing better, and so far fans haven't been camping on our street. Then again, that's setting the bar low. Very low. I want to see the silver lining, but this fallout has inflicted a deep wound on Kite.

He's hurting.

How can I find an ounce of silver in that?

"Kite hasn't confided in you at all?" Ester asks when I return from the bathroom. "Even though you're his girlfriend?"

We're in my room watching *Miss Love & Hate*, a K-drama about a secretary who claws her way up the corporate ladder to get close to the chairman, the person who stole her family's farm for his own business ventures and left them homeless. He also happens to be young, handsome, and gravely misunderstood.

"I'm not his girlfriend." I climb back into bed, carefully avoiding Ester's laptop poised at the edge. "Kite asked me to go out with him. He didn't ask me to be his girlfriend."

"What's the difference? Are you two seeing other people? If not, you're exclusive, which makes you girlfriend and boyfriend."

I don't know what we are anymore.

Are we dating, and if I'm being honest with myself, should we be?

The last thing Kite needs is another scandal.

Last I heard from Mrs. Xu, Kite's isolated himself and leaves his bedroom only to use the bathroom. I wish he was comfortable enough to talk to me. All I can do is be there for him. That might not be much, but if I could ease his burden even a little, I'd go running to him.

"He has to talk to you eventually," Ester muses. Then, as if reading my mind, "He's probably afraid you think less of him for punching O-Kei."

"I don't condone what he did, but I understand why he did it." I watch as Secretary Choi "accidentally" spills hot coffee on Chairman Lee as they pass each other in the elevator. "Can anyone honestly say they've never fantasized about hitting someone out of frustration?"

The difference is that Kite didn't just fantasize about it.

The night is still young when I receive a phone call from Stephanie.

I put her on loudspeaker. "What's up, chicken butt?"

Ester rolls her eyes at my lameness, and I expect a similar reaction from Stephanie.

After a moment's pause, where I can hear her labored breathing, Stephanie speaks, her voice urgent: "Where are you right now?"

"At home?" I throw a backward glance at Ester, who looks as bewildered as I am. "Do you need something?"

"A bottle of aspirin, please!" she says, sounding more and more out of breath. "Where do I begin? I was on my way to—wait, no—that was—"

"Stephanie." I use my stern teacher voice. "Take a deep breath."

All is quiet as Stephanie composes herself. Finally she breaks the news. "Kite went out today, and someone recognized him and leaked his location. I'll give you the details later. You should probably stay with me for a few nights."

Ester whips out her phone and unleashes a shrill scream. "It's true! Someone posted a photo of Kite with Maru. It's trending on Twitter." I stare at her, unmoving. "Get packing! Fans are going to firework your house any moment now!"

Oh. My. Sweet. Tea. Kite is back in the Garden State! Someone spotted him at an animal hospital with an injured cat. The proof is in the photo. It's unclear when he returned, but I bet it was sometime after the first video leaked. The scandal with O-Kei must've taken a toll on him. If being with his family is what he needs, I support him 100%. His health comes first. Fireworks, we don't F.A.P. or F.U.K. Kite has so much on his plate right now. Let him be!

#KeepCalmSPARKOn

32

"I need to explain a few things before you go in."

Stephanie meets me outside as I step out of my car onto her driveway.

I don't bother mentally preparing myself for what I'm about to hear. My mind is still spinning from the news I received an hour ago.

"Earlier today I was on my way to get my nails done and happened to cross paths with Kite. I was driving and he was, um, running from someone." Stephanie stops to make sure she has my undivided attention.

She does.

"Some girl was chasing him," she continues. "She was gaining on him, so I offered him a ride, and then she tried to outrun my car! I lost her as soon as I turned the corner."

"That's what a lovesick fan would do," I tell her, unsurprised. What surprises me is that Kite was outside. The nail salon Stephanie frequents is on a busy road that takes twenty minutes to reach by foot. How did they cross paths?

Stephanie reads the confusion on my face. "Kite was coming back from the animal hospital, the one by that old flower shop. Someone ran Maru over; driver didn't stop."

Fear and dread grip me at once. The thought of Maru lying injured on the road, crying for help, brings tears to my eyes.

"Is she okay?" This time I prepare myself for the bad news.

"She was hit near your house, right down the road. Kite heard her crying and rushed her to the hospital. She's spending a few nights there after her surgery. Anyway, that girl was there, too, and she recognized him, took a photo, and you know the rest."

I sigh in relief. Kite's actions cost him big time, but I'm grateful he saved Maru.

And then I realize the missing detail in Stephanie's story. "What happened after you gave Kite a ride?" I didn't hear any commotion over at the Xus' while packing my bags to come here.

Stephanie shifts uneasily. "I came straight home."

I connect the dots and my mind explodes. "Kite is here, at your house?"

"In my basement. My parents are away on Martha's Vineyard. I have the house to myself until the week of move-in day at school."

I grab Stephanie by the shoulders and shake her. "Have you lost the plot? If this gets out, there'll be another scandal, and you'll be at the center of it! And if word gets out that Kite and I are living in your basement, the rumor mill will have a field day! There'll be headlines about love triangles!"

Stephanie brushes my hands off her. "I planned to give you the guest room, but if you insist on staying in the basement, go ahead."

"Is that the only thing you took away from what I said?" I growl. For someone who sounded shaken over the phone, Stephanie is way too lax about this.

"Listen, I'm aware this could backfire, but"—Stephanie purses her lips—"I thought it would be a good opportunity to bring you and Kite together. The circumstances aren't ideal, but I'm working with limited resources here. Do you want summer to end with Kite quietly making his exit, leaving you with a million unanswered questions?"

"No," I reluctantly cede through gritted teeth.

Stephanie claps me on the shoulder. "Then don't miss this opportunity, not when I wrapped it up for you and topped it with a pretty bow."

"There is nothing pretty about this," I say.

Kite stands at the bottom of the basement stairs, arms crossed. Looks like Stephanie's fantasy of me running into his arms isn't going to play out.

While I was unwinding in the guest room, Stephanie clued him in on my situation, which I'm grateful for, because I didn't want to be the one to break the news. After all that's happened, the thought of seeing Kite puts me on edge. Now that I can talk to him, I don't know what to say. I don't want to feed him platitudes or trivialize what he's going through with empty optimism.

"Mind if I come down?" I ask from the top of the stairs, holding two cups of after-dinner tea as a peace offering.

Kite didn't join Stephanie and me for dinner, so despite my nerves, I came to him.

"Sure," he says.

As I slip into the basement, I steal a quick look at him, and right away I can tell his face is slimmer. He has bags under his eyes, his lips are chapped, and the lethargy in his voice is matched by the way he carries himself: shoulders slumped, eyes to the ground, body leaning against the wall like he has no energy to stand up straight.

I place our tea on the coffee table and sit on the edge of the sofa, reminding myself not to get too comfortable. My eyes instinctively wander over to the grand piano. The velvet drape has been pulled back, exposing the keyboard.

"Were you playing earlier?" I ask him as he crosses the room to stand by the billiard table, putting three or so yards between us.

"Yeah, to kill time."

"I'd love to hear you play," I say a little too eagerly, overcompensating for his lack of enthusiasm.

"Maybe later," he says noncommittally.

It's pointless to act as if nothing's happened. Dancing around the giant pink elephant in the room doesn't help either of us. There's no way to broach this without some discomfort, so I bite the bullet.

"About the video," I begin, hesitating when I notice the subtle flinch in his arms as he shoves his hands into his pockets. "I want you to know that I don't see you differently."

This sounded way more comforting in my head. Hearing the words out loud makes me sound conceited. Why would my opinion matter more than thousands of others? Yet I hope Kite values what I think.

His silence isn't instilling any confidence in me.

"Stephanie told me what happened. . . . Are your parents okay with you staying here?" This seems like a safe question to ask, better than *Are you okay?*

"They know I'm here," he says, a nonanswer.

"Okay," I say, because what else is there to say?

"My dad's going to bring me an overnight bag," he continues, rubbing the back of his neck. "How long will you be staying?"

"As long as I need to, I guess. Hopefully not too long."

Mom and Aunt Mei will be my eyes for the next few days.

They'll tell me when it's safe to come home. I haven't heard of any public disturbances, but I have a feeling it'll take at least a day for fans to show up at the Xus'. Hardcore fans will drop everything to see Kite, no matter the distance. Last year we had oblivious parents carpooling middle schoolers from out of state to see Kite's house. I saw license plates from Ohio, Indiana, and Florida.

"You and me both," Kite says, fumbling with his phone, showing no interest in the cup of tea on the table or the empty spot next to me on the sofa.

He feels so far away. Everything that happened between us before the scandal may as well be a distant memory.

I get off the sofa. "I'm going to head back up. Holler if you need anything."

Halfway to the door, I hear Kite call out to me. A loud, unwavering "Lovely" echoes in my ears and fills my heart with hope. I turn back, and as soon as he has my attention, he freezes up. I linger by the doorway, silently urging him to say what he wants to say.

"Thanks," Kite says, after much suspense, "for the tea."

A smile tugs at my lips.

"Thanks" is as good a place to start as any.

Later that night, when I hear piano music floating up from the basement while Stephanie and I paint each other's nails, I am reminded of all the good and the bad that this summer has offered, and that it's not over yet.

"I'm sorry about everything. I'm sorry you got dragged into my mess. I'm sorry that I'm an idiot who can't talk to you when you're trying to help me. A billion things are swimming in my head, and I don't know what to do with them. Coming home was the best thing to happen to me in a long time. I wanted this summer to be special, but now it's all gone to hell."

Kite's text message to Lulu, sent at midnight and read a second later.

33

Someone somewhere caught wind that my family lives next door to Kite's. Since we are guilty by association, they and their social media followers started spamming Dāngrán Bakery with negative reviews.

But that isn't the worst of it.

I haven't been home for three nights. According to Mom, people of all shapes and sizes are visiting my neighborhood as if it's a hot tourist attraction. The crowd doesn't seem as invasive as last year's, since the police acted early, but they can only do so much by patrolling the area. They can't ban people from walking through a residential area as long as they aren't engaging in disorderly conduct. Mom told me people are playing ding dong ditch, taking selfies in front of Kite's house, and shouting nice and not-so-nice things from their cars. (Sounds like disorderly conduct to me, but what do I know?)

The Xus bear the brunt of it all, but Mom and Aunt Mei haven't gone untouched. I feel bad leaving them to the wolves, so I'm back at the bakery, hoping the situation doesn't escalate.

So far business is normal. Aunt Mei left to see her gynecologist while Mom's out to restock our supply of strawberries.

"I'm surprised people haven't mobbed this place," Stephanie says, sipping her honey green tea while I sweep the floor.

"Don't jinx it!" I shush her. "I had five girls come in asking about Kite. One offered to pay me if I gave her Kite's phone number."

"How much was she willing to pay?"

"Does it matter? I would never give it to her."

"A million dollars could loosen the tightest lips."

"Someone that rich would hire some tech genius to hack Kite's phone."

"You better guard yours before someone steals it," Stephanie says. I instinctively check my back pocket. "Those delulus would commit armed robbery to meet—"

Something goes splat against the shop window.

Confusion passes between us. We turn in time to witness a gaggle of girls outside, pelting eggs at the glass—which I washed this morning.

Stephanie springs into action. The girls are too busy giggling to notice the storm barreling toward them. The front door slams open with the force of a hurricane and nearly sweeps one girl off her feet.

They scatter, all three darting in different directions.

Stephanie grabs a carton of eggs and chases the slowest target: a petite girl in flip-flops. She closes the distance between them before raising her arm above her head, egg in hand. "Stop or I'll make an omelet in your hair!"

The girl stops, nearly tripping herself, and turns. Stephanie and I run over.

I call the nonemergency number while Stephanie enters evil-stepsister mode.

"Wait until your parents hear about this," she says as tears begin to gather in the girl's eyes. "Now talk."

I stare at Stephanie, gobsmacked.

We manage to extract some information while waiting for the police to arrive.

Our little troublemaker, Olivia, is thirteen, lives on Long Island, and has been in love with Karnival since their debut. Kite is her bias. She sent him a letter at the start of the scandal to show her support. Frustrated by his lack of response, she paid a visit to his house earlier today, only to receive a verbal warning from the police officer patrolling the neighborhood.

She thought egging the bakery would get Kite to notice her.

Any attention is better than no attention, apparently.

Her friends tagged along for moral support. They gave her the idea to take her anger out on the bakery. Meanwhile, Olivia's brother, who drove her here without knowing her intentions, is at Pho King Delight, waiting to take the three of them home.

After a sisterly sigh, Stephanie crouches down at eye level with Olivia. "It hurts when your crush doesn't reciprocate, but anger doesn't give you a license to vandalize private property. Why couldn't you vent to your friends over ice cream or bubble tea? Lulu could've made you a delicious taro milk tea, but now you don't deserve one."

Olivia glances in my direction before mumbling an apology.

Turns out, she loves taro milk tea.

I can see the guilt chipping away at her as she calls her brother to explain what happened. On his way over from Pho King Delight, he takes a good look at the mess Olivia and her friends made before apologizing.

Once the police car arrives, we get down to business. I explain what transpired, Olivia confirms my account, and the officer snaps a few photos of the bakery, caked in milky-white film and yellow trails of slime. Mom returns right on time to speak with the officer. She'll be calling Olivia's parents but won't be filing charges. "Not worth the hassle," she says.

Olivia seems like a decent person, albeit misguided and irrational. Her apology was sincere, and she volunteered to wash our window with no help from her brother or friends.

In the end, I make her a taro milk tea to take with her on the trip home.

34

"I can't believe I wasn't there!"

Ester is on the verge of yanking out her hair.

She was with her sister yesterday. I didn't tell her about Olivia until today, after she invited Stephanie and me over for more *Miss Love & Hate*. We were halfway into an episode before I brought up the incident, and now Ester won't shut up.

"Steph got to be all badass while I was eating lukewarm supermarket sushi!"

The three of us are on the living room sofa with Ester in the middle, shooting laser beams at us with her smoldering, mascara-rimmed eyes.

"Badass is not how I'd describe it," I chime in. "Stephanie was downright terrifying when she went all mafia on Olivia."

"My adrenaline was running. I got caught up in the moment." Stephanie dismisses my fears with a wave of her hand. "If Ester had been there, she would've had assault charges brought against her by the end of the day."

"I'm not an animal, Steph!" Ester snaps. "As much as I would have loved to channel my inner assassin and hunt those girls down, I would never beat up a bunch of kids."

"You're right," Stephanie concedes with an amiable smile. "Unlike me, you would've started singing 'Lights Fantastic' with

Olivia." She then trains her smile on me. "Meanwhile, this one here would've screamed 'Heeeere's Johnny!'"

Stephanie now has two people shooting laser beams at her.

"There's nothing wrong with bonding over a mutual interest," Ester counters. "Make love, not war." Throwing one last glare at Stephanie, Ester whips around to face me. "Does Kite know what happened?"

"Oh, we're still talking about this?" I ask, feigning ignorance. "I thought we moved on to the sixties. Power to the people—"

"Answer me!" Ester interrupts.

"You need to chill." Ester's glare hardens to stone, and since I'd rather live to see another day, I go ahead and answer her. "No, I don't think so."

I still haven't spoken much to Kite. Most of my day is spent at the bakery while he plays piano in the basement.

Mrs. Xu swung by yesterday and told Kite he could stay with his aunt and uncle in Connecticut until this all blows over. I expected him to go, but he insisted on staying. Mrs. Xu wasn't keen on his decision, so Stephanie phoned her parents, asked them to speak with Mrs. Xu to give her some peace of mind. Mr. and Mrs. Nguyen couldn't care less about Stephanie housing a K-pop idol so long as it won't jeopardize her place at Barnard.

"I'm surprised the egging didn't make the news," Ester says, taking it down a notch. "Tabloids usually gobble up that kind of tea in seconds."

No major news outlet has gotten involved, thankfully, although a journalism student from Rutgers did request an interview with the Xus regarding the controversy surrounding Kite—which they declined instantly.

"I'm more surprised by Kite's decision to stay in my basement," Stephanie says.

"You do have a swanky basement," Ester adds.

"Mind if I interrupt?" A frosty voice blows through the room.

Standing there in the open doorway is Connie.

"The door was unlocked, so I let myself in," she says, tapping a large envelope against her thigh. "This arrived at my house. It's for Ester."

"Me?" Curious, Ester takes the envelope and screams. "Oh my god, yes, yes! It's here! It's finally here!" The floor shakes as she hops up and down.

Whatever's inside that envelope must be worth a fortune. Ester wasn't this excited when she received her acceptance letter from Rutgers.

"Don't leave us in suspense. What is it?" I ask.

"Shhh, you're ruining the moment." Ester hugs the envelope as she would a teddy bear and murmurs something too low for us to hear. Then, with uncharacteristic restraint, she opens the envelope by its seal to reveal a photographic portrait of Wayne with his signature scrawled on the back. Time seems to slow as Ester stares longingly into his eyes, and then picks up again when she starts pecking his two-dimensional face with kisses.

We all look on as Ester makes out with a piece of paper.

More amused than disturbed, Stephanie remembers to ask the important questions. "So, Connie, exactly how long were you standing there? Long enough to hear everything?"

"Yup," and with that, Connie goes out the way she came.

I hurry after her. "Wait!"

Connie quickens her pace, gunning for the silver car parked across the street. Just when I think she's going to keep ignoring me, she stops abruptly in her tracks and whirls on me.

I brace myself, expecting the worst.

"I don't get it," she says, exasperated, a stark contrast to her earlier indifference. "Aren't you pissed off that some stupid fangirl egged your mom's bakery, and that people are making up lies to ruin her business? How about the fact that you can't even stay in your own house?"

It takes me a moment to realize she isn't blaming me for what happened to Kite. Instead, she sounds worried—about me.

Blinking back my surprise, I decide to be open with her, her own honesty emboldening me. "Of course, I'm mad. Who wouldn't be?"

"Then why didn't you let what's-her-name have it?"

"Stephanie gave her plenty, trust me. Besides, the girl apologized."

"Anyone can say sorry without meaning it," Connie huffs.

"What should I have done instead? Blindfold her, tie a cement block to her ankle, and dump her in a river?"

"The Hudson, preferably."

Sighing, I ask Connie what I originally chased her down for. "Why did you come here to deliver an autograph? I thought you would've mistaken it for junk mail."

"Kai told me he was expecting a package addressed to Ester. He wanted to make sure she got it, so he asked me to give it to her. I'm not that big of a bitch, you know."

Tempted to debate her, I remind myself that, although she and I haven't been on the best terms lately, Connie did go out of her way to deliver something precious to Ester.

"And how are you holding up?" I wonder if, amid all the drama, anyone's thought to check in on Connie.

"How nice of you to ask." Connie crosses her arms and immediately uncrosses them. "Sorry, forget I said that. . . . I'm doing okay. Better than Kai, anyway."

"Is there anything you want to get off your chest?"

"There is, but I don't think you have all day to listen to me."

Rather than agreeing or disagreeing with her, I simply wait, because I know she wants to say more. I can see it in the way her eyes flick back and forth, and how she keeps tapping her fingers against her thigh. My silence is an invitation, and she takes it.

"That weird friend of yours said she 'would never beat up a bunch of kids,' which I find ironic. She totally looks capable of murder. Anyway, what she said got me thinking. . . . Kai's the biggest softie I know. He wouldn't punch someone without a reason."

Looking back at all the years I've known Kite, I don't think I've ever seen him angry, not in the way I've seen others angry, where they turn red in the face, holler at the top of their lungs, and slam every door in their wake. I've seen him stressed and frustrated, and I know he can be cold and standoffish—but never violent.

"I know my brother. O-Kei is no angel, and Kai is not the devil people want him to be. What pisses me off is how O-Kei has been silent this entire time. Kai's dream is on the line, and if anyone should be helping him through this, it's his own damn teammate."

I return to Stephanie's with a better understanding of Connie.

Her pride gets in the way of how she truly feels, but now I know she isn't mad at Kite or me. She's angry at the situation we're in.

If Connie and I can have an open conversation, I'm tempted to try again with Kite, and so I make another trip to the basement.

Maru is the first to greet me when I enter. Her purrs resonate throughout the room, growing louder as I approach a spacious cage furnished with a bed, a litterbox, and two bowls. Stephanie picked Maru up from the animal hospital this morning. Maru broke her hind leg from the hit-and-run (vet said she was lucky to escape with just that) and will be on cage rest for the next six weeks. Kite volunteered to take care of her and the expenses.

I tap Maru on her little nose through the metal bars of her cage. Her *meow* is loud but raspy. "Have you eaten? Should I get you a snack?"

"Don't, she's been begging for treats all day," Kite says, coming up behind me.

"You've been spoiling her, haven't you?" I say, glancing back at him.

"You listen to her cry for an hour." Kite stoops low next to me and strokes Maru's paws through a square opening in her cage.

"Can't we both spoil her after what she's been through?"

"Wayne will never let me hear the end of it if I overfeed her."

"Oh." I pause. "Wayne knows about Maru?"

"I sent him some videos of her." Kite taps Maru on her nose, just as I did, and once again moves to stand by the billiard table while I take the sofa.

"Ester got his autograph. She said thank you."

"No problem."

"So, uh, how are things in South Korea?" What I really want to ask is if his group members are upset with him, for the video scandal and for getting outed.

Kite tilts his head back, exposing the length of his neck, his Adam's apple bobbing as he swallows. "Everyone's past the point of feeling. We just want this to end."

People finding out he's back home isn't a scandal on its own. It's an inconvenience, but not damaging to his career. Coupled with the video leak, however, his medical hiatus is drawing suspicion. Some fans think his return home is a telltale sign he'll resign soon.

Drumming his fingers against the billiard table, Kite starts to speak. "Is it . . . Is it true someone threw eggs at the bakery?" His voice is tight, his jaw clenched.

"Yeah." I don't know who told him, but there's no use lying. "Stephanie and I caught the girls who did it. Everything's resolved."

Kite drags a hand down his face, and his shoulders deflate as he exhales. "I'm sorry this is happening. If only I hadn't gone out that day . . ."

"It's not that big of a deal."

"But what if it happens again? What if next time someone throws a rock or, I don't know, plants a bomb in your mailbox?"

"I don't think anyone would do—"

"You don't know that!" Kite suddenly raises his voice. "The other day some singer in Taiwan found needles in his food after fans found out he was dating! What if—"

"Kite, stop talking and come here." I firmly pat the space next to me.

He's reluctant at first, but then I say *please,* and that one word is all it takes to bridge the distance between us. It's not enough to dismantle the wall he's erected, but I'm reaching out to him and he's reaching back.

Once he's settled next to me, I take his hands in mine and let my honesty guide me.

"You have nothing to be sorry for. I know you didn't mean

for any of this to happen. I'm happy you saved Maru. It was selfless of you to do that, and anyone who tells you otherwise is a cold-blooded monster." My heart races as my own irritation gnaws at me. "I don't know what happened between you and O-Kei, but we all make mistakes. Don't let this ruin you."

"Easier said than done when people are demanding your resignation." Kite keeps his head down as he speaks, his hands slipping from mine.

I press my hand against his cheek, my palm warm against the cool surface of his skin as I wait for him to reject my touch. He doesn't. Gently I turn his face toward me.

"Please don't let this stop you from doing what you love. For what it's worth, I don't care what the media says about you, I don't care what fans say either, and I definitely don't care what they might say about me. What I care about is you. If you give up now, then these last four years, what were they for?"

I wait for an argument to ensue, for him to tell me I don't know what I'm talking about and that this isn't a rom-com where all your problems can be solved with a pep talk.

But he doesn't. Instead, he turns away, blinking rapidly.

"That day when I hit O-Kei . . . earlier we were in the practice room, learning some new choreography. I couldn't get the timing right. If I was too slow or too fast, if my shoulders were too stiff or my elbows too far out, O-Kei would stop everything to correct me."

Something catches in his voice. He stops to clear it.

"When I told O-Kei to let Wayne or Xiaoming coach me, he said I shouldn't burden them just because I'm lazy. I told him I was trying my best and then he"—Kite takes a deep, shaky breath—"he said if this was my best, then my best wasn't good enough and that I might as well go back to America—even though nothing's waiting for me back home."

"That's not true," I can't help but interject.

"I know." Kite tries to smile, but whatever comfort he feels is overtaken by the sad look in his eyes. "O-Kei's criticized me before, but his comments are usually constructive. This time he went too far, and I . . . snapped."

Who wouldn't? Kite's under enough pressure without his own teammate berating him. As Karnival's leader, O-Kei must know how difficult it is when everyone constantly expects perfection from you.

"O-Kei and I did apologize to each other, but things haven't been the same between us. . . . I started wondering if maybe he was right and I don't have what it takes to survive in the industry. I'm not a strong dancer, so I make up for it with my singing. Even then, I get fewer lines than O-Kei and Yoosung, and I have to fight tooth and nail to co-write songs. The negativity, the stress, everything . . . sometimes it feels like too much."

"Have you talked to Wayne and the others about how you feel?" I ask.

"A little, but they also have a lot on their plates. I don't want to burden them."

"You're not a burden, Kite."

"Thanks." His hands find their way back to my own, and his eyes fasten on mine. "I know I've been avoiding you, but I do appreciate having you here."

"And I'm not going anywhere," I say.

"I just don't know what to do."

The thought of Kite leaving Karnival makes my heart hurt,

but this is a decision he has to make on his own, so I let our conversation end there.

We don't speak of it for the rest of the day. Nothing seems to have changed, but when he comes upstairs to help me cook dinner and sits down to eat with me, that little semblance of normalcy is like an unspoken promise.

35

"Are you sure it's safe?" Ester asks, tapping the steering wheel while sizing me up.

We're parked three blocks from my house. We scouted the neighborhood twice and found nothing: no paparazzi, no fans lurking in the bushes, no drones in the sky.

Aunt Mei said yesterday our street was so deserted, you could hear a pin drop. I don't know if Fireworks are on a break or if they had a sudden change of heart and now respect other people's privacy, but it seems safe to at least drop by the house.

Still, I want to practice caution, which is why I paired my plain tee and capris with a baseball cap. I would've opted for something more revealing in this humidity, but the last thing I need is a wardrobe malfunction caught on camera. I can already imagine the headlines: KITE'S NEIGHBOR: A CHILDHOOD FRIEND OR A BUDDING EXHIBITIONIST? I don't care what people might whisper about me, but I don't want to give them gossip material either.

"I'll be in and out," I assure Ester. Stephanie wants to watch *My Fair Princess,* so I'm here to grab Mom's box set.

"I'll be your lookout," Ester says, starting the engine.

We pull away from the curb, and seconds later, a teal bungalow enters my view. Despite our reconnaissance, there's an unfamiliar red Lexus in the driveway that wasn't there earlier.

Ester and I trade looks, mirroring each other's confusion.

I'm not even out of the car yet when the front door of my house swings open and out walks Dad.

"Oh." Ester barely stifles a gasp.

Today's the first Sunday of August, the day Dad and Katherine were scheduled to fly in from California. I thought they'd be in New York. Before I can ask why no one gave me a heads-up, my phone dings with a message from Mom: *Dad dropped by unannounced. Don't come home unless you want to see him. Aunt Mei is there with him.*

Too late.

"Lulu!" Katherine hurries past my dad, taking big strides in my direction. I keep my arms crossed, refusing to budge when she reels me in for a hug. "Happy early birthday! Can't believe you're turning eighteen. Last time I saw you, you were only a high school freshman."

Dad comes up from behind and wraps an arm around her shoulder. His salt-and-pepper hair is stark against her glossy brunette curls, but they're both sporting the same olive tan. His skin is darker than I remember, rough and weathered around his eyes.

"How's my birthday girl doing?" Dad asks, kissing Katherine on the temple.

"As well as I can be," I mutter, arms still crossed. I haven't seen my dad in ages, yet he can't bother to look at me when saying hello.

"Are you doing anything special to celebrate?" Katherine asks, jubilant. "I know this wonderful spa in—"

"I'm fully booked for the week," I lie, startling when Ester hooks arms with me.

"Hi, I'm Ester. You must be Mr. Cheng." She extends her

hand. Dad shakes it, his face contorting as she waves his arm up and down like a jump rope. "I've heard so much about you. Don't mind us! We're just passing through."

Ester pulls me toward the house. We're halfway across the lawn when, from the corner of my eye, I notice Dad massaging his hand. I love Ester.

After grabbing *My Fair Princess* from Mom's room, I find Aunt Mei brewing tea in the kitchen. It irks me that she's playing the role of a welcoming host. If I were Mom's twin sister, I would've slammed the door in their face.

"Believe me, it's a surprise to all of us," she says. "Now play nice."

I groan, stopping as Dad and Katherine crowd the doorway.

"Are you staying for tea?" Katherine asks me. "Kyle's out for a walk, but he'll be back soon. He's a high school sophomore now! Time flies, doesn't it?"

"We're heading out," I tell her.

"Are you sure you can't stay for a bit? I'd love to catch up."

"We're sure," Ester answers for me.

"Maybe next time, then." Disappointment salts Katherine's tone. She turns to my dad. "Dear, the girls need to be somewhere. Let's not delay them." Fixing Ester and me with a smile, she says, "Nice meeting you, Ester, and congratulations on your graduation, Lulu. Sorry we couldn't be there."

I didn't want you there anyway is what I want to say, but I bite my tongue. She seems sincere. Torn between the fact that she's a homewrecker with the nerve to show her face here and that she's shown more interest in me than my own dad, I opt for a simple nod.

Just as Ester and I point our feet toward the exit, Dad suddenly speaks up. "Are the Xus home? I don't see a car in their driveway."

"I think they're out," Aunt Mei says, fetching cups from the overhead cabinet.

"That's too bad." Dad sighs. "I heard Kai's home for the summer. I was hoping to get his autograph." Then, as if the idea miraculously occurred to him, "Lulu, would you do me a favor and get me his autograph?"

My blood pressure skyrockets, and a fire rages in my belly. I inch forward, my mouth a loose cannon. Ester pinches my shirt and tugs me back.

"Tea's ready!" Aunt Mei steps in front of me, blocking my view. "Vincent, why don't you and Katherine take a seat in the living room?"

While Aunt Mei distracts them, Ester ushers me toward the back door. The second we're outside, someone's car alarm goes off. Ester and I loop around the house. We don't see anything, save for the blaring red Lexus.

Then Connie's voice booms over the rose hedge.

By now Aunt Mei and the others are outside. Dad disables the alarm while Ester and I cut across the lawn to the Xus'. A soccer ball whizzes past us, close enough for me to feel the air move.

Connie is armed with soccer balls, and her target is Kyle.

He's crouched by the rose hedge, shielding his head with his arms while soccer balls roll past his feet. Connie must've kicked a ball into Dad's car.

"Kyle!" Katherine rushes to his aid. "Are you all right?"

Connie marches over. I stumble out of her way, and something crunches under my foot. It's a shattered phone hidden in the grass.

"What's going on here?" Dad charges over, chest out, arms swinging.

"Won't you look at that? It's Ms. Li's ex-husband! I almost

forgot what you looked like." Connie's sass is at an all-time high. "And to answer your question, your son was sneaking around my house. I caught him peeping through the window with his phone!"

"Oh my god," Ester whispers under her breath.

"Don't raise your voice at me." Dad shakes a finger at Connie (that'll show her). "I know my son, he would never—"

"That's enough." Katherine's voice chills over, earning everyone's attention. I've never heard her use such a tone before, and judging by my dad's reaction, neither has he. "Kyle, get up and don't make me repeat myself."

Kyle does as he's told. You can almost make out the imprint of a soccer ball on his face.

"I'm going to ask you once and only once. Is this young lady telling the truth?" Katherine stares Kyle down with the intensity of a magnifying glass in the sun. This version of her is light-years away from the one who had to bribe her son to eat dinner with us.

Head hung low, Kyle answers with a weak nod.

Connie smirks up at my dad, and he backs off.

"Let's take this inside," he says, eyes scanning for anyone who might've overheard. "I'm sure there's a misunderstanding—"

"I'm done here." Connie dusts off her hands and heads inside.

"Connie is a firecracker! I have never been more attracted to someone in my life! But Wayne is still my spicy maple cookie."

What Ester is thinking during the drive back to Stephanie's.

36

I trail after Ester as she hurtles up the stairs with the speed of a panther and the grace of a panda and flings Stephanie's bedroom door wide open.

"Oh my god, Steph, you'll never believe what happened!"

Stephanie's lying supine on her king-sized bed, draped in a lavender bathrobe, her face coated in a mint-green mask while two slices of cucumber conceal her eyes (which are probably rolling right now). Lips pressed into a thin line, she mutters, "You found a winning lottery ticket in a storm drain and had to fight off rabid raccoons for it?"

"Close! Lu's dad, like, ambushed her! And then Connie caught Lu's stepbrother sniffing around her house, so she taught him a lesson!"

Stephanie gingerly props herself up by the elbows and removes a cucumber slice from one eye. "I'd like to hear Lulu's version of events."

I make myself comfy at the foot of her bed. "Where to start . . ."

By the end of my recap, Stephanie has exhausted all her facial muscles. Her face mask is now a dried sheet riddled with cracks, especially on her forehead. Even the threat of wrinkles can't stifle her scathing judgment.

"Respect to Connie for defending her fort. A pity we didn't

have Olivia and her eggs for additional ammunition." Stephanie disappears into her connecting bathroom and, after the sound of running water, reemerges with a naked face. "Will the Xus report Kyle to the police?"

"Doubt it." Ester and I didn't stick around for the aftermath, but it's unlike the Xus to escalate, not when family friends are involved. "Dad will probably apologize for Kyle, and since Kyle's already been punished, it'll all be dust under the rug."

Kyle and Katherine are as good as strangers to the Xus, but Dad isn't. He knew Kite and Connie when they were in diapers (probably changed some, too). He should be ashamed of what Kyle did and for yelling at Connie.

"So much for wanting to celebrate your birthday," Stephanie says, brushing her hair in front of her vanity mirror. "Sounds to me like what your dad really wanted was to see Kite."

Today cinched a feeling I already knew to be a fact: my dad cares more about Kyle than me. Visiting my house was simply a covert operation for obtaining Kite's autograph for Kyle.

"At least Kite wasn't home," Ester grumbles, crossing her arms. "Who knows what kind of photo your slimy stepbrother was after! I commend his taste in guys, but—" I narrow my eyes at her. "That's enough excitement for the day. We need some H_2O after all this hot tea."

And then she's out the door.

A second later, she pokes her head back into the room.

"Uh . . ." She lingers in the doorway and signals me over. I oblige, curious as to what could possibly worry her, and find an abandoned tray of coffee at the bottom of the stairs.

I find Kite in the backyard with his jeans rolled up, calves-deep in the pool. He looks back over his shoulder as the patio door squeaks on its hinges. I kick off my sandals and join him on the pool's edge, the coolness of the water a relief against the events of today.

"Thoughts?" I nudge his leg with mine. "Now that you heard everything."

"Can't say it's anything new." He sighs. "I wish people wouldn't involve my family. They didn't sign up for this. Connie's tough, but I know this takes a toll on her."

"I'm sure it does. . . ." I think back to what Connie said the day she delivered Wayne's autograph to Ester's house: *I know my brother. O-Kei is no angel, and Kai is not the devil people want him to be. . . . Kai's dream is on the line, and if anyone should be helping him through this, it's his own damn teammate.* "But she supports you."

Kite touches the back of his neck. It seems like he's rubbing a sunburn, but he's actually blushing. "I don't know how to be a better brother to her. I told my parents I was thinking of quitting K-pop, that it might make everyone's life easier. When Connie heard, she threatened to punch me if I did."

"Your sister has a way with words." Which would I rather face? Negative PR or Connie's fist? "So . . . are you quitting?"

"It's easy to want to." Kite drums his fingers on the pool's edge. "I came home to get some perspective, figure out what it was I really wanted. At first it was nice to feel normal, like I could be just another kid here. But . . . I can't quit. Like you said, if I quit now, what were these last four years for? I can't leave everyone in Karnival behind. Music is my calling." Kite releases a breathy chuckle. "And Connie said if I ever want to punch O-Kei again, she'd do it for me."

"Let's hope that never happens."

"It won't. I know I make O-Kei sound like a bully, but he's more like a strict older brother who gets carried away looking after the group. He was shocked when I hit him, but he didn't try to hit me back."

"What kind of younger brother does that make you, then?"

"Look, I'm still trying to figure out how to be a brother to Connie."

"At least you're not someone's creepy stepbrother. Sorry about Kyle."

After what Kyle did, there's no way in hell anyone's going to let him apologize to Kite in person. Like Dad, I'll apologize in his place, but unlike my dad, I mean it.

"I'm sorry, too," Kite says.

"About what?" I ask, drawing circles in the water with my feet.

"Your dad."

At first I don't understand what he's referring to. Then it clicks.

"Please." I dismiss his concerns with a wave of my hand. "You can't expect much from a guy who couldn't be bothered to attend his daughter's graduation. He said he wanted to celebrate my birthday, but I knew that wasn't true."

Except I didn't know he wanted to see Kite more than me. Only Katherine seemed genuinely happy to see me. Oh, the irony. I could laugh and I could cry, but I won't do either.

"Do you ever miss him?" Kite asks.

"No, why would I?" I all but snap. Kite doesn't shy away from my tone, but my own ears sting at the sudden rush of anger. "Sorry, I can't talk about my dad without getting mad."

"If you want to vent, I'm listening."

"If only my own dad would." I swing my legs, kicking shallow

253

waves in the pool, our reflections rippling. "He only cares about what he wants. He cheated on my mom, lied to both of us for months, then ran off to be with his new family, and now he pulls this stunt."

Now that I'm talking, I can't stop. "He didn't come to my graduation because flying across the country for a once-in-a-lifetime event didn't benefit him—even though I saved him a spot. I didn't want to see him, but I thought if he made the effort for my sake, then he wasn't completely lost to me. Well, he failed that test."

I take a deep breath. "It's when I don't want to see him that he reinserts himself into my life. Even then, he isn't doing it *for* me. Sometimes I wonder if he calls me, hoping I won't answer, because then he can tell himself he tried and it's me who's being difficult. News flash: my life isn't a revolving door that he can enter and leave whenever it's convenient for him. I'm ready to say goodbye to anyone who doesn't think I'm worth staying for."

An odd look passes over Kite's face.

"Do you have any good memories with your dad?" he asks.

The question throws me for a loop. It's strange of him to ask after everything I just said. I want to tell him no, but then I recall how Dad used to drive Kite and me around on the weekends: to the movies, the bowling alley, the mall, and all the birthday parties. He was more like a chauffeur, but he never complained whenever I wanted to go somewhere or wanted to be with my friends (so long as my homework was done). I wouldn't say I have good memories *with* him, but he helped me make them.

"Once upon a time, I liked having him around . . . until he dreamed of something more than Mom and me. So here we are."

"Do you wish things were different? Meaning . . . if your dad wanted to make amends, would you let him?"

"At this point, making amends means giving up what he has, groveling to my mom, and admitting to all the pain he's caused. But he would never do that. And that's perfectly fine. I can live without him. Some people you just have to let go."

Kite soaks in my words. He seems to be concentrating hard on something. Maybe he's searching for a way to cheer me up, or maybe he disagrees with me. Whatever it is, there's something he wants to say.

"I'm sorry for everything he's put you through. I should've . . . been there for you."

"Don't feel bad. It is what it is."

"It is what it is," he echoes back.

After a stretch of silence, he pats my thigh and hops to his feet. "Ester's right. We need some H_2O after all this tea."

Before I can ask him what he means, he dives into the pool, shirt, jeans, and all. I follow his blurry silhouette as he slithers through the water and breaks the surface at the opposite end of the pool. He smooths back his hair. His white shirt, turned transparent, is clinging to him; he peels it off and hurls it over my head, onto the grass behind me.

That is an invitation, and I jump in after him.

"Lulu, I know a lot happened today. I spoke with the Xus, and all is forgiven. Kath really wants to make it up to you. We'll be in New York for the week. If you want to celebrate your birthday with us, I'm only a phone call away."

Voice mail left on Lulu's phone from her dad.

37

"Happy birthday!"

Stephanie and Ester burst into the guest room and leap onto my bed. We spent all of last night finishing *My Fair Princess,* and somehow they have more energy than I do. Too sleepy to give them a piece of my mind, I flop around like a fish out of water as the mattress bounces under the weight of two pairs of feet jumping up and down on the springs.

The smell of pancakes travels up my nose, and I crack an eye open.

Ester hops off the bed and returns with a tray of fluffy pancakes, topped with a square of butter and glossy maple syrup, and a small bowl of mixed berries sprinkled with brown sugar.

"Guess who made this," Ester says, way too close to my ear.

"Cinderella," I grumble, pushing myself upright and rubbing my eyes.

"Close." Stephanie drags a cold towel across my face to wake me up. "It was Kite."

Kite also watched *My Fair Princess* with us before playing a piano rendition of the opening song. I fell asleep to its soothing melody, and now I get this rude awakening (though I can't complain about pancakes).

As I dig in, I take this time to check my phone. Mom and Aunt

Mei wished me happy birthday at four a.m., the time stamped on my birth certificate.

I smile into my fork and clean my plate without sparing a drop of syrup.

✳

Kite's nursing a cup of coffee in the kitchen.

"Good morning," I greet him after brushing my teeth and changing out of my pajamas. "Thanks for the pancakes. They were delish."

"I aim to please," he says, "but I must give credit where it's due. Wayne taught me the recipe."

"I'm seeing a trend here: O-Kei taught you how to make kimbap, Wayne taught you pancakes, and what else?"

Kite sips his coffee contemplatively. "I used to take break-dancing lessons from Xiaoming but stopped when I nearly threw out my back." I wince. "Tell me about it," he says.

It's strange. As much as I love hearing Kite's voice, I can't believe we're talking like this again. So much has happened in the last two weeks, and somehow we landed here. I guess it is true: honesty goes a long way. Any more ups and downs, though, and I might die from the whiplash.

"Any plans today, birthday girl?" he asks.

Suddenly I'm transported back to two days ago, when Dad ambushed me at my own house. After what happened with Kyle, I have Dad on the record, saying Katherine of all people wants to make it up to me. Well, no thanks!

"Are you okay?" Kite waves a hand in my face, and my anger dims.

258

"Sorry, I got distracted." I scratch my head. "I don't have any plans."

"You're not going all out for your eighteenth?"

"Meh, I'd rather relax today." At least then I can spend my birthday with Kite. It's too risky for him to go out, and if that means staying indoors, so be it. "What more could a girl want than breakfast in bed?"

"A lot more. You can afford to be a little selfish, Lovely."

The doorbell rings. I ignore it, thinking Stephanie will answer it (after all, this is her house). When it rings again, I throw my hands up and answer anyway.

On the welcome mat is a gift basket overflowing with miscellaneous items: star candy, chocolate rocks, a cat-themed coloring book, stickers, my favorite perfume, a bottle of sparkling cider, a custom set of bath bombs and candles, wireless headphones, a Korean-English dictionary (weird), a five-thousand-piece jigsaw puzzle of Jeju Island, and a Karnival beach towel with Kite's face on it (also weird).

"Happy birthday! Again!"

The screen door flings open behind me, clipping the back of my calves, as Stephanie and Ester shower me in confetti. A colorful rainstorm obscures my vision before they torture me with tickles until I'm in tears. And just like that, I go from loving my friends to hating them, then back to loving them when they go easy on me in Mario Party.

But the surprises don't end there.

When dinnertime rolls around, while Kite and I get started on the puzzle, Ester manages to work the outdoor grill without incident. Stephanie said to leave all the cooking to them, and by *them,* she also meant Mom and Aunt Mei. They arrive with a checkerboard cake, the same one that was on *The Great British Bake Off*. Mom replicated it for me, and with all the drama that's thrown everything into a whirlwind lately, I'm beyond grateful.

The celebration simmers down before the indigo sky darkens to navy.

Stephanie and Ester clean up, leaving me and Kite to enjoy each other's company. I'm finishing my second slice of cake when we lock eyes in the kitchen. Soon he's standing right in front of me.

I take an instinctive step backward and bump into the kitchen island. He reaches his hand out, and I close my eyes, anticipating a kiss. But our bodies never connect.

He's petting Maru. She's lounging in a carrier behind me. How embarrassing. At least I didn't pucker my lips.

I scarf down the rest of my cake while Kite remains oblivious. Maru preens at his touch, her eyes little half-moons as she shoots a haughty look my way—but I'm not mad, because she's adorable. She could scar my face, and I'd forgive her.

I forget my humiliation and pet her to my heart's content.

"Is it safe for her to be out of her cage?" I ask, eying her bandaged leg.

"As long as I keep her from jumping or running, she should be okay. I thought a change of scenery would be good for her." Kite gently tugs the fleece blanket cushioning the floor of the carrier. Maru hisses at him. "She loves this blanket. She'll lie in it all day."

"She is so spoiled."

Laughing, he strokes Maru's tail, eliciting a rumbling purr. "You have this whole house wrapped around your finger."

"I'd like to be wrapped around *your* finger."

Kite widens his eyes at me.

"I didn't say that!" I frantically search for the source: Ester's peeking in from behind a wall, trying not to laugh. "Don't you have charcoal to scrape off? Get to it."

Now Kite's trying not to laugh. He takes a moment to collect himself before locking Maru's carrier. "I'm heading down." He starts for the basement. "You coming?"

I follow him downstairs. Given the events of today, I can't help but expect another surprise to be waiting for me.

Kite flicks on the lights. Nothing's out of the ordinary.

Part of me deflates, but I try not to look disappointed. I don't want to make Kite feel bad for not reading my mind. Why expect more from an already amazing day?

I relax on the sofa, and, after tucking Maru into her cage, Kite plops down next to me with his iPad.

"There's something I want to show you," he says, tapping the screen.

"Another recording?" I brighten up, eager to be serenaded. Earlier, before we cut the cake, he sang "Happy Birthday" with Stephanie and Ester.

"You'll see." We scoot onto the floor, sitting with our knees to our chest while his iPad sits at eye level on the table. "Ready?"

I look at him, at the unmistakable smile on his face, and smile back. He presses the Video Chat icon, the screen changes, and we're greeted by a chorus of hellos.

Xiaoming, Wayne, and Yoosung appear onscreen, the three of them holding up a giant HAPPY BIRTHDAY banner. They wave at me.

"Happy birthday, Lovely!" Wayne steps into the forefront of the camera, his body taking up most of the frame. "Is it okay to call you Lovely, or is Kite the only one allowed to?" Then, without giving me a chance to respond, he says, "Anyway, we've heard so much about you! Thanks for taking care of Kite. I hope he took very good care of you today."

That sounds highly suggestive.

I want to say something, but I'm silently hyperventilating and can't function right now. I was not prepared for this, at all. Xiaoming, Wayne, and Yoosung are here. Not physically in this room, but they can see me and I can see them. Realization hits me like a meteor crashing through the earth's hemisphere. Stars are parading across my vision, literally.

I'm actually meeting Karnival. For the first time.

Off-camera, Xiaoming shouts, "We're doing Kite a favor! You owe us!" in a mix of Chinese and English.

"Guys, tone it down. She's a little nervous," Kite says, squeezing my shoulder.

"I think . . . I'm having a heart attack," I pant, clutching my shirt.

"There's a breathing exercise I practice before every show, helps chase away the nerves," Wayne says. "Let's try it out." He falls back in line with his teammates and says a few words to them in Korean.

Kite nudges me encouragingly, and together we mimic Wayne's actions. We draw half circles in the air with our forefingers for every breath we take in and for every breath we take out. This whole exercise is absurd yet adorable, and after drawing several half circles, my heart steadies into a normal rhythm.

The camera blurs as Wayne repositions his tablet. "Before our manager catches us, the three of us are going to sing you a song. Any requests?"

"Um, how about 'Happy Birthday'?" It's the first song that pops into mind.

Wayne looks taken aback. "I wasn't expecting that. . . . Well, if that's what the birthday girl wants, that's what she gets." He clears his throat, rubs his palms together, and starts a countdown with his fingers.

Xiaoming begins beatboxing before the count of three, throwing everyone off.

"I didn't know we were doing a remix," Wayne says, dumb-founded. He steals a glance at Yoosung, who seems equally confused. Xiaoming keeps going and doesn't appear to be stopping anytime soon. "Okay, we're winging it. . . . This is for you, Lovely!"

Thus begins a bizarre yet endearing beatbox-rap-but-also-a-cappella version of "Happy Birthday" that has Kite dying with laughter.

"Ige mwoya?" A new voice flows through the speakers, and although I can't see him, I know O-Kei is there somewhere.

Wayne moonwalks off-camera and drags O-Kei into frame. As soon as we see each other, he freezes, surprise flashing across his face before he leaves as quickly as he came.

Kite was too busy coughing into his elbow to witness the last five seconds.

My one-of-a-kind birthday song concludes on a bittersweet note.

"For you, Lovely! Hope you enjoyed that as much as we—Xiaoming did," Wayne says. Xiaoming smiles at the mention of his name, blissfully unaware that Wayne just threw shade his way. "Our manager is calling—peace!"

Yoosung and Xiaoming cross their forefingers over their thumbs to form a V.

And then the screen goes black.

"That was very . . . interesting" is all I can muster.

"I think they forgot who they were singing to," Kite says, his voice cracking as the urge to laugh resurfaces. "I'm never going to let Wayne live that down."

"You know what?" I turn the iPad off and set it facedown. "I think they wanted to cheer you up, and by cheering you up, they cheered me up," I jest, waiting for Kite to phone Hallmark and ask them to hire me.

But because this day hasn't had enough surprises, Kite flicks my forehead before kissing it. His lips leave a warm imprint on my skin. Music fills my ears, and my heart quickens, never knowing when to quit as it races toward him.

"Is this okay?" I ask, leaning into him.

My mind involuntarily flashes to O-Kei, and my chest tightens. It feels wrong to be lost in my own world while people around me are hurting.

Kite tucks a lock of hair behind my ear and kisses the top of my head.

"It's more than okay. I like it when you're selfish."

Hey, Lovely, it's Wayne. Don't mind if I slide into your DMs. O-Kei wants to ask you something, but his English sucks, so I'm playing the carrier pigeon. Kite and O-Kei have been avoiding each other since you-know-what, and he wants to know if Kite hates him. I already told him no, but he doesn't believe me. Your opinion is liquid gold and mine's maple syrup, apparently.

Instagram message from Wayne, sent on August 9.

To O-Kei: Kite doesn't hate you. Do you hate him?

Instagram message from Lulu, sent on August 9.

I don't hate him.

Instagram message from O-Kei, sent by Wayne on August 9.

The feeling's mutual. Now talk to him. Be honest and he will be too.

Instagram message from Lulu, sent on August 9.

38

A knock at the door stirs me awake.

Bleary-eyed, I check the time. It's three a.m.

My mind is foggy with sleep, but I know without asking that Kite's outside the guest room. Only he would be polite enough to knock.

Turning on the bedside lamp, I roll out of bed and comb a hand through my hair before opening the door. Kite stands in the dimly lit hallway with a travel bag slung over his shoulder, the same bag he hasn't touched since the scandal broke. I look him over once, then twice as my brain works. The sun doesn't rise for three hours, yet he's fully clothed, baseball cap and all.

He cracks a shy but hopeful smile, and then I'm diving into his arms, my fatigue fading, giving way to joy. He catches me, teetering on the balls of his feet before finding balance. We share a brief but celebratory laugh, hushing ourselves when we remember Stephanie's next door.

I usher him into my room, our footsteps in perfect harmony as I reverse through the door and stop at the edge of the bed.

"I talked to O-Kei," he says, the warm light of the lamp softening his features. There's a spark in his eyes, a hint of optimism that makes my heart sing. "I'm . . . okay now."

Slipping his bag onto the floor, Kite reels me in by the waist, his thumbs pressed against my pelvis while his warmth seeps through the thin fabric of my pajamas. Wrapped in the scent of freshly laundered cotton, I rest my cheek against his chest and listen to his heartbeat, the steady rhythm a lullaby.

"Thanks for putting up with me," he whispers into my hair. "No more sulking, no more hiding. It's time to move on."

"That must've been one hell of a conversation you had with O-Kei."

"It was a long time coming. . . . I have a bad habit of shutting down when things go wrong. After our fight, I didn't know how to talk to him or if he'd even listen. Turns out, he felt the same way." Kite sighs. It's not the sound of defeat but of acceptance. "The music industry can be rewarding, but it's also lonely and unforgiving. Instead of helping each other, O-Kei and I were competing against each other."

"Do you still feel lonely?"

"Sometimes, when the judgment and criticism are louder than the voices that do matter. Being away for so long, I forgot what it was like . . . to allow myself to be vulnerable. The industry teaches you to strive for perfection, to show only the best version of yourself. Coming home, I had to unlearn that." Kite squeezes my shoulder. "There are things I still can't bring myself to talk about—with you or my family—but I want to do better."

"You're already doing better," I assure him.

Kite ruffles my hair and kisses the top of my head. "I don't know what this summer would've been like without you."

"You probably would've been spending it in someone else's basement."

He laughs wholeheartedly.

I quickly clamp a hand over his mouth. "Sleeping Beauty does not like to be disturbed."

Then his phone goes off, the ringtone blaring. He fumbles through his pockets, only to realize his phone is in his bag. As soon as he silences it, we both freeze and stare at the door, waiting for signs of movement. Several seconds later, we're in the clear.

Kite checks his phone. "Dad's here to pick me up. Guess I kept him waiting too long." He hauls his bag off the floor. "I'll see you at home?"

"Of course."

"Hope Stephanie won't mind if I take the cat."

"Maru's all yours."

As for me, I'm ready to return to bed, knowing I can rest easy now that Kite can, too.

39

"The house feels empty without a K-pop idol in my basement," Stephanie laments, nursing a glass of lemonade in one hand and a copy of *Pachinko* in the other.

We're chilling by the pool in her backyard.

"Your house feels empty because your parents are away," I correct her. "I'm surprised they're still on Martha's Vineyard. Don't they want to spend time with you before college?"

Move-in day at Barnard is a week and a half away.

"Eighteen years under the same roof with them is enough." Stephanie shrugs. "They can visit me anytime, and besides, I have you and Ester. You two are a handful as it is."

"That should be my line." I laugh.

"My house wouldn't feel so empty if Maru were still here. I can't believe Kite took her with him." Stephanie pouts, snapping her book shut.

Kite returned home two days ago.

The Karnival fandom has quieted dramatically. There hasn't been a Firework sighting in days, and the fan mail has thinned out to almost nothing. Most of the K-pop community has been gossiping about Eun-hee, a female idol from Battle Jewels, who was caught out past curfew, drinking at a nightclub. Fans and haters are calling her a party animal (and that's not the worst of it). People love finding reasons to be outraged.

I started sleeping at home again last night.

I haven't told a single soul about my conversation with O-Kei, however brief it was. I deleted all traces of it from my phone. He must've reached out as a last resort. Asking me if Kite hates him might be the most roundabout way to get an answer. I'm baffled yet sort of flattered he valued my input.

"It was fun while it lasted," Stephanie says. "I shouldn't be greedy." She studies me over the rim of her cup. "How much longer will Kite be here for?"

I make a sound halfway between a cough and a sneeze. I wipe my lips with the back of my hand and stare absently at the pool.

"He told me late August."

We're already halfway there.

Stephanie sips her drink and gazes into the woods, her expression melancholic. I know she has more to say but wants to spare my feelings—unnecessary, really.

I always knew Kite would leave at the end of summer. I never thought he and I had forever.

As it turns out, Mr. and Mrs. Nguyen contracted a premature case of empty-nest syndrome and left Martha's Vineyard early. I was leaving right when they pulled into the driveway.

While Stephanie's (probably) bonding with her parents over crossword puzzles right now, I'm back home to an empty house. There's a stillness to the neighborhood, and after all the commotion, I'm not quite sure what to do with myself in this peace.

A string of knocks at the back door yanks me from my thoughts.

Kite and Connie are in my backyard.

I smile instantly. It's a reflex I can't control. Kite and I haven't seen each other since he left Stephanie's. Two days isn't a long time to be apart, but seeing him all sunny, relaxed, and unfairly handsome in the early afternoon light . . .

He is a delightful sight to behold.

I welcome them in. The second Kite steps across the threshold, we lean in for a kiss—withdrawing when we remember Connie. We spare a sheepish glance her way, and she sighs.

"Don't bother acting like it's a secret. I know you guys are dating." Connie gives me a pointed look, and I flinch at the sting of her judgment.

But I deserve it. I lied to her face and have to own up to it.

"I'll be in the living room," she says, shaking the box tucked under her arm. "I heard you like board games. We're playing once you guys are done making out or whatever."

As soon as she turns the corner, Kite and I reach for each other, our bodies drawn together like magnets. We find shelter behind a wall, away from the door and windows, and share one kiss, two kisses, then three more. His presence has renewed something within me, and now I'm craving his touch—which I'm quite verbal about, except I let my hands and lips do the talking.

"That's one way to say hello," Kite says between kisses.

"Do you want to see how I say goodbye?" I say, equally breathless.

"Do you want to see me choke on my own vomit?" Connie calls out.

We laugh and, after another kiss that leaves me weak in the knees and desperate for air, we stumble into the living room.

"Everything okay next door?" I ask Connie as she unboxes a game with cartoon monsters on the cover and KING OF TOKYO printed in bold text.

Kite told me he hasn't seen or heard of any Fireworks visiting the Xus' this week, though I'm not sure if his experience is the same as Connie's.

"Better than before," Connie says, organizing the various playing pieces. "Our recycling bin isn't overflowing with letters anymore, and we now have a cat that scratches everything." Kite coughs into his fist. "Anyway, let's get this game started."

It's quite surreal for the three of us to be here—stomachs flat on the floor with cards, dice, and cardboard figures between us—like it's the most natural thing in the world. I can't remember when we last hung out together like this.

On our second round of King of Tokyo, the house phone rings.

"You going to get that?" Connie asks, staring at the scorecard in her hand.

"Let it go to voice mail." I'm too engrossed in the game to answer it.

Then my dad's voice fills the room.

"Hey, it's Vincent, calling to let you know Kath and I are back in Cali. We let Kyle stay a few more days with a family friend. He's still upset about what . . . happened last week. Lulu, if you're listening, I hope you had a good birthday. Things have been rocky between us, and you don't want to talk. I get it. I've never been good with words, but—"

I scramble to my feet to turn off the machine, cutting the message short.

273

"Sorry. About. That." I grind out each word, my voice fighting through the mortification. I try to iron out the tension locking my body in place, but with two pairs of eyes on me, I'm finding it impossible.

"Can you give us a moment?" Kite says to Connie.

"Sure," she says. "Take all the time you need."

Once we hear the door shut, Kite beckons me to him, his arms like a silk sheet on a hot night. I bury my face in his shoulder as if I can hide from my own embarrassment. We stand in silence, his hand cradling the back of my head while my own hands clutch the back of his shirt.

"He keeps doing this," I finally say. "He left to be with his new family. Why can't he leave for good? I'm eighteen now. He can stop pretending to care about me."

"Maybe he does care, though? His way of reaching out seems insincere, but maybe he's really trying." Kite says exactly what I don't want to hear. "Just because he's not here doesn't mean you have to cut him out of your life."

I take a small step back and look at him. "You weren't there, Kite."

My voice is sharp, more biting than I intended. Kite flinches as if I've slapped him, but he smooths over his expression and waits for me to continue.

"It happened at the start of freshman year." I remember the brutal humidity of picture day and how worried I was about my hair frizzing up. Little did fourteen-year-old me know I'd have much bigger problems to face that evening.

"Mom was making credit card payments when she noticed a bunch of transactions from California—at a hotel, a Louis Vuitton store, and some high-end restaurants. A week earlier, Dad had gone to San Francisco for a work function. Usually he'd put his expenses on his company card, but this time he didn't. Mom asked him about it. He told her he'd forgotten his company card at home and had to use his own, so she asked for proof that his company had reimbursed him."

I swallow hard and keep my voice level. "That's . . . when Dad came clean. There was never a business trip to begin with. He used his vacation days to fly out to San Francisco to see Katherine or, as he put it, 'someone who made him happy'—unlike his family, as he so kindly implied. Then he left to stay at a hotel."

Not once did he apologize for betraying Mom's trust. He didn't apologize for betraying mine either. His actions revealed how little guilt he felt, as if his mistake wasn't that he cheated but that he married the wrong person.

The divorce proceedings were swift as divorces go. Dad informed the judge he was moving to California to marry his mistress. Mom was given the house, the car, and sole physical custody of me while Dad got visitation.

Three years later and the divorce still ignites a fire in me.

Kite drags a hand down his face, searching for words.

I don't know what he's thinking. Whatever it is, I don't need my dad to keep ruining things for me. Today was going so well, but now I'm losing it to my temper—for a man on the other side of the country—and I don't know how to salvage it. This aggravates me, because the last person who should have any hold over me is my dad.

"Like I said before, some people you just have to let go." I put some distance between Kite and me and turn on the TV. "Can you tell Connie she can come back in?"

40

Mom whips up congee the next morning, complete with my favorite sides.

All three ladies of the Li family sit down for breakfast.

"Are we celebrating something today?" I ask, perplexed.

"Should we be?" Mom says, crunching on a mouthful of bamboo shoots.

"It's rare for both of you to be home at this hour." I grab a pair of chopsticks and dig in.

"Making time for your family isn't a crime," Aunt Mei chimes in, sliding a plate of tofu skin toward me, "and seeing your beautiful face is a wonderful start to the morning."

Mom and I roll our eyes.

But I appreciate the sentiment. Last night I sat Mom down and talked to her about Dad and his consistently poor timing. Enough was enough. I didn't want to hear from him ever again. She didn't probe me for all the details. All she said was that she'd take care of it.

"What are your plans for today?" Mom asks me.

"Stephanie's picking me up later," I answer. "We're going to the mall."

"Have fun. Be back before six. The Xus invited us over for dinner."

The second rare occasion of the day, yet it oddly rings of déjà vu.

Stephanie and I stand before our high school, with its brick façade, terra-cotta columns, and tinted windows. Band practice is in session on the front lawn, the drumline grating on my ears, each beat bringing me closer to a headache. Our school was never ranked highly for creative arts.

"Can't believe we spent four years in this hovel," Stephanie says before veering through the staff parking lot toward the track.

"Why are we here?" I ask, trailing behind her. "Correct me if I'm wrong, but this isn't the mall."

"Don't you want to take one last look before college?"

"Not really," I mutter. I said goodbye to this "hovel" back in June.

The gate to the track is unlocked. Stephanie prances in and climbs the metal bleachers overlooking the football field ringed by nine red lanes. She finds a shaded spot at the top and beckons me over.

"This place feels different," she says. "It's not as stifling."

"That's because we're outside," I say. She gives me the side-eye. "Okay, yes, it does feel different, probably because there isn't that dread at the end of every summer where we know we have to go back and drown in more homework."

"Come September we'll still be drowning in homework but as college freshmen."

"With style." I laugh. "Even if you and I are up to our necks with schoolwork, we have to make time for each other. We can't be best friends and not see each other."

"Don't forget, you have Ester."

"Yeah, but Ester isn't a placeholder for you."

Stephanie presses a hand to her heart. "Aw, Lulu."

I'm blushing. I said something sentimental to her without thinking.

Stephanie hugs me. "You're irreplaceable to me, too."

When she pulls away, her eyes are trained on something at the bottom of the bleachers. I follow her gaze and find Ester and Kite standing there. I know Kite well enough to see through his disguise, and at this point, I'm no longer frazzled by these little surprises my friends keep scheming.

"Steph, you and me!" Ester shouts, pointing at the track. "Loser has to buy the winner bubble tea."

"You might as well part with the money now." Stephanie tightens her shoelaces, shoots me a little smirk, and then meets Ester out on the field.

Kite takes his place next to me. He looks around before removing his hat and sunglasses; finally we lock eyes.

Yesterday ended on a sour note. We did continue our game once Connie came back, but the mood wasn't the same. I couldn't keep my emotions in check; my mind was preoccupied.

"Feeling better today?" Kite asks.

I think about how to answer, then sigh. "A little. Sorry for making things awkward."

"It's not your fault. Connie and I are up for another game whenever you are." Kite pauses when I shoot him an incredulous look. "Okay, maybe not Connie, but I am."

And then we kiss. Short and sweet.

"I always wondered what high school would've been like," Kite muses as we watch Stephanie outpace Ester on the track.

"You didn't miss out on much," I tell him. "It's four years of the same routine."

"Routine isn't necessarily bad. What about all those times you and I used to walk to the bus stop together?"

"I do miss those walks," I say, more to myself, inviting those childhood memories into the forefront of my mind. "Still, fifth-grade you didn't dream about high school. You dreamed about becoming a K-pop idol."

"True." Kite taps his foot. "But what if I had gone to high school?"

Here on the bleachers, we're like a normal teenage couple. Kite and I could've shared countless moments like this if he'd stuck with the traditional life script. But best not to get lost in what-ifs.

"Maybe then I would've had a prom date," I say teasingly.

"Not maybe," Kite says. "You *would've had* a prom date."

I tilt my head back and laugh. I don't know why. "In an alternate universe, you and I would've gone to prom together, and we would've been crowned Prom King and Queen."

"I can believe it."

"One way or another, you still would've ended up in South Korea."

Kite stares at me, his expression unreadable.

"Hey, lovebirds!" Ester calls out to us. She and Stephanie are back at the starting line. "Let's see who's the fastest between the four of us!"

I turn back to Kite. "I'll race you there."

And without a moment's hesitation, I'm hurrying down the bleachers, but instead of running toward Ester and Stephanie, it feels like I'm running away from Kite.

By dinnertime, my chest feels tight, like someone's tugging my heart, stretching it taut like a freshly laundered bedsheet and checking it for holes.

Mrs. Xu cooked up another feast, and Mr. Xu doesn't waste a second popping open the wine. I spot some familiar dishes from the last time we all gathered. It's as if we're back in June, celebrating Kite's return.

Shame I don't have much of an appetite. I help myself to bony cuts of Hainanese chicken and manage a small serving of lotus root soup before I start pushing food around on my plate.

"Connie, any idea what college you want to go to?"

"How's the bakery doing?"

"Someone pass the sriracha."

"Did you hear about the new Costco that's opening on . . ."

I'm vaguely aware of the conversations around me; meanwhile, I'm hyperaware that no one is talking to me, which works in my favor, since I don't want anyone asking me why I'm not eating, but still, the lack of parental clucking seems intentional.

Something's amiss, and no one's being forthcoming here.

I bite the ends of my chopsticks, pensive, paranoid, and a bit peeved.

Kite places a hand on my thigh; only then do I remember he's sitting next to me.

"I'm going to catch some air," he says, an unspoken invitation.

I raise a brow at him, and he starts to get up.

Dinner just started. I expect some protest as Kite and I leave the table, but everyone's too busy drinking and chatting to care. Even Connie, who's on the brink of yawning at Aunt Mei's story, seems preoccupied. Of all people, she would be the first one out of here.

I follow Kite onto the front porch. We sit on the top step, surrounded by the sound of insects. Kite lights one of those mosquito-repellent candles, and gradually the incessant buzz reduces to a murmur. The air is balmy, yet I find this moment suffocating.

My intuition is pleading with me, but I can't understand what it's trying to tell me.

"Did something happen?" Kite asks, nudging me. "You seem upset."

"It's just . . . one of those days." I lean into him, his arm open and ready, securing me in place. My paranoia wavers, and my chest begins to uncoil. I take in the evening air, welcoming the breeze as it sweeps by in small fleets.

We sit like this for a while, the moment enveloping us, unshaken by the fear of someone spotting us. Kite snakes a finger under my chin and tips my head back, drawing my eyes away from the sky to focus on him.

He's luminous in his own way, and unlike the stars, I can touch him.

I close my eyes. His nose brushes against mine, and his lips come to rest against the shell of my ear.

"My manager called," he says, barely above a whisper. "He wants me to catch a flight back this Sunday."

This time, I can't keep the frown off my face. The harder I fight it, the deeper it carves itself into my face.

I throw his arm off me and rush to my feet. He catches my hand and entwines our fingers, his palm slippery with sweat. My sweat. I snatch my hand back, regret lancing through me as I glimpse the pained expression on his face.

This Sunday. That leaves us six days—barely if he departs in the morning.

Silence stretches between us.

This was bound to happen, and finally, it's happening.

"Are you ready to go back?" I ask, knowing that what he wants doesn't matter.

"I am," Kite says without hesitation.

"Oh, well, that's good." I sound like a robot. "Did you already buy your ticket?"

"I did. Listen, we can—"

"Wayne will be so glad to have you back. Tell him I said hi when you see him." I don't know what I'm saying, but I keep going. "And don't forget to send me a photo of all the fried chicken you'll be eating once you're—"

Kite takes me by the shoulders, the drop of his hands weighing me down like an anchor. "Lovely, don't worry, we can make this work."

My mind goes blank. "Make what work?"

"Us," Kite says, cupping my face in his hands.

He wants to try long distance. The idea always seemed impossible.

"Kite . . ." The words catch in my throat, and I feel myself slipping away.

POSTED BY MYLIGHTKITE ON AUGUST 14.

This is to all the traitors who turned their back on Kite and wanted to see his career crash and burn: Kite might've hit rock bottom, but the only way forward is up, and Kite will fly higher than before. Kite hasn't resigned despite your outrageous demands. I bet he'll make a comeback soon, and all you fake Fireworks can do is watch him soar.

#FireWorks #FlyHighKite #hatersgonnahate #stanwithkite

41

"You rejected him?"

Stephanie and Ester stare at me, gobsmacked. We're playing Uno on the soccer field as I recount the events of last night.

Kite actually wants us to last. I didn't know what to say except that I was sorry, I couldn't see it happening. He tried to be a good sport about it, but the disappointment was palpable, so heavy I felt it prying us apart.

"Our friendship didn't work long distance. How could we make a relationship work?" I tell them the same thing I told Kite.

Ester abandons the cards in her hands, scattering them across my lap, and shakes me. "How could you break that poor boy's heart?"

Stephanie eases Ester's iron grip on me. "She made the right call. Long distance or not, they would never last."

I roll my eyes. "Wow, thanks."

"Do you want me to validate you or not?" Stephanie tosses her cards onto the grass. "LDRs are so much work for so little gain."

"Don't talk like you're speaking from experience," Ester snaps. "Just because you don't want to be tied down doesn't mean Lu has to be single."

"And you pushing so hard for Lulu and Kite to be together isn't a product of your own projection?" counters Stephanie.

"Ladies, this isn't the time to be fighting," I interject.

"You're right. This is the time to decide if Kite is worth fighting *for*!" Ester exclaims.

"What am I fighting exactly?" I ask, shrinking under her shadow as she looms over me.

"Against the odds!" Ester says, as if it couldn't be more obvious. "Give me something to be happy about. Give me the love story I need!"

"She wants no part in your fantasies," Stephanie says, earning herself a glare.

"Lu didn't want to treat Kite as some summer fling, but now that he asks to be serious, she bails! Where's the consistency?"

Kite and I knew he'd leave in August. Even when he was thinking about quitting Karnival, I never actually believed he would. I never let myself consider a future in which Kite stayed in America, I couldn't. I was prepared to say goodbye.

Last night changed everything.

What will the future look like if Kite and I stay together?

The uncertainty unnerves me. I don't want to take Kite for granted, but who's to say he won't lose interest once we spend enough time apart? He's going to be busy with his music, and I'll be busy with school. I can't imagine that whatever free time he does have will be dedicated to me, and then we need to account for the different time zones. As harsh as it sounds, at the end of the day, he's the same person who left his friends and family behind four years ago. That's a long time to never see or hear from someone. If I wasn't worth the effort then, why am I worth it now?

"Kite isn't your dad, if that's what you're worried about."

My eyes slide over to Ester.

"You're worth the effort. Your dad might not see it, but Kite sees it, I see it, and"—Ester glances at Stephanie—"Steph sees it, too, despite what she said about how you two would never last. She's just trying to make you feel less guilty for rejecting Kite."

Her resolve gives me strength, but I can't dispel the worry lurking inside me.

I look away, searching for a distraction.

"I'm going to be straight with you," Stephanie says, her only warning before she drives the knife in. "Ester and I, we notice things. Like how, at the start of summer, you kept downplaying how much of a Karnival fan you are and saying you didn't care that Kite was coming home."

I run a nervous hand through my hair.

"Should I also mention how you kept denying you were in love with Kite, but as soon as he asked you out, you jumped at the chance?"

I purse my lips and cross my arms.

"There's no shame in wanting to be with Kite. Don't lie to yourself."

"It's not shame," I finally say, my stomach twisting. I take a deep breath as the tightness in my stomach slithers up my chest, balling into a knot at the back of my throat. I screw my eyes shut and press a hand to my forehead. "It's exhausting to . . . hope for something and then all you get is disappointment."

Until this summer, I had given up on the idea that I would ever see Kite again.

Distance makes the heart grow fonder, but it also eases heartache.

Out of sight, out of mind. When you have friends, family,

school, and other obligations, it's easy to distract yourself long enough to move on.

I had convinced myself that I could be content by simply being Kite's fan. But the truth is, after all these years, I never stopped missing him. So, yes, I downplayed my enthusiasm whenever Kite came up in conversation. I didn't want to get my hopes up at the news of him coming home in case he didn't remember me or want anything to do with me.

But he did. He remembered me and so much more, and then I found myself wanting . . .

"Why think about someone who isn't thinking about you?"

"But Kite *is* thinking of you," Stephanie insists. "He wants to do long distance."

"And when he gets too busy again?" I chew on my bottom lip, my eyes stinging with tears. Ester reaches for my hand. "Then what?"

"Do you think Kite's feelings are that flimsy? You don't think he thought about all this before suggesting long distance?"

"He probably did put a lot of thought into this, but say we do long distance and things don't work out. Where do we go from there? Are we still going to be friends?"

Or will I lose him for good?

"That's a question you can answer when you get to it. If you don't trust Kite, then save yourself the trouble. But he seems to trust you. Take that for what it's worth."

That afternoon, as I'm leaving the house to hit the bookstore for Chinese and Korean language workbooks, a sound draws my attention across the lawn, over to Kite's bedroom window, where a redbird noisily flaps its wings. Before I can look away, the window suddenly cracks open, and Kite comes into view.

He's like a princess out of a fairy tale. I half expect a deer to gallop out of the brush and a family of rabbits to gather below his window while he sings to them.

Then he spots me staring.

I panic and scurry away.

This isn't me. I rejected him. The least I can do is own up to my decision. I have only a few more nights with him. Am I going to spend what precious time I have left avoiding him? If you want to end summer vacation devastated, that's how you do it.

But I can't be around him right now. I thought I knew what I wanted and where I was going, and I couldn't have been more wrong.

42

Mom finds me in the dark, sprawled across the sofa with a pint of ice cream, the pastel tones of *Miss Love & Hate* throwing muted pinks and blues across the living room.

"Honey, you're ruining your eyes," she says, flicking on the living room light. She mutes the TV, scoots me over, and makes room for herself on the sofa. "Why are we eating ice cream alone and feeling sorry for ourselves?"

"Because it's midnight and I can't sleep," I murmur, hugging my knees. Mom looks at me expectantly. "And . . . Kite's on my mind."

"Of course, he is." Mom loosens the blanket around me and tucks herself under it. "It's your decision in the end. While I never dated a celebrity, I understand your hesitation."

"But?"

"But I don't want you missing out for the sake of practicality. Marrying your dad"—she studies her ring finger, probably thinking of the gold band that once adorned it—"was a practical decision. We dated all through college, waited until we were financially stable, it was all very by-the-book . . . and we all know how that turned out."

"Um, Mom, this isn't very encouraging."

Mom acknowledges me with a sympathetic nod. "My point

is, safe decisions aren't always the best decisions. Your dad and I didn't get married thinking we'd be divorced years later. Yet here we are. I was happy while it lasted, and I'm happy now with you and Mei."

"You don't regret marrying Dad, even after everything?"

"I don't. That doesn't mean I'm not upset about how things fell apart between us, but if I were given the chance to undo everything, I wouldn't. Otherwise, I wouldn't be here with you." Mom bumps shoulders with me and winks.

Knowing what I know now, would I rewind time back to the day Kite asked me out and turn him down? So much has happened since. We would've missed out on so many memories, good and bad. As torn as I am right now, I would have regretted rejecting him then.

Kite left everything behind to chase his dreams. He gave up his past and his present for the future, but he *did* come back. He didn't forget me, and now he's asking for a future together. Stephanie's right. I should give him more credit. I was living a life without him as much as he was living a life without me. Four years is a long time. Two months can't replace them, and yet, we've never been closer.

I think about Kite and what's worth hurting for.

I think about my dad, his new life, and his empty hellos.

And then I think about what it means to say goodbye.

The sun is high in the sky when I text Kite to meet me at the playground.

He hasn't responded, but I'm here and will wait for as long as I have to.

I thought about holding off until later, but why keep stalling when I've already wasted enough time? I'm willing to incur the wrath of Fireworks by dating Kite—what's one more risk?

Dangling upside down on the jungle gym, I connect my forefingers and thumbs to form a camera frame and watch as a lady strolls by with her fluffy dog, followed by a cyclist blasting music from his phone. I shift the frame and capture a moving figure in the distance flickering in and out against the morning sunbeams. By the time I recognize him, I'm untangling my legs from the monkey bars and landing clumsily on my feet.

Kite's sprinting down the road like he's gunning for an Olympic gold medal.

I meet him halfway, running so fast I need to dig the soles of my sneakers into the ground to stop myself from colliding into him.

He's not wearing any disguise, not even his sunglasses. His hair is damp, his bangs clinging to his forehead, and not only is his shirt on backward; it's inside-out. I may have caught him right after he got out of the shower.

Combing back his bangs, Kite takes a moment to catch his breath, but before he can voice a syllable, I kiss him. I couldn't find the right words last night and I can't find them now, so I let my body speak for me.

I kiss him like it's the last one we'll share, but not because this is goodbye.

This is only the beginning.

As lovely as a summer breeze
With a heart full of song
You come running to me
And in a loud, joyful voice
You tell me home is this way

English lyrics to "Lost & Lovely," written by Kite the night before
his flight.

43

The morning of Kite's flight, I'm up bright and early. He'll be over for breakfast in a bit. I told him to come hungry. Knowing Mom and Aunt Mei, they're going to pull out all the stops.

After I get dressed, Aunt Mei asks me to take out the trash and water the plants in the backyard. Once that's taken care of, I find Mom and her clamoring in the kitchen. Every burner on the stovetop is occupied, the electric kettle is steaming, and the oven is ticking.

"Do you need help?" I walk up to Mom as she rigorously stirs a pot of congee. I examine her forehead. "Are you sweating?"

"Everything's under control," she says, out of breath. "I put some laundry in your room. Put it away before Kai arrives."

"If you say so . . ." I retreat to my bedroom, and instead of finding a stack of clothes on my bed, I find Kite—along with a full table spread.

In the time it took me to complete two simple chores, Mom, Aunt Mei, and Kite must've set everything up. Judging by the gingham tablecloth, the fresh floral centerpiece, and the fine china Mom reserves for fancy occasions, they didn't cut any corners. Someone also tidied up my room (nothing spoils a romantic breakfast like a dirty bra on the floor).

"Speedy table setting should be a competitive sport." I peck

Kite on the lips before taking a seat across from him. "You know how to surprise a girl in the bedroom."

"Not just any girl," he says. Such honeyed words would usually fall on oblivious ears. With him, I can't help but listen.

Aunt Mei waltzes in, holding a carafe in each hand. "Are we having coffee or tea?" she asks, the satisfaction of pulling off a surprise evident in her smile.

"Depends. What's for breakfast?" I ask. Congee and coffee don't exactly mix.

"Anything and everything: congee, pancakes, bagels, eggs, sausage, ham, bacon, and fruit. I can make you an omelet—your choice."

"What's with this first-class service?" That's a lot of food to feed two people. Even counting Aunt Mei and Mom, that's still too much.

"Stephanie and Ester will be over shortly." Aunt Mei pauses to register the stunned look on my face. "They'll be in the dining room. Your mom's also bringing food to the Xus."

"In that case, I'd like my eggs sunny-side up and my bacon slightly crispy, with fruit on the side and a cup of coffee, too."

"I'll have congee, a side of sausage and eggs, and tea, please," Kite says.

In the hour that follows, everything feels like a dream. The coffee is more aromatic, the strawberries taste sweeter, and the eggs and bacon on my plate are smiling. I feel weightless and giddy, the world is a soft shade of pink, and everyone seems to sparkle in the daylight.

But when Kite checks the time, I remember he has a flight to catch, and the rosy hue of the world recedes.

"Your flight is at eleven-thirty?" I say it like it's a question.

"Yeah, my parents want to get to the airport by ten."

"That's late by parental standards; usually they'd want to arrive two hours early."

We already agreed that I won't be accompanying him to the airport. I want him to spend the last hour with his family.

Stephanie and Ester pop into the room wearing their Sailor aprons. Aunt Mei gave me the heads-up, but I didn't hear or see them until now.

"Are we finished here?" Stephanie asks. "Does anyone need refills?"

"I think we're done," I say.

It's a quarter to eight. Kite will have to get ready soon.

As Ester gathers up our plates, her eyes zero in on my closet. I'm half-listening when she says, "Did Lu ever show you her Karnival fangirl collection?"

It takes me a second too long to realize what she said, and by then, Kite's shaking his head and eyeing me curiously.

"Can I see?" he asks.

I can't bear to tell him no. Not today. While Stephanie and Ester clean up (and giggle to themselves), I retrieve the shoebox buried in my closet.

"These are just some small things I collected a few years ago," I tell him, blushing as he sits next to me on the floor. I look back, making sure Stephanie and Ester are out of the room before I remove the lid.

Inside the box is a heap of stickers, photo cards, key chains, and enamel pins, along with a T-shirt and a scrunchie with Karnival's logo printed all over them. Kite shuffles through the photo cards, laying them out neatly. As I count them one by one, I realize nearly half are of Xiaoming.

I scream, throwing myself on top of the cards so he can't see them.

"It's not a big deal, Lovely. Xiaoming's a handsome guy." Kite tugs my arm, laughing. When I don't relent, he scoots over and sits me up so that my back is flush against him. "Let's add another photo while we're at it."

He holds out his phone, positioning the camera so both our faces are onscreen. We take enough photos to replace my entire collection, and by the time we're done, my facial muscles are spent.

Massaging my cheeks, I fall back into Kite, making myself comfortable between his legs while his chin comes to rest on my head. We fit perfectly together.

"What are you thinking?" I ask, closing my eyes.

"About how much I don't want to let go," he says, arms tightening around me.

"Same, but someone has to." I focus on the rise and fall of his chest instead of how empty my hands will feel once we part. "Rock, paper, scissors?"

"You need hands to play, and mine are busy." Kite smooths my hair back and kisses my forehead. I shift my body to better look at his face, and in turn he hooks a finger under my chin and meets my gaze. "I promise to write you."

"Even when you're tired and all you want to do is sleep?" I stop to think. "Scratch that, I don't want you sleep-deprived. I don't need to hear from you every day. I can wait, as long as I know you're taking care of yourself."

"Writing to you is taking care of myself."

My heart is so full of affection, it's overflowing.

I finally told Kite about my doubts and fears the other day.

He understood where I was coming from. Long distance has its challenges. Romance and stardom come with even greater challenges. But he promised to do everything he can to make us work—so long as I wanted to make us work as well.

And I do. I really, really, really do.

I trace a finger along his jawline before trailing it with kisses. He smiles, I smile, it's never-ending.

"Did you pet Maru goodbye?" I ask him.

"I did. I told her I'd miss her, and that Connie will be taking care of her from now on. My bedroom will be hers."

"How did she take that?"

"She rolled over and fell asleep, so pretty well, I guess."

Footsteps approach and stop shy of my bedroom door.

"Kai, your parents are outside," Mom says.

"I'll be out in a minute." Kite takes my hand. "Ready?"

"Ready."

Stephanie and Ester are outside with the Xus. Connie's loading the trunk when Kite and I join everyone on the driveway, our hands still entwined.

"Have a safe trip," Stephanie says, giving Kite a friendly pat on the back. "My basement is always open when you need it."

Ester wedges herself between them. "Good luck in Korea! Let us know when you'll be doing a world tour. We'll definitely see you there, right, Lu?"

My friends give me a meaningful look.

"Of course," I say. Contrary to how I felt when rumors first circulated about a world tour, I'm eager to see Kite perform onstage.

Who knows? A concert might be when we meet again. In the meantime, emails and phone calls will have to suffice. "I expect no less than VIP tickets."

"Nothing but the best for you ladies," Kite says, laughing.

"Think you can spot me in a crowded stadium?" I ask, stepping forward as Stephanie and Ester slink back.

"I'll find you." Kite squeezes my hand and I squeeze back.

No matter where we meet, I know without a doubt that when we do see each other again, sparks will fly. I won't deny the pain distance brings and the fear that accompanies it, but I have Stephanie and Ester, and so much more.

"Bye, Lovely." Kite starts for the car, his fingers slipping from mine.

"Talk to you soon." And then I let go.

ACKNOWLEDGMENTS

Writing is a journey with countless ups and downs. *Fireworks* is not the first book I've written, but it is the spark that rekindled a dying flame. While its original draft was an individual endeavor, this book would not have been possible without the help and encouragement of many.

To my agent, Lynnette Novak, thank you for championing Lulu and Kite's story. Words cannot express the depth of my gratitude.

To my editor, Alison Romig, for believing in this story and believing in me. Your kind and insightful feedback took this story where it should've been from the very beginning. As a slow reader and an even slower writer, I am amazed and envious of your quick turnaround.

To the wonderful people at Underlined: Wendy Loggia for acquiring this book, Casey Moses for her on-point cover design, copyeditor Candy Gianetti for her eagle eye, interior designer Jaclyn Whalen for her lovely typesetting, proofreader Tamar Schwartz for reviewing and revising, and everyone who helped to get this book out to the world. A big thank-you to all!

A special shout-out to artist Mikyung Lee for her stunning and adorable cover illustration.

And finally, to my twin sister for listening to my ramblings throughout this whole process, and for being my painfully honest beta reader when I need you to be.

In her fellow matchbreaker, has she found her perfect match?

Turn the page to preview a humorous and heartfelt romance from Underlined!

CHAPTER ONE

Camp Time: Sunday. July 17.

I've been waiting for this moment my entire life. For the first time ever, I get to be a Camp Starling counselor. The first and last time.

My cursive loops on the blank page of my camper's journal. This one has a purple leather cover with a tree embossed on the front. A lone bird soars in the right corner, which is what drew me to this specific journal. I don't take choosing the perfect camper's journal lightly. This one will stay with me over the next two weeks and document all the camp moments I never want to forget. That's especially important this year.

A lump tightens my throat as I lie on the bottom bunk in my empty cabin, staring up at the wood planks of the bed above me. The other counselors aren't here yet. It's just me and one big secret that presses in on me from all sides. I put my pen to paper and prepare to unload that secret—that's what journals are for—when I hear a rattling noise outside.

My spine straightens. What kind of bizarre sound was that? It reminds me of the obnoxious way my mom's boyfriend Dave shakes cubes of ice in his glass—only louder. The rattle is followed by a loud *SHHHHHHHHH*.

The only other people on the grounds right now are my mom—the owner of Camp Starling—and Dave, who gets to serve as assistant camp director just because he's dating my mom. Camp Starling is a camp for all ages to enjoy nature at its best. The next two weeks are designated specifically for teenaged girls and boys ages twelve through fifteen. Sixteen and up—me!—get to serve as camp counselors.

I hear the noise again and briefly wonder if it's my best friend, Nora. Nora is going to be the counselor in the cabin next door to mine. It's early, though, and Nora is a fashionably late kind of friend. I, on the other hand, view arrival times as a rule never to be broken. Actually, I view all rules as unbending lines in the sand.

The rattle and *SHHHHH* noises start again. I still myself and listen. It almost sounds as if it's right outside my cabin. Unable to contain my curiosity, I leave my journal to walk over and peek outside the door. There's no one there. Just Blue Lake, which is little more than a hop, skip, and a jump down a stone path ahead of me. To my left there's nothing but woods because Chickadee Cabin is the last before an expanse of tall pines and oaks. To my right . . .

I pull in a sharp breath. "What are you doing here?"

Hayden Bennett whirls to face me as he stops walking away

from my cabin. He has a surprised expression, as if he had no idea anyone else was here. Even though we've had plenty of classes together over the last couple years, I wouldn't say that Hayden and I are friends. He's that guy who's cute in theory, but who's always in trouble. I know this better than anyone because my mom is the principal of our high school. Usually when I stop in to see her, Hayden will be sitting outside her office, inside it, or he'll just be leaving. It's not that he does horrible things. He's just perpetually tardy, turns in his assignments late, and doodles on everything except paper.

I cross my arms over my chest. "This is private property," I tell him, waiting for an answer to why he's standing outside Chickadee Cabin. Camp Starling isn't even in the town where we live. It's a thirty-minute trip if my mom's the one driving. If I'm behind the wheel, it's more like forty because I only just got my license and I'm a cautious driver.

Maybe Hayden is a counselor here. I seriously doubt he filled out the application, though. Even if he did, my mom would never choose him. *Must be good with kids* is also a requirement. And from what I've seen, Hayden lacks people skills in general.

Case in point: instead of making conversation right now, he's just standing there. He kind of looks nervous, which is different from his usual apathetic demeanor. Even when he's outside my mom's office at school, he's slouched in the chair with his long dark bangs hanging over his eyes like he's just waiting to go inside to . . . what? I don't even know because I am never that unfazed about anything.

As I watch him, his eyes are wider than I've ever seen them, drawing me in to the color of his irises. They're brown. His gaze shifts from side to side. His feet are shifty too, making him look like he's ready to bolt. I notice the fabric messenger bag on his shoulder. It looks heavy and there's a bright green stain seeping through the canvas material. Before I can ask more questions, Hayden starts to back away.

His eyes dart around anywhere except to meet mine. What was he doing right before I peeked out of my cabin? I'm certain he was the source of the strange noises. "Hey, Pais. I, uh, didn't know anyone was here yet."

"Just me and my mom, *Principal* Manning," I tell him, emphasizing the word *principal* even though my mom takes that hat off during the summers. I'm just trying to ignite fear in Hayden's eyes. He doesn't look scared, though. Just suspect. "A few of the camp counselors are starting to arrive too." The counselors arrive one day before the campers. It gives us a chance to bond and review the rules before we take charge.

Hayden steps back and I can tell he's about to jet. I don't want him to go until I figure out why he's here to begin with, though. "We have counselor orientation this evening. Camp starts tomorrow," I tell him, trying to stall. "Today is Camper's Eve."

The skin between Hayden's dark eyes pinches softly. "Like Christmas Eve?"

I shrug. "Camper's Eve is what my dad used to call the afternoon before all the campers arrived for the first day. It might as well have been Christmas to him. He loved Camp Starling." I can feel my eyes suddenly burning and I know they're glistening. Now I'm the one who wants to retreat. I don't talk about my dad much, and this is why.

Hayden looks mildly interested. "Used to? What does he call it now?"

Hayden didn't start attending my school until my seventh-grade year, right after I lost my dad. I guess he doesn't know my story. Why would he? I'm surprised he even knows my name. Or at least the first syllable of it. "My dad died when I was twelve."

Hayden looks at me for a long moment. Then his gaze drops to his feet. I notice that he's used a pen to draw all over his white Converse shoes. There's so much ink, they're practically black. I make out tiny streets and a cityscape. I think maybe there's a dragon on the toe of his other shoe. I look up at him again and his gaze swipes to the bag on his shoulder.

"My dad is gone too," Hayden says. "He doesn't have a good excuse. He just bolted one day." He shrugs like it's no big deal. Maybe it's not for him, but not having my father around is a huge deal to me.

"You never answered what you're doing here," I say more forcefully this time.

"I, uh, was just driving around and saw this place. I guess I wanted to see what it was."

He must think I'm gullible to buy such an obvious lie. No way would he waste gas to drive thirty minutes from his home for no good reason. "The Camp Starling sign at the front entrance should have clued you in that this place is a camp. At least for now," I mutter.

"What do you mean by that?" he asks.

Oops. I didn't mean to say that out loud. I shake my head. "N-nothing. Nothing I can control at least."

Hayden's gaze catches and holds mine. "You have more control than you think. Adults just like you to think you don't."

I watch him for a moment, wondering if he's right. If I could somehow reverse the huge tidal wave that's about to sweep my life off its axis. Once my mom makes up her mind, though, her decision is cemented. There's no wiggle room to compromise for what I want.

"A starling is a bird, right?" Hayden asks then.

I have to admit, I'm surprised and a little impressed that he knows this. "A starling is one of the most intelligent birds," I say. "They've actually outperformed tamarin monkeys in intelligence tests."

Hayden blinks.

I know a lot of random information about birds. It was my dad's thing and now it's kind of mine too.

"Wow. That's cool."

"Yeah." I quickly drop my gaze and deflect the attention back on him. "What's in your bag?" I take a step forward, but he takes several steps back, nearly tripping over his graffitied shoes.

"I'm sorry," he says again, looking at me for real this time. "I didn't know this was your mom's place. See you around, Pais."

"Paisley," I say, correcting him. Apparently he thinks he's

too cool to use my full name. He doesn't seem to hear me, though. He's already walking, half running, away. I watch as he veers off the path and into the woods that eventually lead to a fence that he'll need to clear before leaving the property. I have no doubt he'll be able to. He's an easy five foot ten, whereas I'm only five foot four standing tall. There's a parking lot beyond the fence. I'm guessing that's where his car is.

Again, I wonder what he was doing here and what that mysterious noise I heard before stepping out of my cabin was. I watch him disappear and another thought comes to mind. Since Mom and I are moving away from our hometown of Seabrook next month, I'm pretty sure that was the last time I'll ever lay eyes on Hayden Bennett.